A. ANTHONY

The Gate Drop

Risk the fall

Contents

Acknowledgments — iii

1 Stephanie — 1
2 Axel — 6
3 Stephanie — 13
4 Stephanie — 20
5 Axel — 35
6 Stephanie — 43
7 Axel — 54
8 Stephanie — 60
9 Axel — 74
10 Axel — 80
11 Stephanie — 87
12 Axel — 98
13 Stephanie — 102
14 Axel — 113
15 Stephanie — 118
16 Axel — 126
17 Stephanie — 134
18 Axel — 145
19 Stephanie — 155
20 Stephanie — 159
21 Stephanie — 170
22 Axel — 182
23 Stephanie — 196

24 Stephanie ... 205
25 Axel ... 223
26 Stephanie ... 228
27 Stephanie ... 236
28 Axel ... 241
29 Stephanie ... 247
30 Axel ... 252
31 Stephanie ... 259
32 Axel ... 262
33 Axel ... 268
34 Stephanie ... 279
35 Axel ... 290
36 Stephanie ... 298
37 Stephanie ... 309
Epilogue ... 315
Acknowledgments ... 320
About the Author ... 324

Acknowledgments

Author's note

At the end of the day, this is a work of fiction. While every effort was made to portray the sport as accurately as possible, certain details, events, and situations have been altered or exaggerated to better serve the story and it's characters.

Content Warning:

This book contains explicit sexual content, strong language, and depictions of injury, accidents, and the physical risks associated with professional motocross. Some scenes may be intense or triggering for certain readers. Reader discretion is advised.

Spotify

Apple Music

SMX Cheat Sheet

Supermotocross is broken down into three parts:

SUPERCROSS:

Stadium races, tighter tracks. Main focus is rhythm.

Avg Schedule: Practice, Qualifying, 2 heat races, LCQ(last chance qualifier), 15 min 250 main moto, 20 min 450 main moto

PRO MOTOCROSS:

What some call the outdoor season. Larger, spread out tracks

Avg Schedule: Practice, qualifying, consolation race, two 30 minute main races for each class

PLAYOFFS: Three rounds

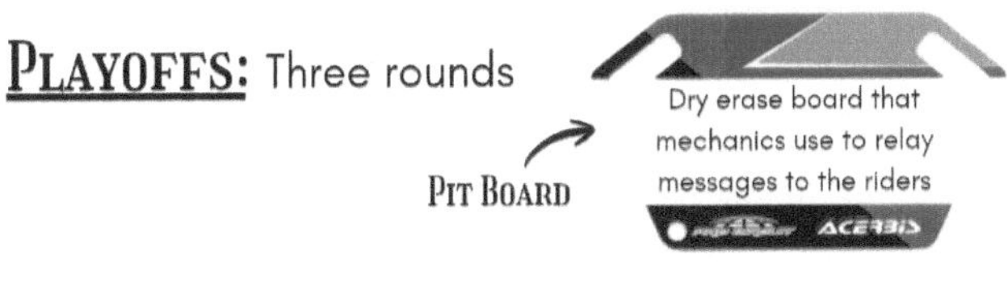

PIT BOARD

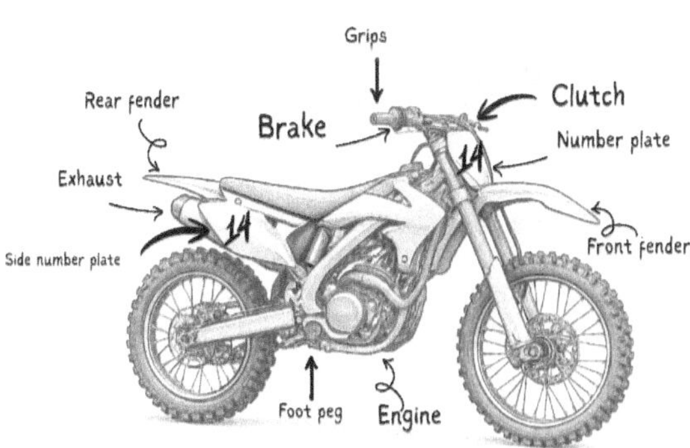

CLASSES: 250 Lights / 450 Premier

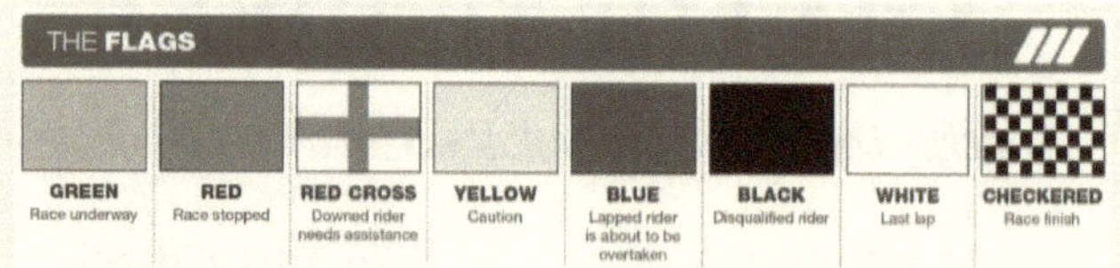

Line: A specific way around the track or through a particular part of the track; can vary with changing course conditions

Holeshot: Taking the lead into the first turn of a race

Rut: A deep groove in the dirt that forms when bikes keep riding over the same spot.

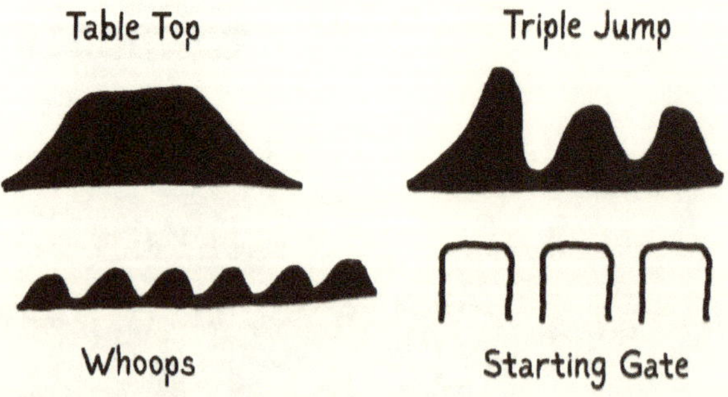

1

Stephanie

etting out of your parents' shadow is like clawing out of a six-foot grave. It's tough, dirty, and impossible. I even moved across the country to escape it. And right now? I almost convinced myself I'm not watching the race.

My back is to most of the televisions lining the airport bar, except for one screen behind the bartender. My suitcase is wedged against my shin like I'm prepared to bolt. My phone is face down on the counter, screen dark, notifications ignored.

Just don't look.

I tell myself like it's easy.

The bar smells like citrus cleaner and spilled beer. Someone down the counter laughs too loudly. A flight attendant nurses a glass of wine like it's medicinal. Normal nightly airport things. Then the crowd on the television surges to its feet. My fingers tighten around my glass before I can stop them.

The bartender glances up, reaches for the remote, and turns the volume up despite himself. Engines roar through the speakers. A few people cheer. Someone groans.

Supercross isn't exactly mainstream airport entertainment, but chaos has a way of drawing an audience.

"Last race of the season," the guy next to me says. He's already half-drunk, Yankees hat tilted back on his head. "You into this stuff?"

"No," I say easily.

It's a good lie. Smooth and practiced.

On-screen, a green bike and a red one are locked together like they're magnetized. Kawasaki versus Honda. I know the colors, the makes, the brands, without really looking. I know the posture, the aggression, the way one rider cuts a line like he owns the track and everyone on it.

My chest tightens.

I shouldn't care. I worked very hard not to care.

The green bike dives inside. The red one slams the door shut, not letting him pass.

The bar erupts.

I look up despite myself, just in time to see the green bike clip, wobble, and disappear off the track in a spray of dirt.

"Oh shit," someone mutters.

The rider doesn't get back up right away. I can't help but hold my breath until I see movement. He shoves himself to his feet. He rips his goggles and helmet off and throws them across the track, nearly hitting a flagger in the process. Crew members rush in too late, hands out, voices useless.

He doesn't look hurt. He looks down right furious. But, at the same time, he looks contained and focused. It's like he's already decided who's responsible.

Dirt flies nearby as riders cross the finish line. The fallen green bike remains in the dirt as it's rider storms away. Fireworks and flames explode. The announcer, crowning the red bike as their champion.

Rad Carson.

I don't need the commentary. I'd know that name anywhere. But, the celebration doesn't start yet. The Kawasaki rider stomps into the pits, and I wince as he gets right up in Rad's face. Too close without hesitation. I feel the tension crawl up my spine.

Oh no.

Hands grab shoulders as one shoves the other. Rad's helmet comes off. A fist cocks back while they continue to push each other. The broadcast cuts away before the fight goes too far. The last thing on screen is Rad's ruffled hair and winning smile.

A woman two stools down whistles. "Someone's getting fined."

That's optimistic.

My phone buzzes on the bar. I already know who it is without even looking.

Mom: *Did you see that?*

Of course she did. She always sees it.

Me: *Yes.*

I flip my phone, face down, harder than necessary. The guy in the Yankees hat eyes it, then me.

"Bad day?" he asks.

"You could say that."

He nods, like that explains everything, and turns back to the screen.

I signal for the check and pull my wallet out. My credit card slides across the bar. The bartender squints at it, then at me.

"Carson," he says. "Any relation?" He adds nodding to the TV.

"No," I say too quickly. My smile feels brittle.

He shrugs, uninterested, before he turns to process my card. I drain my drink, the burn welcoming. Around me, people are already pulling out their phones. They're already replaying the footage, speculating, and laughing like it's entertainment instead of blood and bone. I don't need to check social media to know it's on fire.

That rider, the one on the Kawasaki, didn't just lose. He refused to accept it.

And now he's *my* problem. All because I said yes to a job, in a field, I thought I was going to leave forever.

By the time I reach the gate, I don't even need my phone. I already know the headlines. Some stories write themselves.

I drop into an empty seat and finally let myself exhale. This was supposed to be a clean break. A short flight and controlled return. I wasn't supposed to have overlap between the world I left and the one I'm trying to build.

I open my phone just long enough to send a text to my best friend, Lex, telling her I made it to the gate before quickly locking it again. It's short-lived when my phone starts buzzing.

Unknown number

I stare at it for a few moments before answering it.

"Yes?"

"I'm sure you already saw the end of the race," a male voice says.

I look up at the flight attendant beginning to usher people onto the plane.

"Hard not to."

A beat of silence.

"I know you're not officially on until next week," he continues, "but something came up."

I tighten my grip on my carry-on.

"What kind of something?"

"An opportunity," he says carefully. "Or a problem. Depends on how it's handled."

I exhale slowly as I close my eyes, the image flashing anyway—dirt flying, a rider standing stiff and furious. Not reckless but worse, volatile.

"I don't do damage control for egos," I say.

"We're not asking for damage control," he replies. "We're asking you to show us how you handle pressure before we expand your role."

There it is.

The test.

Memories surface. Years of being watched, measured, evaluated. Proving myself twice as hard just to be taken seriously. I'm getting really tired of that shit. No more.

I straighten.

"Fine," I say. "Send me what you can."

"We'll go over the rest in person," he adds. "Consider this... a preview. See you in two days."

The call ends.

I step into line, adjusting my bag over my shoulder. It feels heavier now, loaded with expectations I didn't ask for, but something else hums beneath it. Curiosity. Challenge.

Whatever they're throwing at me, they clearly think it matters.

But despite it all, I smile to myself.

Well, this will be interesting.

2

Axel

People talk about adrenaline like it's chaos. Like it's this wild, uncontrollable rush that takes over your body and leaves nothing but wreckage behind. For me, it's the opposite. Adrenaline is control. Absolute and unforgiving control. The kind that sharpens every sense until the world narrows down to throttle, balance, and instinct.

Was it easy? Hell no. Nothing about this ever has been. I fought for every inch of ground that brought me here. I've lived and breathed two wheels since I was in diapers. Before I could spell my own name, I could tell you the difference between a good line and a bad one. I've missed birthdays, holidays, normal childhood shit people take for granted. I've broken bones, lost friends, buried parts of myself in the dirt just to get back on the bike the next weekend.

I'm in the 450 class now. The bikes are heavier, meaner. They don't forgive hesitation. The second you stop respecting it, it humbles you. This is the class that separates the boys who *like* racing from the men who survive it. Who understand that fear isn't something you outrun, it's something you ride with.

And having a machine like that underneath me? 50-plus horsepower responding to the slightest twitch of my hand, vibrating like it's alive? That's the closest thing I've ever known to peace. Out there, nothing else exists. No past, no outside noise, no doubts. It's just me, the bike, and the line ahead. Perfectly controlled, or not at all.

This is my third year with Kawasaki and I'm determined to have my best year yet. To win a championship, even when the team has had a losing streak for the past eight.

Walking into the meeting, I knew it wasn't going to be good. The air conditioning in the office building is blasting like it's trying to do more than just cool me down. The 450 team manager, Jim, and assistant manager, Kevin, are sitting at the large wooden desk with their arms crossed.

"You two look like a set of parents after they found out their kid isn't going to college," I scoff as I sit down. Jim, with his shorter stature and signature sunglasses perched on his bald head, folds his hands and sets them on the desk.

"This isn't funny, Milano. The sponsors aren't happy."

That makes two of us.

"They are considering ending your contract," Jim says sternly.

"Seriously?! I didn't do anything! Did they watch the race at all? Did they see Rad cut me off and fuck me over?!" I sit up straighter and put my hands on the armrests.

I look to Kevin. His peppered short hair and matching trimmed beard show his years of experience. His facial expression unfazed, as he chimes in.

"You threw your helmet, left your bike on the track, which gained you a lot of penalties right off the bat. *Then,* to top it off, you almost punched Rad in the face and said some pretty foul words on national television."

"The bastard is lucky I didn't-"

"*Axel-*"

"-but Nationals is in a couple of weeks! You know I'm better at the outdoor races, Kevin."

I lean back, fingers locking behind my head, forcing myself to breathe.

"I know. I know. After kissing an embarrassing amount of ass, they agreed to keep you. But that was your last free pass. No more temper tantrums. No more penalties. One more incident and you're gone."

His voice is firm, but the edge wobbles. He doesn't love this any more than I do.

I fight the urge to roll my eyes and settle for tapping my foot like a ticking bomb. The situation pisses me off, but the message is clear. My career's on the line. I don't want to start from scratch with another team, not when I was that close to winning with this one. I gotta break this cycle. The staff's solid. The guys are good. So, I need to suck it up. Play nice. Be professional. Even if it tastes like shit.

Fuck me.

"Got it. Message received," I say as I stand to shake their hands to make up for my unprofessionalism.

"Oh, and one more thing," Jim says while trying to hide a smirk. "We hired you a personal PR representative to try and do some damage control. Your little freak-out is trending on social media and not in a good way. I know you hate the media and interviews, but you have to cooperate and work with her if you want to keep racing for Kawasaki."

"You've got to be kidding.." I mumble shaking my head with

irritation.

"Her name is Stephanie, and she will meet with you here at the Foxhole tomorrow."

"Awesome," I say flatly. I walk out of the office before I decide to do something stupid.

"Be nice!" They both shout after me.

"Yeah, yeah," I say to myself.

I really thought the slap on the wrist was it, and I'd be in the clear like the past. But, the rest? This has to be a joke. All this bullshit just because I got a little mad. Okay, maybe I had a major breakdown, but still... I don't need my own PR. If they knew the real story, then they wouldn't have pushed this new hire on me.

I'll just accidentally lose track of time and miss the meeting, problem solved. I could avoid her at all costs. But, the compound is only so big and that'll just delay the inevitable...damn. Maybe I'll just get her to quit. Bingo.

My head continues running through ideas about how I can get out of this mess as I walk through the Foxhole. It's basically a seventy-five acre Kawasaki training headquarters on the West Coast. Teams typically have their main hubs in either California, Florida, or the Carolinas, where it's warm all year round, giving riders an advantage. Personally, I'd take the California heat over southern humidity any day.

I walk up to the massive building that holds the heart of the Foxhole. The sun is still partially hidden by clouds, but I can feel the heat coming off the gray metal siding. The music blaring from inside the huge warehouse makes me smile.

Ben.

His six-foot, toned body, from years of hard work, is standing at his designated workbench with tools and parts spread before him. The aroma of cleaning materials surrounds him as a rag sits on his shoulder. His light brown head bounces to the music as he's completely in his element.

He's been my mechanic for years now, but my best friend for way longer. We were neighbors growing up and bonded over our love for two wheels. Even though he's a decent rider, his true love is the inner workings of the bike. That's where his true talent shows. When we were little, I'd wreck the bikes and he'd "fix" them. We've been the best team and inseparable ever since.

"Hey!" I half shout so that I don't scare the shit out of him. He turns around and lifts his chin towards me in greeting. His forearms flex as he wipes his hands on the rag. My bike waits on its stand, clean like it's never been ridden, the side number plate pulled off. The light above it hits just right, washing over it in a way that feels almost sacred.

14

The white plate with black numbers looks perfect against the bright green. Too perfect for a number that still feels like a loss I can't outrun.

That number one plate should be mine.

"How'd the meeting go?" Ben breaks me from my thoughts.

"Shit. Sponsors almost bailed, and I apparently have my own personal PR lady now." I complain, as I sit in the short mechanics chair that's nearby.

Ben grabs a socket wrench and mindlessly twirls it in his hand, as he shrugs his shoulders.

"At least you're not off the team."

Easy for him to say.

"Yeah, but who knows what torturous things I'll have to do now. I hate interviews and all that shit, man."

"Hey, maybe the new chick will be hot or something," Ben smirks.

"My luck, she'll probably look like Stacy." We both shudder at the thought.

"Hey, she was super nice though," Ben says defensively.

"If she was so nice, why didn't you ask her out?"

"Maybe because she had teeth missing and was old enough to be my mother?" We both burst out laughing. Ben always sees the good in people and balances out my negativity.

We then worked in comforting silence while we did the standard maintenance on the bike. I know it's not "my job," but it allowed me to focus on the task at hand and clear my head. I was starting to feel a little better about tomorrow.

When the bike was put back together, I clapped Ben on the shoulder and made my way to my little "on-campus apartment" in the bunkhouse. I claimed one of the top rooms for obvious reasons. While the balcony is nice, the rooms are pretty generic. I never personalized it. Didn't need to. With this profession, you never know when you'd have to leave. But, right now, it's home, since I don't have the luxury of a real one.

Once I get cleaned up, I walk out to the balcony to watch the remaining riders on the track. My hands grip the railing while the final water droplets evaporate off my bare chest. The last rays of sunlight begin to peak above one of the jumps. Slowly, the sounds of powerful engines get less and less until the track is empty. I lift my phone to take a picture. There aren't many words to describe it, so I just posted it on Instagram with no caption. It doesn't take long before the comments start pouring in.

"I hope you're getting extra practice in!"

"Rad doesn't even need to practice to be able to beat you."
"The view of you is better ;)."
"How does second place feel??"
"Wanna join Honda yet?"
"I hope they gave you your binky back after that race!"

"Fucking trolls.." I shake my head and walk back to the bedroom, plug my phone in, and set it on the nightstand. I stretch out on the bed, hands behind my head, staring at the ceiling. I've had the same routine for three years. Why do I have this feeling impending doom? Like a shoe is about to drop. I shake it off. I should get some sleep before I have to play nice.

Or not.

3

Stephanie

"That flight seemed longer than usual."

Cue the opening line of *Party in the U.S.A. by Miley Cyrus* playing in the background.

The baggage claim felt farther away than it actually was, my stiff legs not helping.

I should have upgraded for more leg room.

It's mid-afternoon, and the California heat is already bearing down. When it's only May. I guess I need to get reacclimated, and the time change is going to be a bitch for a second.

New York's weather was starting to grow on me, surprisingly. Not having it growing up, I was able to see the beauty in the snow. Even though it took three winters of freezing to death to finally see it. I rip my sweatshirt off and drape it over my suitcase.

I hear Lex before I see her. Walking out the entrance doors, I find her arguing with the airport staff. *Of course she is.* I smile to myself. She's always had that fire. Inside and out. Her big curly red hair blows slightly in the wind along with her bright yellow sundress. One hand is on her hip while the other is pointing to the car and then back to him.

I'm tempted to hide so I can witness how this plays out, but I wave instead. She finally sees me and squeals, which makes the man almost jump out of his skin.

"There she is!! I told you!" Her slender pointer finger jabs him in the chest.

The poor guy shakes his head in defeat or annoyance, I'm not sure, and walks away.

"Do you *have* to cause trouble everywhere you go?" I say as I hug her.

"Who would I be if I didn't?"

I laugh as we load my things into her pristine, vintage, baby blue, Volkswagen Beetle. I slide on my all black shades and my seat belt. Lex pulls down her visor, checks her makeup, and grabs her big gold sunglasses. She takes her time, like she wasn't just yelled at for parking here. After finally ignoring the beeping behind her, she peels out of the airport, driving like it's a Mustang instead of a punch buggy.

Cliche by mgk blares as I gaze out the window. I lift my face towards the sky, soaking in the sun. It feels good to be back with my best friend, in my home state, but I can't help but think about tomorrow. Do I know what I'm doing? Yes. Am I worried about the dynamics? Also yes.

I already know my family isn't happy, so seeing them every weekend during race season will not be fun. My mom has left me a voicemail stating as much, full of her disapproval. I look over at Lex, who's singing way out of tune, her red hair blowing out of the window. I wish I had her carefree attitude.

"You're not vibing. Why aren't you vibing?" She tries to yell over the music.

I start fidgeting with my hands as I take a second to answer. She reaches and turns down the music.

"Don't tell me you're nervous about the job?! You're going to kick ass! And hopefully get laid. You look like you need to loosen up a bit." The back of her hand hits my thigh, and I give her back a small forced smile.

"First of all, this job is a big deal! I need to focus on my career and avoid my parents," I point my finger. "And by the way, I am NOT getting laid, not happening!"

"You know you are always welcome to stay with me as long as you need! Plus, the extra bedroom has sat empty for months. You know I have a bad history with picking a roomate," she winces. "And thirdly, why not?! You'll have plenty of options I'm sure! You're hot! Just save one for me! I can't seem to find a decent guy anywhere."

"You can have them all. They are definitely not my type..." We instantly look at each other and start bursting out laughing.

I might have had a crush on a guy in high school that rode dirt bikes. But, it was short lived when he didn't know how to change the air filter which is one of the easiest things to do.

We both bring up embarrassing memories, reminiscing, and laugh the rest of the way. It proves that no distance or time could change our friendship. My mood quickly shifts to something more positive.

We pull into the parking lot, and my eyes land on my new home for the foreseeable future. The apartment building rises high above the street, sleek and impressive. It's smooth, glass, exterior catches the late afternoon light. The windows shimmer like mirrors, reflecting the sky and nearby trees so perfectly it's hard to tell where the building ends and the world begins.

Stepping inside, I'm greeted by a wave of cool, conditioned air and the faint scent of polished wood. The lobby stretches out wide and open, it's ceiling soaring overhead as if it belongs in a hotel rather than an apartment complex. Tall palms and leafy ferns surround the space. Clusters of plush, modern furniture upholstered in soft neutrals are staged in various corners. Everything seems designed to impress. The lobby makes visitors pause for a moment and just *look*. A place not uncommon in Southern California.

We get into the elevator with several other people who don't look all too happy with the lack of room we caused them. I try to look sympathetic as I awkwardly put my suitcase in front of me.

I forgot how lovely people can be here.

Lex makes sure to give everyone the biggest smile as she reaches over to press fourteen. Dodging each person as they tried exiting the elevator was a challenge in itself. I sigh in relief when we finally make it to the apartment door.

I set my sunglasses on the small table in the entryway, catching my reflection in the small mirror above it. For a two-bedroom apartment, it has plenty of space. The open concept main area matches the lobby's modern style. The kitchen is all up to date with granite countertops, modern fixtures, and stainless steel appliances. My eyes gravitate to a large Keurig on the counter, and I almost kiss it. I'm a bitch without my coffee.

I step down into the living room and see the large 75-inch flat screen TV centered on the wall. The electric fireplace below gives the space a cozy feel. The sectional couch dominates the space, giving you the perfect balance to either watch TV or the floor-to-ceiling windows. It has the type of view that makes you think you have your life together.

The apartment is split in half with a bed and a bath on both sides. Since this is technically Lex's apartment, she already has the room to the right, obviously. Just like her motto. She's always right. I smile.

I head left to my room and drop my suitcase by the bed. The room is the perfect size with two dressers, a queen-size bed, and a decent closet. I was so relieved when she told me it was furnished. No hassle of moving furniture from my parents' house and more importantly, no more pink.

Although I planned to get my own place, I am eternally grateful to Lex for letting me stay here. I'll be on the road every weekend for races anyway, so she'll still have her space.

Her dad gifted her this apartment when she started college. She has since graduated early with multiple degrees and has started her own tech company. She doesn't just have the beauty, but she also has the brains to back her up and has since doubled the money her dad gave her.

I collapse on the bed, thankful that I can finally relax, when my phone starts ringing. Well, that was short-lived.

Why the fuck is my mother calling me?!

I groan.

I glance at the clock on the nightstand. 5:00 pm. I'd better answer it, or she'll get mad and keep calling me.

"Hello?"

My mother's shrill voice fills the room.

"Where are you? Your flight should have landed by now."

"I just got to Lex's apartment."

"You're still friends with that bimbo?! New York should have at least gotten you some better people to associate with. Why didn't you come home?"

Why would I come home to that?

My hand grips my phone so hard I could break the damn thing. I don't respond, choosing silence over retaliation.

"Hello?! Stephanie?!"

I take a deep breath.

"I told you that I was staying with her, Mom. I'll stop at the house in the morning before I head to the Foxhole."

"Before you go work for a different team than your own family. I don't understand you, honey, I really don't. I tried seeing if Honda has an open PR position, but they are fully staffed at the moment. Even with the tons of money this family brings in! Ugh! I'll keep trying, though."

"That's okay. I'll figure it out," I say tightly.

Meaning, I won't change a damn thing.

"Alright, Hun, I'll see you in the morning! Make sure you wear red!" She must think she's hilarious because she's still laughing as I hang up and throw my phone down on the bed.

Her typical negative comments are nothing new. She never liked any of my friends growing up. I wanted genuine relationships, and I didn't care if they were rich or where they came from. But, my parents didn't agree. So, at the end of the day, Lex has been the only one willing to deal with my shit storm of a life, and I'm beyond thankful for her.

It goes to show you that a "picture-perfect" family is never perfect. It's a farce. Social media does a great job of adding to the facade of happiness. So, don't be fooled.

It's another reason why I wasn't allowed to post anything until my mother approved it. She had to make sure we looked good. Say the right caption. I guess I should give her some credit. The schooling, this career hopefully, it's been so easy, so natural, like I was made for this. Or groomed. Hard to tell.

She also drilled into our brains that once something is out there on the internet, there's no going back, so we had to really think about everything we posted. It took the complete fun out of it. Now I only use my personal accounts to creep, or for work research purposes. You could say I did both, on who I think is going to be my new coworkers, before I drifted off to sleep.

4

Stephanie

"Tell me again, why, I said I'd go home this morning?" I say to Lex as she makes me a fresh coffee. I yawn, grabbing some creamer out of the fridge and forcefully sit down at the island. The lack of a good night's sleep doesn't help the inevitable of seeing my parents. The unfortunately familiar feeling of anxiety makes every movement slower. It's always there at the worst times.

"Because you're dumb." Lex shrugs her shoulders nonchalantly.

"Yeah you're right," I admit. "It's just hard for me to say no sometimes."

I'll complain about my parents, rebel even, but a part of me still wants to please them. I still end up going back even though I regret it every time. It's a constant cycle that I can't seem to break. I'd talk to Rad about it, but he's a guy and just brushes everything off. Plus, they go easier on him anyways.

"You'll always have me!" She bats her eyelashes at me.

"Always," I smile at her gratefully, knowing I'd be lost without her. I lay my empty mug in the dishwasher. My signal that it's time to go.

I walk towards the entryway, taking one last look in the mirror. My long dirty blonde hair hangs in waves over my black polo. I'm also sporting dark jeans with short black combat boots. Professional enough but practical for a motocross setting.

"What are you still looking in the mirror for? You look hot!"

"Thanks Lex. Wish me luck!"

"With the job or seeing your parents?" she smirks at me.

"Both," I chuckle.

Twenty minutes later I'm looking out of the window of the Uber at the end of my parents driveway. I thank the driver as I step out. I figured I could at least pick up my car that I've left here for four years. I can see the red 2016 Honda Civic parked down the driveway. My parents could have bought me a mustang, but I refused to have anything fancy. My goal was to keep the attention on me to a minimum. It's better that way.

I walk up to the fence to buzz myself in. The gate clicking open like it's granting me an audience. Every house on the street is over-sized and over-confident. The manicured lawns and pristine hedges are as green as their money and just as smug. The kind of neighborhood that smells faintly of fertilizer and entitlement.

Yet, I annoyingly can't deny it. My childhood home is beautiful. The white siding still gleams like it wouldn't dare show age or dirt on it. The black shutters stand at attention while the wraparound porch looks as if it can be used for a magazine shoot or a carefully staged family memory. The large, multi-car garage being the only place allowed a little breathing room.

My dad, Paul was a world renowned Supercross champion and ended up starting his own business, Carson Machining, after he retired. He supplies after market and upgraded engine parts to factory teams. He met my mom, Diane, at a bar one night after a race which led to her being pregnant with Rad. Now she helps manage the business and flaunts the benefits from it. The cliche, one night stand story, except it landed her with his last name and the house with the picket fence. Some call their relationship love at first sight. I call it a business transaction.

My feet begin ascending the porch steps, the wood barely making a sound. I glance down at the simple and modern welcome mat. I hold in a breath, raising my fist towards the door. My heart jumps slightly when my mom swings it open. The cameras most likely warning her of my arrival.

"You're here!"

Her perfume hits me before she does. *Gucci.* Overly priced, with heavy floral and sharp sweetness.

"Yep. I made it. Is Dad here?"

"No, he's at the shop. He sends his love!"

Not surprised. I'd be at the shop too.

I walk in to the grand foyer and see that nothing has changed since the last time I flew in for the holidays. It's like it was plucked from a modern HGTV show, with white everywhere. White walls, white couch, white counter tops, no color to be seen. Still not my style. I like to see some personality, some personal touches, *some* color at least.

I want to avoid staying here any longer than possible, and realistically, I can't, *which was my plan,* so as soon as my mom leaves the room to grab me a water, I bail.

"I'm going to grab some things from my room and I'll be

right back!"

I climb the spiral staircase, my steps echoing down the hall towards the last room on the left. Muscle memory guides me there, like my body remembers the house better than my mind wants to. My fingers brush against the white door frame before it finds the handle.

The room is exactly how I left it. Pink walls close in around me, untouched by time, as if someone decided I'd never grow past them. A queen-sized poster bed dominates the space, dressed in a pink comforter that's been fluffed and smoothed into submission. Trophies and medals line the shelves, their metallic shine dulled just enough to feel like relics instead of victories.

God, I still hate pink.

I drift toward the desk and pick up the only picture frame left behind. Rad and I, barely more than kids, stand shoulder to shoulder in matching moto gear. His arm is slung around me, easy and protective, with a dirt track stretching out behind us like the future was wide open and uncomplicated. We're smilling. *Really* smilling.

We looked happy.

I was happy.

Everything was simpler back then. Before pressure, expectations, and whatever it was that slowly pulled us in different directions. Somewhere along the way, Rad grew quieter, harder to reach, hiding behind a practiced facade every time I saw him. It got old, pretending not to notice.

Still... I know he's in there. My same brother from the photo. Even if I have to dig to find him now. I set the picture frame on my bed as I turn to my closet.

I find a duffel bag and start filling it with whatever I might need back at the apartment. I grab extra clothes, shoes, all things that I'll sort through later. It's all practical, automatic, until my eyes snag on a flash of purple peeking out from the top shelf.

The bag slips from my hands and hits the floor with a dull thud as I reach for it. My fingers close around soft, silky fabric, familiar in a way that makes my chest tighten. I pull it down slowly.

My favorite riding jersey.

Mostly purple, cut through with black zigzag patterns that once felt bold and fearless. It still smells faintly like dust and adrenaline. Like early mornings at the track and late nights pretending I wasn't exhausted.

I hesitate, then reach up again and grab the rest of the kit. The pants, gloves, everything, before I can talk myself out of it. I'm not sure why I need it. It's not like I'll be riding at all.

Last, I slip the picture frame into the bag, tucking it carefully between folded clothes, and zip it shut. The sound feels final.

With my arms full, I take one last look around the room. The pink walls, the trophies, and the old version of me frozen in time. It feels like I'm finally closing an old chapter but I fear the book is still not over yet. I take one last look around the room before turning away and heading back downstairs.

"So, you really aren't moving back home?" My mom's concerned tone makes me slow my steps. I hesitate. I really can't move back home. I would literally go insane and need therapy. I take a deep breath.

"No, sorry mom. I love the apartment and it's closer to work. Plus, I'll be away every weekend anyways." The rehearsed response falling flat.

"Ah, where the enemy lives. Don't let them brainwash you."

A bit dramatic I'd say.

I turn my head as my eyebrows shoot up. It's a fucking Motorsport racing team, not a cult. But, my mother has always been extreme.

She makes it like I went against the family instead of just getting a job after graduating college. She was hoping I'd become a lawyer or a doctor or something. But, I didn't, and like always, she has to make it negative. It's about making the team look good, not tearing down others. I would never intentionally hurt them or make them look bad but she never listens long enough to understand that.

Looking at the clock, I see its 8:30 am. I'm supposed to be there by nine. *Perfect timing.*

"I gotta go Mom! I'll talk to you later!"

Maybe.

"Remember what I said! Don't forget about your family!"

Annoyed, I grab my old set of keys and haul my bag out to the driveway. The red bullet sits there, slightly dulled by the few years of sun and neglect, like it's been quietly judging me for abandoning it. I toss the bag into the back seat and slide behind the wheel, greeted by the stale scent of dust and upholstery.

The keys feel heavier than they should, dragged down by a ridiculous number of keychains. The race tags, cracked plastic charms, each little piece a reminder of my teenage years. I release the breath I was holding when the engine comes to life without hesitation.

I plug the address into my phone just in case, put the car in drive, and point the Civic towards Burbank. I mentally cross my fingers, silently hoping this wasn't a bad idea. I didn't even question if the car still ran or needed an oil change, nothing.

The short drive seems like a lifetime until I hear "Your destination is up ahead on the right."

I sigh in relief when I see a dirt road that everyone else would just drive by. I breath in, expanding my lungs, as I begin this new start.

Driving down the long entrance, I'm amazed by the size of the place. It seems like it's situated in the middle of nowhere but the city is just ten minutes away. Sporadic trees line the driveway and the angle of the sun makes me pull my visor down. I glance in the rear view mirror to see the dust trail behind me. It feels good to start something new, something of my own. I hope it'll all be worth it.

Situated at the entrance of the parking lot is a large metal sign with *The Foxhole* written in bold black and white letters. A green fox head and a dirt bike are painted behind it.
Cute.

I park at what I'm assuming is the office building, and look in the mirror to make sure my makeup is still decent. It's minimal, but an eyeliner smear would be unfortunate on my first day, even in a male dominated space.

I wipe my hands on my thighs to make sure they aren't clammy before I shake anyone's hands because *that* would be embarrassing. I grab my purse and step out of the car. My hand quickly flies up to my forehead in an attempt to shield my eyes.

Damn it's bright.

A bell chimes overhead as I pull open one of the double doors and walk inside. My eyes take a second to adjust as I'm greeted with a warm smile. A middle aged woman with short brown hair, sits at a simple wooden desk looking like curse words aren't in her vocabulary.

"Good morning, darlin! You must be Stephanie. I'm Sharon. You can head back to the conference room. Jim and Kevin will be in shortly." She flashes me a sweet smile as I give my thanks and walk back the hallway.

I find the room empty as I enter. I sit in one of the chairs and set my purse at my feet. My left hand mindlessly twirls the checkered ring on my right. Multiple Kawasaki posters line the wall and a small projector sits at the center of the long table.

Just a few minutes pass when my new bosses walk in. I stand to greet them.

"Good morning. I'm Jim, the 450 team manager, thank you for coming on such short notice," a shorter bald man says as he reaches over the table to shake my hand. I almost chuckle when I notice the sunglasses tan line hes sporting, stark contrast to his professional demeanor. I look over at the taller man who's graying beard and friendly smile greet me with a more gentle handshake.

"I'm Kevin, the assistant manager. You must be Stephanie. Welcome to what we call the Foxhole!"

They both have black Kawasaki polos on with an authoritative aura about them. But, you can tell in their eyes that they have soft hearts. Jim's is just a little more hidden. On the phone and in person. They gesture for me to sit as Kevin begins speaking like a little fan boy.

"Stephanie Carson... You're dad was a great rider. I remember his last championship win where he was ahead by seven seconds the whole race! The way he was able to conquer any whoops section still amazes me," he says as his face lights up like it's Christmas morning.

Yeah, yeah I've heard it all.

"And we use a lot of his parts for the bikes," Jim chimes in.

I internally cringe.

Is that why I got this job? I should have used an alias or some shit.

They gesture for me to sit back down as Jim waves his hand cutting straight to business.

"But enough of that. Your resume shows you achieved both a degree in public relations and communications. Being fresh out of school we understand you don't have much experience in this specific profession but we know you've at least grown up in the moto world. We wouldn't normally jump to hire someone this young, but honestly... we need the help."

Well, that's... comforting...

"We have a rider that needs some redemption in the public eye," Kevin chimes in.

My heart starts beating faster even though I shouldn't be surprised. I already know where this is going and who it is.

"One of our top riders, Axel Milano, didn't end the Supercross season in a positive way. I'm sure you saw what happened."

I nod my head.

"We need your help on improving his image. Interviews, social media, whatever you have to do. We need Milano in tip top shape for Nationals and with *no* incidents. He's got a temper, that one," They both shakes their heads in agreement. "If you're successful then we'll expand your duties and you'll be able to assist the whole team".

You can tell they truly don't want to lose him. Especially, when they're taking a gamble on me. I give them a small understanding smile. This season will be a test for not just me and my future in this field, but him as well.

"It won't be easy," Jim's serious tone makes me question what they aren't telling me.

"I'll do my best," I say confidently, despite the warning. "Where can I set up shop and start working?"
They look at each other like it was something they didn't think about prior to my arrival. Jim hesitates while Kevin covers for him.

"The Foxhole is at your disposal! Whatever works for you. We don't currently have any office space as of now but the mess hall has WiFi. You can also work from home some days as well and obviously you'll be on the road working remotely, for the races. Please let us or Sharon know the days you do work from home and if you need anything."

"Awesome, thank you," I smile.

"Do you have your own laptop or computer?"

"Yes, I have one."

"Great! I'm looking forward to you working the Carson magic!" Kevin says enthusiastically, rubbing his hands together likes he's at the casino. "We've heard great things!"

Carson magic.. yay.

"He's an amazing rider that we can't afford to lose," Jim adds. "Here's his schedule, and your ID lanyard. We told him he has to meet with you at ten this morning and that he has to give you a tour of the Foxhole as well," Jim says, smirking at the last part, surprising me with the glimpse of humor.

I give them a half smile, grab the paper out of his hand and look over it, accepting my personal assignment.

"Should I wait in here? Or head out to the track?" I say as I glance at the clock on the wall.

"He'll come in here. He should be about done with morning practice," Jim answers, checking his watch.

"Great! Thank you," I say. Kevin places his hand on the door frame as he looks back, hesitating a moment.

"Fair warning. He isn't entirely too happy about this whole situation."

"Understandable," I shrug as they leave the conference room.

So, Axel isn't happy about this whole thing, who would be?

I begin to brainstorm. It shouldn't be too difficult. This is child's play compared to dealing with keeping my family's image intact my whole life. One motocross rider shouldn't change that.

Right?

After being engrossed in my notes, I suddenly feel like it's been awhile so, I look at the clock again.

10:45

He was supposed to meet with me almost an hour ago. Where is he? I look over the paper again with his schedule on it.

Axel Milano's Schedule

0630: Breakfast

0730: Hydrating and stretching

0900: Motocross track practice

1100: Lunch

1230: Strength and Conditioning

1400: Motocross track practice

1600: Cool down and recovery

"Fuck this shit."

I start gathering my things. I'm not going to sit here and wait for God knows how long. I'll find him myself. He's probably trying to get out of this whole thing like a damn child. I yank the door open with a huff. I'm mumbling to myself as I pass by the front desk.

"Oh you're still here! Whatcha need honey?"

"Oh nothing, Axel was supposed to meet with me but he never showed so I guess I gotta go find him."

"He's somethin that one!"

Sounds like it

I walk outside and look towards the tracks. They are definitely not hard to miss. According to the schedule he should be either getting off the track or heading towards the mess hall. Since I didn't get a tour, I walk towards the track with the shortest distance from the office building.

Memories flash as the sounds of exhausts and the smell of race fuel hits me, the closer I get. Even though there are only a few bikes, it's still hard to tell who is who and it doesn't help that I can see only part of the track.

Must be a motocross one.

I look around deciding my next move. I peer to my right and see an observation tower. *Bingo.*

My boots stomp in the dirt as if I'm on a mission. In no time, I'm climbing my way up the stairs, my purse swaying on my shoulder. I'm too distracted and angry that I almost bump into someone when I make it to the top.

"Oh sorry!" I say breathlessly as I look up into a set of deep brown eyes. A middle aged man stands there in a green T-shirt, cargo shorts and flip flops. His floppy fisherman's hat is pressed in at the sides from the headset. His goatee moves up and down as he chews his gum.

"Don't worry, sweets! How can I help you?" He reaches and flips up the microphone.

"Hi, um, I'm looking for Axel Milano. Today is my first day and I'm not sure where everything is yet. He was supposed to meet with me over an hour ago. I figured up here would be a good place to start and give me a good vantage point. I'm Stephanie." I stick my hand out to shake his.

"Ah, you're the new girl. I did hear you are the one to have to deal with this sore loser," he says dropping my hand as he smiles. He jabs a thumb over his right shoulder. "I've had the, uh, *pleasure* of working with him for the past two years. I'm Rick, his spotter. He's currently by that rhythm section over there talking to Ben, his mechanic."

I grab the edge of the railing and look down onto the track. My eyes scan the multiple mounds of dirt until, I finally see the man of the hour. *Axel-freaking-Milano*. He's sitting on his bike like he doesn't have a care in the world. Like he didn't have a meeting to attend to. His dark, short, wavy hair is slick with sweat, his strong jaw clean shaven. He's wearing black and white gear and his black helmet is hanging on the handlebar.

Is it because he's a pro rider? Does he think he's hot shit? If so, that doesn't excuse his lack of respect for other people's time. I don't care who you are.

His left foot is propped on the peg and his right foot is planted on the ground. His mechanic, Ben, is holding a pit board with his head tilted like he's explaining something to him. It seems like Axel is listening intently, until I see his head start to turn. It's almost like he senses that something is off. Time slows as our eyes finally meet for the first time. I attempt to wave but he quickly looks back to Ben, ignoring my existence. My hand awkwardly falls back to the railing.

Oh hell no.

My hands grip the wood, knuckles white.

"Asshole," I mumble to myself before spinning around.

"Thanks Rick!" I yell over my shoulder as I storm towards the stairs to start my decent. He's not getting out of this that easy.

5

Axel

*O*h she's pissed.

Who I'm assuming is Stephanie, my new personal babysitter, is stomping her little black boots this way. Her long blonde hair blowing behind her like Medusa herself. Her right hand is gripping the purse on her shoulder, like a weapon that I'm sure she'd use against me. Let's see her try.

"This otta be good," I mumble to Ben.

I give her my most charming smirk as I look her up and down, hoping it makes her uncomfortable. From what I can tell, she has all her teeth at least.

Slight upgrade from Stacy

Ben tries not to react the closer she gets. The bike still idles underneath me. She walks right up to us with no hesitation. "Axel Milano?!" She raises her voice, competing with the bike's engine.

"Depends who's asking," I respond sarcastically as I cross my arms over my chest.

The restraint she's having to not roll her eyes is almost impressive. I uncross my arms, resting my right hand on the throttle and wait.

"Answer the-"

I twist the throttle, exhaust roaring to life as it completely erases her words. Flames appear in her eyes as she looks from me to my hand.

My smirk grows.

I might actually make this bitch quit on her first day. I let off the throttle and wait for her to speak again. But, instead she steps closer, her legs grazing the front tire. A small cloud of dust forms as her purse drops to the dirt.

What the fuck is she doing?

All I can do is watch as her hand slowly reaches over the handlebar. Her bright green eyes lock onto mine, and she...

No fucking way...

...kills the engine.

She just turned my fucking bike off. Without even looking. Never in my life...

The silence that remains is deafening. From the corner of my eye I see Ben's eyebrows hit the sky. Her lips quirk as she tries to contain her amusement.

The balls on this woman.

"Anyways... I'm Stephanie, your newest PR manager and you missed our meeting this morning."

"Oh, was that today?" I say innocently as I look at Ben. He gives me the *you're on your own* look and begins his escape.

"I'll, uh, take the bike back to the shop. I'm Ben, Axel's mechanic, nice to meet you." He shakes her hand like the goddamn gentleman he is and she smiles back at him. I shake my head and swing my leg over the bike, my feet hitting the dirt. He turns his head with his back to Stephanie and winks at me before he swings his own leg over the bike, riding away towards the shop.

Bastard

I reluctantly accept this minor defeat but it doesn't mean I'm going to be nice about it. Without saying a word I start walking towards the mess hall.

"Where are you going?" she calls after me as she bends down to grab her purse.

"Lunch," I toss over my shoulder.

"Great," she says coldly. Her smaller footsteps following behind me. It's a tense silence, my riding boots being the only sound. I take my time to prolong the awkward silence. I catch movement to my right but pretend I don't notice. I smile when I hear Stephanie's startled squeal behind me.

Heeehawwww

"Shit! A donkey?!"

I glance over my shoulder at her, attempting to not sound amused.

"Yeah, that's Marvin."

"What is he doing here?" She asks.

"Kevin rescued him. He lives here on the compound and gets to do whatever he pleases. Careful though, he might steal your food."

She nods her head and waves awkwardly to Marvin as we continue on. His gray ears twitch in acknowledgment.

I speed up slightly the last few steps as I see the glass door to the bunkhouse. I know it's childish but damn I can't help it.

I hear her huff as she swings the door open and steps inside after me. I keep a straight face like I didn't just let the door shut in her face, as I gesture around the room.

"This building is what we call, the bunkhouse. There are apartments that riders stay in through those doors and this room here, is the mess hall. There's also a gym on this main floor."

I grab a plate and get in line for the buffet. Stephanie, like a shadow, is right behind me.

"And in case you're wondering, my room is on the second floor." I give her a wink while she looks even more annoyed.

"Unnecessary information but thanks," she retorts.

Ouch

My attention goes back on the buffet. Multiple trays are lined up and each holds a variety of food. Some riders are on specific diets so there's always plenty of options. We silently grab some, then a drink and sit at a table near the windows.

"So, Mr. Milano. Is there a reason why you missed our meeting this morning?" I about choke on my Gatorade. *Mr. Milano...* that's...something.

She isn't afraid to jump right into it. I'll give her that. I lift my eyes and see that she's staring me down. Her piercing green eyes, unblinking. Her blonde waves resting in front of her right shoulder, elbows on the table. Her fork is leaning on the edge of her plate, food untouched.

I stare back, letting myself really look at her. After a few seconds I glance down at my food like it might hold all of the answers. Something is off, but I can't place it. The green eyes sure they're different and uncommon. Paired with the dirty blonde hair? Nothing unusual. She looks around my age and the moto community isn't *that* big.

Would I know her?

Maybe she looks like one of the girls from a few weekends ago. Tracy, I think her name was? I get them confused or don't care to know their names. Nah, that's not it, I would have remembered those eyes and that attitude for sure.

"I told you I forgot," I say, finally answering her.

"Moving on then. I assume you know why I'm here? What my job entails?" She quirks an eyebrow at me as she picks up her fork.

"You work for PR right? I'm your little assignment for the season. You are supposed to *fix* my image in the public eye, or some shit. Even though I don't need it."

I shrug nonchalantly even though there's a little tap at the back of my brain.

Damn she seems so familiar. Where is she from..

"Apparently you do need it if Jim and Kevin hired me. I watched your little freak out at the last race by the way."

"That wasn't my fault!" I sit up straighter as I slightly raise my voice. She gives me a look as I glance around the mess hall. A few heads glance over at my outburst. I shake it off and go back to my unfazed opponent.

"Then you had to have seen Rad run into me and force me off the track," I say more calmly. Then the wheels start turning.

Wait a minute

I look more closely at her features, her damn eyes, the way her mouth quirks. The way she's already managed to get under my skin. It can't be. I begin scouring through my memories. One after another until I'm forced to go back to the painful ones. And...

Yep. There it is.

Realization hits me like an oncoming train...

It all makes sense now. Why wouldn't it be her? She looks just like him. *Rad.* Fucking Rad Carson. I fucking hope I'm wrong...

"What did you say your last name was?" I cut her off, my tone instantly shifting. She notices.

"I didn't say." Her confident demeanor wavering slightly.

"What is your last name?" I say more sternly, returning her glare that she started this conversation with. She gulps, confirming my suspicion.

"Carson," she says with defeat and a bit of annoyance, at me or the situation I'm not sure.

"Son of a bitch!" My hand slaps the table.

I knew it! My mind starts racing.

Did Rad set this up? Did she lie and tell Kawasaki a different name? Did they not know she was related to Rad? That she was a fucking blood sucking Carson? The rich, entitled family? The family that just so happened to ruin mine?

A fucking game. And I refuse to play it.

"It's not what you think!" she says quickly.

"Not what you think?!" I scoff. "You think I'm fucking stupid?"

"I was hired to do a job. Plain and simple. And I'm determined to do my job well, regardless of who my family is and how *you* or anyone else feels about it." Her words fade as she glances out the window.

"Yeah, sure," I counter sarcastically.

There ain't no fucking way I'm going to work with a Carson. Not happening. She looks at me with her puppy dog eyes as she tries to convince me she's not full of shit.

"I promise I'll do my best to help you. I've already started making a game plan for moving forward. We'll begin with taking some pictures and videos for social media and I'll set up some interviews. We'll meet daily to go over your public image and get you ready for Nationals," she rambles on, pulling out her notes but I can't focus on any of it.

"I refuse," my deadly calm voice taking her off guard.

"You refuse," she repeats my words back to me like she's never been told no in her whole life.

"You heard me. I don't need anybody, especially a Carson."

Hopefully she takes my harshness and runs. Runs far away.

"Obviously, you do," she says. Her attitude returning. She begins to stand and gather her things.

"You got my plate right?" she says as she gestures to the table.

I say nothing.

"Thanks. I'll see you tomorrow morning."

She smirks as she meets my glare, and leaves me sitting there feeling stupid once again. I really thought I had the upper hand this time. I figured out who she was and she still didn't care. But, this time I'm not letting a Carson ruin the life I've taken years to build.

I watch her strut out the door before I forcefully grab her goddamn plate, like the bitch I am apparently. I will not work with her though, not happening.

Time to pay Jim and Kevin a visit.

I stomp like a child that didn't get their toy and head across the compound to their offices. I walk right past Sharon who looks confused.

"What are you up to darlin'?" She's a sweet lady but I'm too pissed to acknowledge her.

I knock on Jim's door since it's the first office I come across.

"Come in!"

Luckily, Kevin is in there too. When I'm in the mood, I call them "Schmidt and Jenko" from 21 Jump Street. I think it's quite fitting sometimes. They both look surprised when they see me.

"Did you know?!"

"Calm down Milano. What are you talking about?" Jim raises his hand and gestures for me to sit down.

"The damn Carson that's infiltrated the team!" They both look to each other with amusement.

"Ahh I see. You figured out Rad's her brother and Paul's her dad," Kevin says casually like it's no big deal.

"You knew?! Why didn't you tell me? You know how I feel about them." They don't know the whole truth but still.

"Of course we knew. Her last name was on the application," Jim says with a slight smirk as he starts typing on his computer. Kevin stands beside the desk and crosses his arms.

"Although I am a fan of her dad, her family isn't the reason why we hired her. She's actually qualified and we feel she's what we need to get you back on track."

"What if she's really here to get inside knowledge to use against us? To help *her brother* for Nationals?"

They both burst out laughing which, pisses me off even more.

"You're really full of imagination aren't you?" Jim shakes his head and stops typing to look at me. "In all seriousness, there is no debate. It'll just be for the season that you'll have to work this closely with her."

Well, this was no use and it's obviously not going the way I want it to go. I don't care if it's one day or a whole season, it's not happening.

"Whatever." I stand abruptly and storm out the same way I came with my tail between my legs.

"Be nice!" They echo, their tone amused.

If they won't fire her then I'll go to plan B.

I'll just make her so miserable that she quits

6

Stephanie

Using an alias sounds more and more tempting as the years go on. It would almost be easier to be honest. I could start over, truly make a life for myself.

The damn Carson name always makes people treat me differently. It's like a personality was forced upon me just by knowing who my family is. I was never given a chance to be... *me* until I went to college. At least in New York their focus was on other sports. I was able to finally breath.

I figured Axel wouldn't be too thrilled to work with me, but to absolutely refuse? And be a total dick about it? Not what I expected. All over a childish rivalry.

But, I'm determined to make something of myself. To not care what people think anymore. I'll do the best I can with this assignment, so that it won't matter what my last name is.

I make my way back to my car, thankful that the red exterior sticks out, since I never got the complete tour. I collapse onto the seat and toss my purse in the other, mentally exhausted from the roller coaster of a first day. I put on my sunglasses to represent the shade I was thrown today and pull out of the lot. It can only get better.

Right?

I try to keep a positive mindset as I drive back to the apartment and call Rad. I need answers.

"Finally call to congratulate me?" Well, he's as humble as always.

"Yes and no. First of all, congrats on keeping the number one plate. I knew you'd do it!" I say with my rehearsed overly enthusiastic voice. "And two, did mom tell you about my new job?"

"Thanks sis! You seem excited about it as always. And, Ahhh yes, it's all she's been bitching about for a week straight. How's team green anyways? Still mad they lost? Or...?"

"Well, thanks to you, I get the pleasure of working with your buddy Axel Milano."

"You're shittin' me! Ask him how second place feels." He can't contain his laughter at this point.

"Not funny Rad! He is downright refusing to work with me, because I'm related to you!"

Utter bullshit

He pauses and puts the act on hold.

"He is? That, uh, sucks." He clears his throat. "If it's too much for you, you can come work with us. I'm sure I can convince them to hire you."

Even Rad wants me to jump ship. Does no one have faith in me or what?

"I think I'm going to stick around here for a bit. I'm determined to change his mind."

"Well sis, in all seriousness, he's not a bad guy. I heard he hasn't had it as easy as the rest of us."

"What do you mean?"

"It's a long story," he clips.

"Oh, okay then," I say as the silence invades the car.

I get the feeling he either doesn't want to tell me or he's a guy that has the inability to give details. On the other hand it isn't my business to know anyways so I steer back to a lighter conversation.

"Any tips on dealing with a difficult rider?"

"Yeah, never let him get the upper hand," he says sounding grateful.

"Oh I can do that." I smirk into the phone.

"Let me know if you need anything!" he throws in, saying our goodbyes before we hang up. I smile knowing that I'm one of the rare few that sees the *behind the scenes* side of Radley Carson. He may put on a front but he's not heartless.

The next morning I arrive at the Foxhole with determination. Thankfully, it's cloudy, so the heat isn't too unbearable. I head straight for the tracks knowing he will most likely be there.

I catch sight of Ben first. His light brown hair is disheveled around his headset. He has a black T-shirt on that's fit snugly around his biceps. His kind eyes find mine as I stand next to him.

"Good morning Benji. How's Mr. Moody today?"

"Benji?" he chuckles beside me as he looks onto the track.

"I know we only met yesterday but you look like a Benji to me," I say with a slight cringe hoping I didn't just creep him out. He doesn't seem to care as he shrugs his shoulders, his smile not faltering.

"And for Axel? He's been better."

It looks like his mind goes somewhere that I can't place. *Interesting.*

I follows his eyes and spot Axel, in bright neon gear, launching over a double jump. Time slows as the bike whips sideways, before landing perfectly on the other side. He then takes the outside of a turn, picking up speed as he crosses a straight away, leaving ruts in his wake.

Just a few seconds is all it takes to see how powerful motocross is. To feel it. The pure discipline and strength you need to conquer it. Knowing from personal experience, it's why I chose to return and take this path for my life. Yes, I can ride a dirt bike, but I was never meant to race one. Did I want to at one point when I was a kid? Yes. Did my parents allow me? Hell no. Rad was their sole focus. At the end of the day it's hard ass work but as a hobby? It sure is fun.

We continue to watch for several more laps until he veers off the track towards us. Stopping in front of Ben, he takes his helmet and goggles off and hands them to him. Ben trades him with a water. I see a glimpse of a tattoo beginning on his right forearm. As he starts drinking, I watch the sweat drip down Axel's head and neck. One drip seems to go extra slow as it disappears under his jersey.

Of fucking course.

"I thought I told you I wasn't working with you?"

His cold voice breaking me out of my trance.

"I thought I told you, that I don't care," I fire back, as I give him an overly dramatic smile while putting my hands on my hips.

"Starting today, I'm going to be in charge of your social media, interviews, and get you ready for Nationals. Which is in less than two weeks. If you still want to race that is."

His eyes seem to darken as I explain each item on our agenda. He may not be happy about it but he has to get over it at some point. I'm not going anywhere.

I hand him my phone and he gives me a confused look.

"I need your credentials to log into your social media accounts so I can manage them. Sounds creepy, I know, but you're going to have to trust me."

"Sounds suspicious to me." He quirks an eyebrow.

"Would you like me to get Jim and Kevin to confirm or??" I hate using the *I'll tell the bosses* threat, but he needs to know I'm not bullshitting.

"I'll do it, but I still don't trust you Kill Switch," he sighs.

"*Kill Switch?*" My head tilts in confusion. This is karma isn't it? I gave his mechanic a nickname so he gives me one in return.

"Yeah. For killing the engine on my bike yesterday."

Ohh yeah, I hit his tiny red button and knocked him down a peg. Annoyance turns to pride knowing I got under his skin.

"Don't like when people push your buttons?" my cocky tone flat out ignored as he continues to use my phone.

My first two days here and I've already managed to get a nickname from my assignment.

Better than sweetie pie or something like that.

"Done. Don't make me regret it."

He hands me my phone and proceeds to put his helmet back on. And before I know it he's onto the track, continuing his practice.

I take the opportunity to pull my camera up for action photos. I managed to snag one of him in mid air coming off a jump which makes me quite pleased with myself.

"You do realize we have a photographer right?" Ben says sounding amused.

"I assumed but couldn't pass up the opportunity being that I haven't met everyone yet," I shrug. "Plus I want to start working on his socials as soon as possible." *Maybe I'll turn the picture into a meme after the season is over.* I smile to myself.

Ben leans over and speaks softly.

"And just know that I apologize for Axel's behavior. He still hasn't gotten over his trust issues."

My heart squeezes a little but I stand up straighter. *That's the second time I've been warned about something.*

What's his secret?

"I would never intentionally hurt him. I hope you know that. Carson may be my last name but it doesn't define who I am."

Ben nods his head in approval and we get back to work. The track buzzes with determination and also… freedom. You can tell they live for the sport.

On one of his breaks, I see Axel talking and laughing with a 250 teammate who I believe is Watson Mays, with the light brown hair and baby face.

Perfect

I lift my phone, snapping the heartfelt moment.

"Good eye," a soft voice says behind me.

I turn to see a red headed young man peppered with freckles. He has wire rimmed glasses and a shy, almost apologetic smile. He clutches his camera with both hands, the strap hanging around his neck like it's there to give him something to hide behind.

The photographer himself.

"Thank you! I was wondering when I'd get to meet you. I'm Stephanie, the newest PR specialist."

"Hi…I'm Casey." He awkwardly waves with one hand quickly placing it back on his camera.

"Nice to meet you. If you get any good shots of the grump

master please send them my way."

His mouth quirks in a small smile as he nods his head in understanding. I give a small wave as I pass him, saving him from a handshake that he probably wouldn't want.

I run to my car to grab my laptop and head to the mess hall. It's mid afternoon so the lunch rush is over. I work better with less distractions, anyways. I claim a table by the window and pick food that's easy to eat so I can multitask. I open my laptop and start with Instagram.

"Let's see what we're working with," I mumble to myself even though I might have already peaked at it the other night.

Pulling up his profile I see he has over a hundred thousand followers which isn't bad. His bio is short and sweet, Team Kawasaki, Moto Life, number 14, 25yrs. A photo of him on his bike is his profile pic. Classic and typical.

I start to look at his posts which aren't that many or often. His last post was two weeks ago before the final race. He finished first in Denver so the photo was obviously him crossing the finish line with his fist in the air. I check the comment section. Most of them are good, standard and some are a little harsh. They must of been added after the final race because they said *how does second place feel? Rads the better rider anyways* and so on.

Ouch

Axel responded with, *Fuck you.* and *Your mom rides pretty well ;)*

I shake my head.

Funny guy, I see.

Looking through my phone at the photos I took today, I go back and forth with which one I want to post. I love the one with Watson but end up going with an action shot since that's what he's mostly posted in the past. I add the caption *Ready for Nationals.* We gotta ease into this new era of his.

I switch things over to TikTok. His profile pic is the same as Instagram but his followers are more, five hundred thousand. I scroll through his videos which are a mixture of the typical race videos and some are of him talking face to face to the camera. I decide to go back to using my laptop so I can see them better. I watch the most recent one.

He sits in a chair in what looks like a hotel room. He has a plain black T-shirt on and a black chain, cross necklace. All paired with dark blue eyes that tell a hidden story.

A pure defeated and angry look is evident. He starts recapping the final race. His free hand waves around as he talks, his multiple scattered tattoos show on his forearms. But, even the tattoos do little to cover up the strong muscles as they flex with each spoken word.

Muscular, tatted, asshole. Got it.

I check the comments as the video replays. Most of the comments are negative unlike Instagram where it's mostly positive. It goes to show you that the more followers you have the more hate you receive as well.

His eyes draw me back in, even though he is explaining that everything was all Rad's fault. He doesn't apologize for anything and it lines up perfectly with his freak out on TV. Posting something in the heat of the moment is never good. And it's out there in the world, *forever.*

This platform needs some more work. I write down some notes on what I want to tell Axel. The first item is for him to not respond to negative comments. I proceed to edit and post a video of him *ready for Nationals,* echoing Instagram's caption, and hope it works well for the first step.

Next, is to practice for interviews and do some research. I look up past videos to see how he responds to certain questions and how fans respond in the background.

From my perspective he downright refuses certain questions and has even walked away from a motocross reporter at one point. The crowd obviously, boo's and yells afterwards.

Yeah, that can't happen if you want to improve your image. I hear the glass door open and look up to see, yours truly. Axel struts in, neon gear still on, and walks to the back of the room. His chunky boots on the smooth floor breaking the silence. He disappears behind a door, not once acknowledging me. I look at the time on my laptop, 6:00pm.

Oh yeah, he lives here.

I do a quick check on the posts I did and read a couple comments.

Not bad...

Guess, I should start heading back to the apartment. I begin cleaning up my table and pack my stuff away when I hear a deep voice.

"Why are you still here?"

I pause, slightly startled, but quickly recover and push my chair in. I look up to find a freshly showered Axel. He's wearing a black Kawasaki T-shirt and gray shorts that end a couple inches above his knees. His black hair hangs in short waves just above his brow as the same black cross necklace from the video hangs around his neck. He runs a hand through his hair and I witness tiny drops of water fling off of in slow motion.

Asshole.

"I work here, remember?" I say trying to look unfazed. It's just normal clothes. Nothing exciting.

I throw my purse over my shoulder and show him the ID

lanyard around my neck. I know they said its just for show when you're here but it's my second day and not many people know me yet. He glances at the badge unimpressed.

"While I have you, I wanted to go over some things with you."

"Like you'd ever have me," he scoffs.

"It's an expression. Ever heard of it?"

Holy hell this guy is infuriating. He ignores me once again and turns around. I reach and grab his arm before he can get too far. He looks down at my hand and I quickly pull back.

"Wait! It's just a few things," I say quickly, trying not to sound desperate.

"I need to eat."

He looks exhausted and I *almost* feel bad for delaying him.

"No, this will be quick and then I'm leaving."

He crosses his strong forearms and I can't help but admire the detailed skull tattoo on his right arm. I glance back up at him as he gives me a pissed off look but lets me proceed.

"Your Instagram looks good. I posted one action photo from practice today. TikTok on the other hand needs a little more work. You have more followers, which is good, but you have more negative comments to accompany it. The video already has a fair amount of views, which is a plus. But, stop responding to negative comments. Better yet, don't even look at the comments. Next, we have to go over in person interviews and practice typical questions and responses. If you want to look better to the fans you can't walk away from certain questions."

I raise an eyebrow at him with a knowing look. He doesn't even flinch as I continue.

"So, tomorrow I'll meet you here for breakfast and we'll go

over some questions before you go to the track."

He doesn't say a word as he turns his back to me and heads for the food. It's like I'm dealing with a toddler.

Bastard

"See you bright and early!"

I yell to him before I walk the opposite way. The door closes behind me and I smile.

He's going to love torture first thing in the morning. I'll make sure of it.

7

Axel

"Ughhh."

The blaring sound of my alarm brings me out of a deep sleep. I blindly reach over, halting the sound.

6:00am

The same time every training day. The only time it can differ is race days and rest days. But, even then I'm up early. My internal clock from this constant life, betraying me from ever sleeping in.

Being a pro motocross rider is a lot like other pro sports. You have to consistently stay in shape. You can't slack off or else it'll show on the track. Having less of an off season helps, when you don't even have the time to fuck off. Motocross is practically all year round at this point. The amount of strength and stamina you need to control the two-wheeled machine beneath you is unimaginable. So, not putting in the work isn't just being lazy it can be deadly.

I pull a shirt on over my head hoping it strangles me. I don't want to speak to her. I know she's going to talk my ear off and fuck up the rest of my day. Unfortunately, I can't avoid her or

54

else she'll find me like a damn attack dog.

I enter the mess hall like I have all the time in the world. My steps are slow as I take in the room. It's buzzing with riders and staff walking every-which-way making it difficult to grab my own food and find Stephanie. *Find* her, like it was even difficult. Not, when she's sitting in the center of the room begging for attention.

Her blonde hair is braided and resting on her right shoulder. Her eyes are focused on her laptop. A plate consisting of a bagel and eggs untouched beside her. Steam from her coffee meeting her eyes when she takes a sip. Her lips are on the rim of the mug, right as I approach the table. Her eyes quickly slide up to meet me and the control I have to keep a straight face in the next several seconds is astronomical.

She starts choking instantly and what a wonderful sound it is. I mean this isn't the first time I've made a woman choke, causing tears to form in her eyes, but there's something about this particular situation that does something to me. Revenge, karma, whatever it is, just made my black heart warm and fuzzy inside.

I try my best to keep my face in a neutral position as she tries to recover. I sit down across from her and pick up my fork. "Something wrong?" I say smugly.

"No. No. I'm good," she manages to say while she tries not to look at me.

"You have thirty minutes."

I actually have forty-five minutes but she doesn't need to know that. I see her glance at the clock and then her eyebrows scrunch.

"You don't have to be at the gym until 7:30."

Fuck

She memorized my schedule, already. Of course she did.

"Creep," I give her a disgusted look before pinching my shirt. "It's just normal clothes you know? Nothing to get all hot and bothered over."

She scoffs, practically choking again. It's almost like she hates how attractive I am. I could use this to my advantage. Nothing chases a woman off faster than insults and heartbreak.

She breaks me out of my planning to discuss the dumb interview crap. I don't see the point in it.

"You have to stay calm and if you don't like a question then try dodging it with something else, like thanking the fans or your team. Everyone feeds off of your reactions and positivity."

"Be fake and happy. Got it."

She ignores my sarcasm and continues on. I do my best to act like I'm not paying attention. To not notice how vibrant she is when she's doing her job. To not notice *how* she says the words and not what she's actually saying. But, it must be working, because with each short response I give her she gets more and more frustrated.

"I know you think I'm full of it, but I really am trying my best here. Believe it or not, I want more for my career."

Wow. She looks sincere, actually. I almost care.

"Did you not enjoy your life or something?" I say as I guarantee she had a cushy one.

"I went to college across the country, and don't work for Honda, so what do you think?" She quirks an eyebrow at me.

I shrug my shoulders as I take my last bite. She shuffles her stuff around to try and look busy, clearly affected and uncomfortable. Good.

"Anyways, I'll go over all of this with you before the first race, that way you're prepared. You know their first question will be about the results of Supercross, but I'll be there to help you."

I scoff at her as I stand up, ending any further conversation.

"I have to go grab my water and hit the gym. Thanks for cleaning up my plate for me."

I smirk as I leave her dumbfounded. Payback sweetheart.

This might actually be... fun.

The short walk to the gym does little to shake my thoughts from the woman behind me. I snag water from the table that's by the doorway. The gym is standard with various types of workout equipment, with one wall being a giant mirror.

Walking in, I see that Watson is already on the treadmill doing a steady jog. He's a nice kid that's racing in the 250 class. He's still in the early stages of his racing journey, but he has a lot of talent. You can tell he's someone that has his heart in the right place, but he still has a lot to learn. He is always the first one in the gym and I give him credit.

We give each other a head nod and get on with our own routines as I see AJ enter the gym. I put my headphones on and hit shuffle on my gym playlist. The first song is *Headstrong by Trapt* to hopefully set the tone for this session.

I start with a series of stretches, eyes locked on my reflection to keep my form clean. Every movement matters. Skipping this part is how guys tear something on the first lap and spend the rest of the season watching from the sidelines. Tight muscles don't forgive mistakes at high speeds, and the track exposes every weakness. I drink my water as I go, measuring, knowing dehydration turns reactions sluggish, and your grip weak.

The routine is second nature now. The muscle memory built

from years of knowing the difference between being prepared and being broken. It's automatic, the same way survival is.

By the time I finish stretching, Watson's already moved on to weights, metal clanking behind me, AJ refills his water, as I head for the treadmills. I punch the speed up higher than I need to and let my mind wander somewhere safer, like food, dirt bikes, anything that isn't her. But, it's short lived, knowing she has now infiltrated my everyday life. And this is just the beginning. The next song that plays almost makes me laugh with how ironic it is.

I Hate Everything About You by Three Days Grace.

I'm not surprised by how this morning went. Annoyed, sure. But not surprised. I honestly thought being a dick would scare her off a little. Most people back off when you make it clear you don't want them around. Apparently, she's not most people. That just means I'll have to try harder next time. Push more, be colder, and lay on the asshole charm thick.

The posts she put up don't help. I saw them earlier. They are clean, straightforward, the kind of updates I would've written myself if I'd bothered. No unnecessary flair or digging for attention. She didn't touch anything she wasn't supposed to, didn't mess with my account or overstep. That should be reassuring and it is, technically. But, that's the problem.

A small, irritating part of me almost wants her to handle more. Almost, wants to hand things off and focus solely on riding. But I don't. I can't. She's a Carson and, Carsons don't get the benefit of the doubt.

Not from me. Not *ever*.

I learned that lesson the hard way, and I'm not interested in relearning it.

Still, no matter how much I tell myself to shut her out, it

doesn't work. The thought of her keeps slipping in where it doesn't belong—uninvited, persistent. It pisses me off more than it should. Enough so, that I don't bother checking the distance as the treadmill keeps rolling beneath my feet. I increase the speed and just run. I run faster and longer like I can burn the irritation out of my system.

Five miles later, I finally hit the stop button and hop onto the rails, chest heaving, heart slamming against my ribs. My lungs feel like they're folding in on themselves as I grab my bottle and drain it without thinking, swallowing until there's nothing left. Sweat drips down my face, splattering against the belt. I tug the hem of my shirt up, wiping at my jaw and neck, but it's useless.

"Fuck it."

I peel the shirt off and toss it aside, heat still rolling off my skin. I feel guys' eyes on me, but I don't bother looking their way. If I can't run her out of my head, then I'm about to have a major problem.

8

Stephanie

It's press day.

I give one last look in the mirror, taking a deep breath. The first race weekend jitters evident, but I let it fuel me. "Here goes nothing."

Even though it's only a two hour drive, we arrived at Fox Raceway last night. The Pro Motocross season consists of outdoor races so everything starts earlier compared to the stadium races in the winter and spring. The riders need any extra minute of daylight that they can get, and it doesn't hurt to be early.

After the half hour drive from the hotel, I stand at the entrance to the pits. It's only 7:00am, but fans are already parking, setting up canopies, and firing up their grills. One of the event's staff members checks my credentials before letting me enter.

I spot the Kawasaki semi truck and wince. Of course it's parked near Honda's. Why can't they be on opposite ends of the parking lot? That would make my life so much easier. My head whips back and forth scanning my surroundings, acting like it's late at night and that someone is going to kidnap me or something. *Ridiculous.*

The trailer already looks busy. The bikes are sitting outside under the canopy, mechanics working on them, and the staff delegating. I just reach the roped off area when my father's voice booms behind me.

"Is that my daughter I see?!"

I was so close.

I turn around to see him walking towards me. He's got a Honda ball cap on, his credentials around his neck, and a big smile on his face. He gives me a quick hug and pulls back.

"I was hoping I'd see you before the race. How's the team treating you?"

"Great so far."

Except that infuriating certain someone.

"Good. I'd have to have a word with Jim and Kevin if it wasn't."

He pretends to act all serious and I give a half smile. I peak around him.

"Where's mom? I figured she'd be here."

"She's still getting ready at the hotel. You know how she is when there will be cameras around."

Not surprised.

"Well, I better head in. I have to do interview prep. Tell Rad I said hi and good luck."

"Sounds good, Hun. Talk to you later."

Well, that wasn't horrible. I turn back towards the truck and see Axel glaring at me through the doorway like a scary movie.

What the hell is his problem?

Jim and Kevin greet me as they pass by. I enter the trailer. Axel is now sitting on a couch with shorts and a Kawasaki polo.

His right ankle is propped on his left knee.

"Getting some tips to fuck me over this weekend?"

Okay then

"Well good morning to you too, sunshine. If you are talking about the chat I just had with my *father*, then you have nothing to worry about."

I sit beside him just to annoy him more. He crosses his arms so that his elbow digs into me. I refuse to move and push *my* elbow back into him like we're damn kids, stopping shortly after, when I realize how ridiculous it is. I forcefully set my phone down beside me and turn towards him.

"What's your deal?" I say sharply but quietly. "Rad cuts you off once and suddenly you're hostile to his entire bloodline?"

His jaw tightens as he stares straight ahead.

"There's more to it than that," his words clipped.

"Then explain."

"Not today."

We sit in silence for a moment. I know men don't talk about their feelings, so I'm not surprised that he didn't pour his heart out to me. I only just met the guy a week ago. And especially if I'm an "enemy" of his. Today isn't the day to mess with a rider's head, so I don't push any further.

"Let's go over questions," I say instead.

"Fine." He straightens.

I pick up my phone, holding it like a mic, slipping into reporter mode. I even exaggerate my voice so he gets the picture.

"Axel Milano. How do you feel going into this weekend after losing the Supercross title?"

He stares at me like I've lost my mind.

"I'm giving you the full effect," I grin.

"I can tell."

"Well? Answer."

He sighs. "I'd say... pretty good. I enjoy outdoors and I always want to win. Past races don't change that."

I blink. "That was... actually good."

"Surprised?" His eyebrow lifts.

"Yeah. Why can't you do that live?"

"Because, *live*, I don't care."

"This weekend, you should," I say pointedly. "They'll try to rattle you."

He nods once, giving me the bare minimum. I have a feeling it's not going to get any easier when it comes to him.

The press conference later that morning is exactly what you'd expect—long table, flashing cameras, riders lined up under sponsor banners. Axel sits stiff, arms crossed, jaw set, answering questions with minimal effort. Controlled, irritated, dangerous. And frustratingly compelling. My page, full of notes already.

Race day is a blur of preparations, qualifying and interviews. Members of the 250 class and 450 class sit at one table under the Kawasaki awning, signing the posters in front of them. Families wait in line while kids jump with excitement. Their faces shine, while their tiny hands hold sharpies, just happy seeing their idols up close and personal. Girls show up in droves, and I absolutely do not notice how Axel's smile sharpens when they flirt.

Nope. Don't care.

Before we know it, it's time to head to the starting gate for the first moto. Ben hops on the back of Axel's bike, the crowd cheering as they go by.

The sun is already blazing overhead, unfiltered and relentless, forcing me into my sunglasses as heat radiates off the dirt track. Dust hangs in the air, clinging to my skin, so I twist my hair into a low bun to keep it off my neck and out of the way. I walk with the rest of the staff thankful I haven't broken an ankle on the uneven ground.

The gate is crowded with forty riders and their mechanics. This is the first of two, 450 motos. Each race lasts for thirty minutes. You get so many points depending on what place you finish. The best average calculated after both motos, wins.

Axel was one of the fastest qualifiers which gives him a better spot in the gate. Today he's sporting a light blue jersey, matching pants, and his signature black helmet. Ben is talking behind him, holding his goggles. I walk over to them to make sure Axel's okay after our talk yesterday.

"You ready?"

He twists, looking back, like he's surprised I'm there. I smile at Ben and he gives me a nod.

"Yeah, I'm ready," Axel says as I'm suddenly pushed forward, my hands flying out.

What the hell?

Luckily, it wasn't hard enough to make me fall head first into Axel's rear tire. I turn around to see who the asshole is. One of the Red Bull girls, with her blue booty shorts, stands there with a smug look on her face. Her long, picture perfect, bleach blonde hair hangs over her picture perfect fake tits.

"What do you want Bethany?" Axel says coldly.

She definitely looks like a Bethany.

Ben's eyes widen as if to say, *oh fuck,* and pretends he's fixing the goggles, but he's not fooling me.

"I just wanted to say good luck today," she says seductively. "I'm free tonight if you want to hang out."

Her voice making me wish I would've went face first into a tire or ran over by one of these bikes. She then leans over and sets her hand on the rear fender and speaks more softly.

"It's been awhile you know."

Ohhh

"We'll see."

He looks up and then turns around, dismissing her. His tone indifferent. *Bethany* makes it a point and winks at me as she struts away. Flicking her hair in a pure Regina George motion.

Bitchhhhh

Obviously these two have a history and frankly I'm not surprised. Good body or not, it's probably as enjoyable as fucking a pit board. Same personality at least. And this is all that I gathered from just meeting her. But I digress. He can be with whoever he wants to be with.

I attempt to bring my scattered thoughts back to reality. I look at Axel and awkwardly wish him good luck.

"You going to wish me good luck sis?"

I didn't realize Rad was that close. He's sitting two positions over and I had no idea. He probably just witnessed the whole Bethany encounter as well.

Awesome

"Hey Rad. Good luck out there."

"Try to sound more sincere next time!" he laughs back at me.

"Be careful, okay?"

I'm definitely more sincere with that. You never know when a race will be your last.

"Always."

He nods and puts his helmet on, locking in. I take one last glance at Axel and instantly regret it. Daggers aimed to kill are what I see. Guess speaking to any member of my family is a no go? I hold back from showing him my middle finger and move to stand behind the barriers to wait for the gate drop.

The fans are up against the track, spread out around the perimeter. These outdoor races let you get up close and personal which they love. I don't blame them. Looking around, it is as exciting as I remember. The nerves, the engines, the crowd, the warm weather, how can you not love this atmosphere?

The gate drops and it's pure chaos. Forty riders fight for the holeshot, a few crashing before they hit the first turn. Eventually the riders spread out among the track with Axel, Rad, and Zane, Yamaha's top rider, in the top three. Axel and Rad battle back and forth throughout the whole race. They focus so much on each other that Zane, the veteran, speeds right past them to win the first Moto. Axel then coming in second and Rad in third.

After moto one, the three of them make their way onto the small stage for the interviews.

I hold my breath the entire time Axel speaks.

"Axel, congrats on finishing top three in the first moto. Did losing the Supercross championship make any impact on your performance today?"

"No," his tone a tad harsh paired with a dramatic pause, causing me to cringe. "It's a new motocross season and I plan to win every race."

"Sounding quite confident! Speaking of confident lets move to Rad Carson.."

I can finally breathe again. He didn't do too bad. but I feel a few of the other team members glance towards me. Almost like they feel I'm already failing. I could be overthinking it.

But, at least there's room for improvement? We have one more moto and hopefully only one more interview to go.

"Are you Stephanie Carson?"

I turn to see one of the Pro Motocross staff members.

"Yes?"

"We would like for you to come up to the booth, to do an interview with the commentators before the next moto. If that's alright?"

They're asking *me* for an interview? My job is to watch *other* people do interviews and prep them for it.

"I, uh, am busy working as this is my first race with the team. Is there a chance to do it at a later day or time?" I ask.

"They are aware and have already informed the team managers for you. They promise that it'll be quick."

He seems sincere as my mind goes back and forth while the surrounding crowd does little to help my anxiety with the decision.

But, at the end of the day, how can I say no? Would it hurt the progress I'm trying to make? I know how these people work.

So, I follow the gentleman up to the booth where the prized pair is. Cal and Scott have been the main announcers for years, not giving up their spots for anyone.

Scott greets me first with his Australian accent as a staff member hands me a headset.

"Ms. Carson! Thank you for joining us!"

He gestures to a seat opposite him and Cal. I put my hands in my lap while I start twisting my checkered ring. They never bring women into their sanctuary. What could they possibly ask me?

"Of course! You can call me Stephanie," I say as I notice

how they are just going to throw me live on camera with no warning. Good thing this isn't my first time.

"Welcome race fans! We have a special guest here today, Stephanie Carson!" I give a rehearsed wave to the cameras. "If you don't know, she started working for Kawasaki this season. For public relations correct?"

"Yes! I help riders with their communication skills, social media and public appearances."

Time to go back to my training and schooling. That's why I say *riders* and not *rider*. Yes, I lied and I'm technically only helping one rider. But, I refuse to sell myself short or have them thinking of me any less. My back becomes straighter as I make sure to sound confident and to look at the camera periodically like the seasoned robot I once was.

"This isn't your first time around dirt bikes is it?" Cal chimes in with a smirk.

I know where this is going so I might as well play along.

"No, this is quite normal for me. I grew up surrounded by all things moto. My dad is Paul Carson and my brother is Rad, who you may know."

Both of their eyes light up like the ball just dropped on New Years.

"Your dad is one of the legends! I remember him winning many races at this very track back in the day."

"And Rad seems to be following in his footsteps!" Scott adds.

"Yeah he's doing great!" I say with as much enthusiasm as I can muster, as I adjust the microphone. I give them my best smile, hoping this is almost over.

"Currently, as the viewers know, Rad's racing for team Honda, which is who your dad raced for as well." I nod my head in agreement. "Why didn't you try to get with them? You could have made it a whole family affair."

Scott tries to say it jokingly, but I know how these two operate. The only reason I'm up here is to gossip and get views. Well, I'm not going to fall for it. I'll "joke" right back and beat them at their own game.

"Well, actually, I was trying to get a job up here." My face a mask of seriousness as my eyes look from Scott to Cal.

Crickets.

"When you both retire of course," I say, lifting the mask, plastering on an innocent smile. Even though taking one of their jobs would be so satisfying, I would want to earn it. *Note to self.* I might just add that to my lifetime career goals.

They both awkwardly laugh, looking slightly relieved. Little do they know I could easily do their job. I may not have raced, but I know all the ins and outs of motocross. And I can actually form a sentence unlike these two sometimes. Apparently you just have to be a former motocross racer, be in the clique, and have a dick to be able to commentate. So, making them sweat, even for a brief moment, has made my day.

"You had us there!" Cal says pointing at me. The tension easing as we chuckle together.

"Thank you, Stephanie for chatting with us. I'm sure you gotta get back to the team," Scott says.

"Yes, thank you!"

I walk out of the booth, well tent, smiling to myself until I practically run into the ice queen herself.

My mother.

"I did you a favor and there you go and ruin it!" she whisper shouts at me.

So, that's why they even knew who I was and why I was there. I should have known.

"*You* set up the interview?" I throw back at her.

"Of course I did," she says cockily. "Figured if you got on TV, and showed those Carson good looks, Honda would want to hire you on."

"Wow, thanks." My words short as my brows lift, my jaw tight.

"You're welcome!" she tosses back sharply.

I walk past her and make my way back towards the gate. The riders are starting to set up for the second moto. I try to play it cool, but I went from a high to a low real quick. I'm fucking pissed, too to be honest.

I try to keep my head down to hide my whiplash, but I glance up and lock eyes with Axel. He's standing beside his bike, putting his gloves on. His face is still peppered with dirt as his jersey clings to his built frame. All things that should distract me from the bullshit that happened but it ends up making me more pissed.

Fuck him. Fuck the dirt.

I sound like a child right now. Wow.

Ben starts to push the bike towards the starting gate. I wonder if they even heard the interview. Sometimes they play them over the speakers. But, with all that's going on chances are low with anyone even hearing it. Hopefully not since Axel's walking straight towards me.

"What's wrong," he says sternly like its more of a demand than a question. And why in the hell did it hit me straight in the vagina? How did he even know? I guess I didn't place my mask back on well enough.

"It doesn't matter," I shake my head.

"Apparently it does, when you storm down here to tell me how I should act when I should be telling you that."

Ouch

He's not wrong, though. I shouldn't let stupid shit get to me and listen to my own advice. But, he doesn't understand what I've dealt with my whole life.

"You're right. You're right. I was just caught off guard. Anyways, thank you."
I ramble and give him a small smile. He, of course, doesn't return it. In race mode I'm sure.
"Go win your race, Milano."

He nods and walks away. I stand there a moment until I suddenly feel like someone is watching me. I peer over to see bitchy, I mean *Bethany* giving me looks that could kill Satan himself. I give her my cheesiest smile and wave at her like she's my best friend. She gives a look of pure disgust and turns around.

Bitchhhhh

Fans begin to cheer as the bikes start their engines. The smell of dirt and race fuel fills the air. The sound of the gate dropping making my heart beat faster. There's so many riders in one tight area that I can't tell who's gotten ahead or who's fallen off the track. I try walking up the closest hill to get a better view.

My eyes scan the track, searching for flashes of green and red until I finally spot Axel and Rad buried in the middle of the pack. For a split second my stomach drops, but thirty minutes is an eternity in motocross. There's plenty of time to recover. Plenty of time for things to go wrong as well.

Lap by lap, they start to carve their way forward. Both of them ride with the same ruthless efficiency. They hug the inside of the turns, launch down the straightaways and, skim the rhythm sections like the dirt barely touches their tires.

There's no wasted movement, no hesitation. Winning isn't just the goal, it's the expectation.

By the time the pit board flips, they've clawed their way into second and third, the crowd feeding off of the battle building between them.

They trade positions through the next few laps, neither willing to give an inch. My heart hammers every time they come through my line of sight, bikes nearly overlapping as they push harder and faster. Then, with two laps to go, everything shifts.

Axel gets tangled with a lapper, someone already a full lap behind, and the delay is just enough. Rad slips past, clean and decisive, opening a gap Axel doesn't have time to close. Axel throws everything he has into the final lap, riding on the edge of control, but luck isn't on his side today.

Rad crosses the finish line first. Axel follows in fourth. Somewhere along the way, Zane goes down, a crash that drops him back to eighth.

When the points settle, Rad stands on top.

Which means Axel won't be happy.

My nerves spike instantly as I start down the hill toward the podium. Rad grabs the champagne, already grinning as he steps forward to spray his team and the fans below. Axel stands stiff beside him, runner-up trophy clenched in his hand, posture tight and unreadable. From a distance, he looks composed.

But I know better.

And the post-race interview is only seconds away.

"Axel, congrats on making podium! What was going on in your mind out there?"

Here we go

"Things were going well," he starts, jaw tight, voice clipped. "I had the pace. I was closing the gap, lap by lap."

He exhales hard, the smile disappearing mid-sentence.

"But between lappers who didn't know how to get the hell out of the way, blue flags that might as well not exist, and a track that broke down into a one-line mess, I didn't get a real chance to race for the win."

The crowd murmurs.

"I'm not saying it wasn't possible," he adds, eyes flashing. "But when you're fighting traffic, bad decisions, and conditions all at once, it stops being a race and turns into damage control."

He shrugs, sharp and frustrated.

"So yeah—it cost me today. I'll own what I need to, but a lot of things out there made it harder than it had to be."

The mask slides back into place just enough to pass.

"We'll reset and come back swinging."

I wince. It could have been worse, I guess.

9

Axel

I scroll on my phone looking at race footage, posts, and comments, not able to relax.

Why do I do this to myself?

Overall, the fans weren't happy with my loss and how I handled it. Like they would feel any different in my situation. And if anyone knew the shit I've been through? They wouldn't think twice about my behavior.

I checked the posts that Stephanie did. Still, no secret comments, DMs or anything suspicious. As far as I can see, she hasn't lived up to her last name... yet.

I go back to scrolling on TikTok but pause when I see a clip of Stephanie in the announcers booth. What the hell is this? I check when the video was posted.

Yesterday

When would she even had time to go up there? I watch closely and turn the volume up. It starts out with Scott and Cal's typical smug faces. Stephanie is to the right of them with her annoyingly, pretty smile. She exudes confidence. It's disgusting.

Hearing their questions breaks me out of my trance. I scoff when they just *had* to ask about her family and why she wasn't working with them. The whole interview is odd if you ask me. They rarely bring people in the booth with them, especially women. But then again, she is a Carson.

"Wait what did she just say?"

I replay the last few seconds.

"Well, actually, I was trying to get a job up here."

The look on Scott and Cal's faces is priceless. It even puts a small grin on my face. And I never cared for the politics or trying to "fit in".

Questions begin to swirl in my mind. Is she smarter than I think she is? What game is she playing? And why in the hell does seeing her smile make my pants tight?

My thumb hovers over her contact, demanding to do something bold. The name "Kill Switch" in all caps waiting there for me. When she gave me her phone to log into my social media, I might have added my number, texted myself, and then deleted the message. Don't ask me why. Call it a fail safe. I'm surprised she hasn't asked for my number anyways due to this "improving my image" bullshit. But, whatever, I hit send anyway.

Me: Nice interview

I smirk picturing how she'll react. A few minutes go by when I get a response.

KILL SWITCH: Mr. Milano? Really??

How do I have your number in my phone??

Me: You thought riding dirt bikes was my only skill??

KILL SWITCH: Gross

I huff a laugh. If I was desperate and willing to show her,

she might actually enjoy my other skills. It'd probably be the first time she felt satisfied in her life, too.

Speaking of someone that felt a little too satisfied, my phone pings with a text from Bethany. A chick I fucked because she was hot. Something that all riders try to do... lay a Red Bull girl. Unfortunately, she liked it too much and thinks I actually have feelings for her.

Was I desperate enough to fuck her a couple times? Yes. Even though it was boring it was convenient what can I say? But, it's a new moto season and I don't need any dumb shit to get in my way.

"Missed you last night. You free today?"

Even though, I've used her to "recover" in the past, I have my own plans.

I'm not blind. I saw her push Stephanie before the first moto. She must feel the need to mark her territory, like a fucking chihuahua. Well, news to her, no one owns me.

"Hmpf, yeah fucking right," I say as I leave Bethany on read, hoping that she'll move on. I go back to other text thread with Kill Switch.

KILL SWITCH: Anyway, speaking of interviews.. we should go over stuff today

It's like having your parents make you study after you told them you have a test tomorrow. It's your own fault you told them. Now I have to accept the fact that I fucked up, all because my bored self got in the way. I try to ignore the slight pulse increase at the thought of her coming over. *Fuck me.*

Me: Fine

KILL SWITCH: Where are you?

Me: The bunkhouse

KILL SWITCH: I'll be over in 20

Not sure how I feel, I throw on a fresh t-shirt and shorts and head down to the mess hall.

"I just need food that's what's wrong with me."

Stephanie

"You gotta take me to one of these races. They sound like so much fun!"

Lex is sitting on the couch, listening to me recap the race like it's a reality TV show. Her eyes are wide, a smile lighting up her face, as she waits for each detail. All she's missing is the popcorn.

"You do realize you can watch the race live on TV, right?" I raise an eyebrow.

"Yeah but it's way better when you explain it," she winks at me.

"Only because I give you the juicy details," I smirk.

"Speaking of... how's the hottie on the green bike?" she wiggles her eyebrows, clearly amused with the current thorn in my side.

"Good 'ol Axel Milano... He's difficult to say the least," I huff as I sit down next to her.

"Difficult *not* to look at you mean?" she gives me a sly smile and it makes it really hard not to return one.

"No," I stand abruptly. "He's infuriating!" I begin to pace. "He's treating me like shit on purpose and I don't entirely know why," I pause to glance at her and sigh. "And yesss he's attractive." I continue my pacing and rambling. "It's bullshit actually. Not that I'd ever entertain that idea, because he's a rider and I've sworn to never go there. AND most importantly, my job is on the line. If I don't get him under control, I'm jobless after the season is over."

"Ugh! You and that stupid rider rule!" She waves me off. Lex is grouped with the majority of people that don't understand how difficult it is for women to gain respect in the moto world. But, I love her anyways.

"That's what you got out of all that?" I ask as my phone beeps.

Lex glances down at it on the coffee table and squeals.

"What is it?" I ask before looking myself.

Mr. Milano: Nice interview

"Wait?! Is that him?!"

I cautiously pick my phone up.

"It looks like it, but I never got his number. How did he..." I trail off.

Wait a damn minute. Did he really manage to do this in the two seconds he had my phone to log into his social media? Why wait till now to reveal the move he played me with? Also, I thought he hated me?

Men confuse me.

"What's that look for?" Lex questions.

"He said nice interview," I look at her, still puzzled.

"What?! Did he know we were talking about him?" She can't contain her excitement.

"I do have to go over things with him," I say as my wheels start to turn. This could be an opportunity.

"Go see him!!" Lex says with way too much excitement.

"I told him I'll be there in twenty," I gulp.

"You better go!" She's gestures to her coffee and TV remote to show that she'll be fine by herself.

I take off to gather my purse and check myself in the mirror while mumbling about why he even texted me in the first place.

"Maybe he likes you?!" she yells after me.

"Good one Lex! He hates all things Carson."

"Maybe you can change his mind? Ruin his sex life because he'll only think about you?" she adds and I laugh. When pigs fly.

"Keep dreaming!" I toss over my shoulder as I close the door behind me.

I leave the apartment building with, shall I say, nerves?

"What is wrong with me?"

10

Axel

I claim a table by the windows, like I didn't have a choice, and pick at my food. I try to enjoy it. I really do. But even without her here, my brain insists on running worst-case scenarios. Her sliding into the seat across from me. Those perfect lips moving while she tells me what I should do, how I should say it, how to not tank my own career. Helpful. Necessary. Maddening.

Congratulations, Milano. You've officially let someone live rent-free in your head.

Every bite tastes worse, the longer I sit there. She's like a fly that won't get the fuck away. Keeps buzzing, keeps landing, no matter how much you want it gone. The only difference is, this one has opinions. And eye contact. And apparently unlimited access to my thoughts. It's bullshit.

Then the door opens.

Not surprised.

She walks in, right on cue, like my irritation summoned her. Dirty-blonde hair falling in loose waves, sunglasses perched on her head like she didn't just step out of my mental spiral. Her white shirt and jean shorts are casual and effortless. Completely unfair. Because somehow she still manages to look like a problem I didn't order.

Our eyes lock immediately, because the universe has a sense of humor. She smiles, with an easy confidence, like she already knows I'm annoyed and doesn't care. I wouldn't be surprised if she enjoys it. She heads straight for me, drops her bag onto the chair beside her, claiming the space like it was always hers.

Fantastic.

Just what I needed. A front-row seat to the very thing I'm trying to get away from.

"How are you today?"

Is she fucking serious?

I almost spit my water everywhere. I lost the first race of the season, to her brother of all people. I'm angry as hell, but do I tell her all of that? Does she actually care how I feel? Of course not, so I give a typical answer.

"I'm fine."

She raises an eyebrow at me like she doesn't believe me, but moves on anyways.

"I was thinking we should schedule an interview or do some sort of event to make up for the lack of emotional control that you so lovely have."

The corner of her mouth quirks up at an attempt to try not to smile. Is she amused with herself? Of course she is.

Hilarious

But, her confidence in herself brings me back to when she shut my bike off. She thought she was so damn clever. It did catch me off guard, I must admit. But, right now, it also gives me a perfect idea.

"I know an event we can do here at the Foxhole."

"Really?"

She sounds surprised and excited. For now.

"Motocross is mostly a male dominated sport, but I know a lot of women and young girls are getting more interested in it. So, let's host a female only class," I say with sincerity.

I actually feel pretty proud about my idea. I'll be even more proud knowing how jealous she'll be when I teach a bunch of women how to ride a dirt bike. My suspicion confirmed seeing the way her body froze for a split second, before she quickly recovered and acted like it's a great idea.

"And how did you come up with this idea? Desperate to get a date or something?" her words holding a slight bite.

If she only knew I could of had one today but I'll leave it be. Don't want to give her flashbacks of almost face planting in the dirt.

"Of course not. This would be a great opportunity for kids too. And you're the one that gave me the idea in the first place since you know your way around a bike."

I give her a knowing look and she blushes, but shakes her head.

"I think this is something we could definitely do. I'll let Jim and Kevin know and start lining everything up."

She pulls out her laptop and starts typing away, already knowing what to do. Damn, I thought she'd be at least a little more hesitant on the idea. I see the way she looks at me sometimes. I know she finds me attractive so hopefully there are some hot chicks in this class to make her jealous. If not, then settling for a thirsty cougar will have to do.

The longer she works with me, the harder it'll be for her to resist me. When she can't resist me anymore, and I give her what she wants, then that's when I'll rip her heart out.

Easy and simple.

That's what I'm telling myself anyways.

***

The fact that she pulled this entire class together in two days is impressive. I'll give her that. Jim and Kevin didn't hesitate to green light it. They never do when something looks good on paper.

The turnout is insane. Way more women showed interest than we expected, but we capped it at twenty. It's better for it to be more organized and focused. Real instruction instead of chaos. The ages range from five to mid-thirties, a mix of nerves and excitement lining the edge of the track. If this works, it could turn into something bigger. A regular thing.

I didn't think much about it at first. Something I'd probably never admit out loud, but I'm not blind either. Watching their faces light up when they throw a leg over a bike for the first time hits somewhere familiar. That wide-eyed excitement, the hunger to learn, the adrenaline before they even twist the throttle. It's the same feeling I get every time I ride. Everyone deserves that. And whether I like it or not, it's good for the future of the sport.

No one will ever know the *other* reason I suggested it. Nope. I'll just put my foot right in my mouth.

The petty, stupid, but effective reason.

I'm helping a five-year-old get balanced on her bike, steadying her handlebars while she beams up at me like I just handed her the world. I can't help but smile with her, because that kind of thing tends to make an impression. It would on anyone watching as well. I glance toward the edge of the track and there she is, arms crossed, sunglasses on, staring straight at me like she knows exactly what I'm doing.

Gotcha.

The rotations start. My teammates and I cycle through the group, adjusting grips, correcting posture, offering encouragement. Casey is there, at the ready, with his camera.

When I stop in front of a woman around my age, a brunette with long lashes and a nervous smile, I slow things down. I place my hands over hers, guiding her grip, keeping my tone calm and steady as I explain throttle control.

And I can feel it.

Eyes on me.

Good.

I swing onto my own bike to demonstrate gearing, the engine idling beneath me. When I glance back, Stephanie's watching closely still. Her stance is serious and focused. Almost like she's already dissecting everything I'm saying.

So naturally, I decide to be an asshole.

"Got anything to add, Carson?"

I emphasize her last name, hoping it lands. The girls immediately start whispering. I picture Stephanie's eyes widening for half a second before she recovers, slipping on that polished smile like armor.

She walks straight up to my front tire and plants herself there, completely unfazed. The bike's still running, so she raises her voice just enough for the group.

"Hi ladies. I'm Stephanie Carson. I've never raced, but I know these machines pretty well. I'd love to add to Mr. Milano's lesson on gears and shifting."

Mr. Milano.

Why the hell does that sound so good coming out of her

mouth?

She glances back at me, lips twitching like she knows what she's doing to me, and gestures toward the bike.

"As you can see, Mr. Milano has the bike running. Arms crossed. Both feet on the ground. If he twists the throttle—"

She motions for me to demonstrate. I rev it, hold it, then settle back.

"—and it doesn't move, he's in neutral."

Then she moves.

Fast.

She steps to the side and slams her sneaker down on the shifter putting the bike in gear.

The bike jerks forward and I scramble, grabbing for the clutch and brake at the same time. The engine stalls instantly.

Silence.

Then there's me sitting there feeling like a rookie. The girls stare at her like she just performed magic. My teammates snicker and try not to laugh.

"So remember," she says smoothly, "pull the clutch in before putting it in gear when you are sitting still. And remember first gear is down on most bikes, like this one."

Applause breaks out. She looks back at me, pulling down her shades, and *winks.*

She showed me up. *Again.* In front of everyone. And instead of pure rage, something darker curls in my chest—something sharp and unwanted. A pull. A challenge. Like she just flipped a switch I didn't know existed.

No woman has ever gotten under my skin like this. They've always folded under the pressure. And it's infuriating. My jaw tightens as I meet her eyes, something heated and dangerous sparking between us.

She has no idea what she just started.

11

Stephanie

The trailer is busy as I push my hood down, the steady patter of rain hammering against the awning overhead. Some people thrive on weather like this. Others look like they're already regretting every life choice that led them here.

Pennsylvania isn't easing us into it either. This is going to be a full-on mud race. The kind that turns bikes into dead weight and races into survival tests. Winning is hard enough under perfect conditions. Add rain and churned dirt, and it becomes a battle of strength, balance, and pure stubbornness.

My eyes track the movement inside the trailer and land on Axel. He's practically glowing, mud already splattered up his gear as he laughs with Ben and the rest of his team. He looks relaxed and confident, like this is just another day at the office. Apparently, nerves aren't something he struggles with. Our eyes meet and he gives me a stern look.

I don't know what that look means, but if I had to guess, he's still annoyed about earlier this week. It has to be about me showing him up. He tried to embarrass me and it backfired spectacularly. Men never take it well when a woman beats them at their own game. It's almost endearing. *Almost.* I smile to myself. I don't feel bad about it either.

That class wasn't about him. It was about the girls. It was about showing them they belong here just as much as anyone else. The looks on their faces...the excitement, the confidence, *that* mattered. And yes, the moment Axel jerked forward on his own bike was priceless. I might treasure it forever. I also wanted to show the girls that they can kick some ass in this sport too, no matter what role they play.

The response online has been insane. The team's DMs are flooded. Articles are everywhere. Axel's face is plastered across half of them. Girls are constantly asking when the next class is. Other teams are even floating the idea of doing their own. Whether he realizes it or not, Axel might've started something big for women in motocross.

And maybe picked up a few dates along the way.

I snort softly. Was that his plan? To make me jealous? *Please.*

You wouldn't catch me anywhere near his strong jawline and stupidly toned body—

I pause.

"Get it together, Steph," I mumble to myself.

He's just like every other arrogant asshole rider. Just a coworker.

It's only a light sprinkle when qualifying starts, the kind that looks harmless until it soaks straight through everything. The track is already slick, mud clinging to tires and boots like it has a personal vendetta. Axel flies through it anyway, earning him the fastest lap. Not surprised. That puts him dead center for the gate drop, the best possible position.

Ben is on him instantly—scraping, spraying, and knocking chunks of mud off the bike like he's in a race of his own. Axel walks closer,completely caked, mud streaked across his jersey, splattered up his chest and thighs, even crusted along the edges of his helmet. When he pulls it off, along with his goggles and gloves, the only clean things left on him are his eyes, his chin, and his hands. Everything else looks like it went ten rounds with the track and lost.

And yet, he's glowing. His shoulders relaxed and an almost smug look on his face. He drops into a folding chair beneath the awning like he's at the beach, except the rain is tapping steadily overhead.

I take the seat right beside him, close enough to feel the heat still rolling off his body. He notices immediately and leans away, subtle but deliberate, like proximity to me is somehow more dangerous than the mud, the rain, or the chaos waiting out there. I bite back a smile. Good. If I make him uncomfortable without even trying, I must be doing something right.

"At least you know what you can do after racing," I say surprising him.

He freezes next to me.

"What?"

"Teaching. You're great at it. Almost as good as me," I say smugly as I cross my ankles.

"Ha-ha, real funny," he says sarcastically.

"No, seriously, the class went really well. It's going viral actually, thanks to you."

"That's good," he says as he starts fidgeting with his riding boots.

I can tell he's not used to helping others and getting recognized for it. Humbled almost. I like that. Rad would have been bragging up and down about it. It's refreshing.

"You like mud races?" I ask him even though I know the answer.

His eyes light up and he stops fidgeting immediately. He doesn't hesitate as turns slightly towards me.

See?

"There's nothing like them. The shear challenge they bring. Even the best riders have trouble which makes them unpredictable. The amount of strength to ride through the deep ruts and to just make it to the finish line is insane. I usually need two days to recover from them but it's always worth it."

"I think you're going to win today." I smile and nudge him.

"You think so? How?"

"I just have a feeling."

This race is one of the craziest and muddiest I've ever seen. Bikes bog down as riders get stuck. Mechanics slide trying to help them. It's utter chaos and everything motocross is supposed to be. Especially when I glance over and see Bethany look downright miserable. She looks pissed as she attempts to fix her hair, the weather literally raining on her bitch parade.

I wonder if her fake tits would help her float or sink in that pond over there?

It takes a rider everything they have to get through a lap with no slip ups. Rad was leading in the beginning of the first moto, but after one of the turns, his bike slid right off of the track which quickly put him behind.

The veteran, Zane, on the blue Yamaha has led a lot of laps. His lengthy experience evident the whole race. But, through all the muddy set backs, Axel is in the lead. He's riding like this is just a normal race day.

Halfway through the moto, his bike tipped over. He was able to get back on and keep going without losing any positions. I couldn't stop watching him as he dominated the whole way to the finish line.

The first moto left a haze to the track. The combination between the bikes moving slower while they are caked in mud can make the bikes start to smoke underneath them. The mechanics scramble to spray the mud off of the bikes so they don't overheat for the next race.

Some riders change into new gear. Others, like Axel, keep their same mud covered gear on. He could be superstitious or he just doesn't care about the mud. The warmer temperature balancing out their wet clothes.

I stand with the team in the pits thankful I packed my rain jacket. It's starting to rain again as the second moto starts. The gate drops and tires instantly slide. The race and the track conditions seem to be even more chaotic then the first. If that's even possible. Bikes are going down left and right.

One rider launches off a jump with a little too much con fidence and lands straight into a puddle the size of a kiddie pool. He disappears in a violent splash of brown water, bike and body swallowed whole. I snort before I can stop myself. It's brutal out there, but it's also impossible to look away. The crowd feels the same. Their cheers rise above the rain, raw and relentless, feeding off every crash, every save, every near miss.

Riders trade positions constantly, fighting the track as much as each other. Mud turns every corner into a gamble, every straight into a slow-motion tug-of-war. Except Axel. Lap after lap, he's steady, controlled, and unbothered.

By now, he's nothing but a moving silhouette, his bike and gear so coated in mud it's impossible to tell what color either of them started out as. He slides through a corner, back tire stepping out just enough to make my heart stutter, then snaps it back into line like it's instinct. Rad is right there behind him, close enough to taste the roost, the mud stretching every second until it feels elastic.

Final lap.

Rad makes his move over the rollers, pushing hard and desperate. The track answers by swallowing his bike whole. The front end drops into one of the deepest ruts and that's it. He's stuck and there's no saving it, no muscling out of it. Axel sails past and crosses the finish line while Rad is still fighting the earth itself.

Minutes later, the race is technically over, but the chaos isn't. Riders are still stranded all over the track like abandoned toys. I turn just in time to see a skid steer rumbling toward Rad, its engine growling as loudly as his mood. He's livid, arms flailing while his crew tries to coordinate with the operator. Someone slips. Someone else nearly eats it. His mechanic goes straight down into the rut they're trying to escape. I press my lips together, failing miserably at holding in my laughter.

At least he's okay. And honestly? If you need heavy machinery to get your bike out, you eventually have to laugh.

"You think this is funny?"

My mothers voice ripping the smile right off my face. I'm surprised she'd risk her Jimmy Choos getting dirty.

"Look around. You have to admit that needing equipment to pull his bike out of the mud is *somewhat* entertaining?"

I glance back at her and cross my arms. She stands there with her perfect blonde hair and makeup while holding an umbrella. Her face is scrunched up like she couldn't believe the sky dared to rain today. She only comes to these races for appearance. Once Rad is done racing I'm sure she'll be happy to stay in her climate controlled office.

"Was that Axel Milano that won? He's on team Kawasaki right? Who you work for?"

"Yeah, why?"

I scrunch my eyebrows at her, confused by her question.

"Just keep your distance with that one."

"Again, why?" I say watching Rad's bike finally get free.

"Just stay away from him."

I look back to see her already walking away.

Well that was weird..

Did she have to be so creepy and mysterious? The thing is, I can't stay away from him when my sole assignment at the moment *is* him. Not that I was letting my guard down to begin with, but I really have to keep that wall up then. At least until I figure out why I need to in the first place.

I slowly make my way to the post interviews and celebrations. My short rain boots having little traction. Axel shines through his mud covered gear as he stands on the stage. This race is what he needed to boost his confidence. His interview is flawless. Seeing him smile makes me feel things that I refuse to unpack, even after talking to my mother.

"I'd like to thank my mechanic Ben, and the team for this win. Mud races are always my favorite and I'm determined to keep the momentum up for the rest of the season."

Couldn't have said it better myself. He's still smiling as he climbs off the stage and makes his way over to the crew. I try taking a step as he walks up to me, but my foot slips. I instinctively grab the closest thing I can, which happens to be the six foot, muddy, dirt bike rider in front of me.

We fall.

Hard.

Next thing I know, I am looking up into his navy blue eyes. His bare hands planted on the ground near both sides of my head. My hands that are trapped between us still clinging to his jersey. I start feeling the cold mud seeping into my scalp from my hood falling down. His weight presses down on me, but I don't seem to care. I should be concerned with my clothes that hopefully wash clean when I get home. But, I can't seem to worry about a damn thing. I'm deep in that ocean, drowning, and can't seem to break the surface.

"New legs?" he says dryly.

"Excuse me?" I stutter.

"First time walking in the mud?"

I clear my throat to try and mask the embarrassment that's creeping up my neck.

"Would you believe me if I said no?"

He starts to get off of me and the emptiness I feel without him makes me feel even more ridiculous.

Did I not drink enough water or caffeine today? How hard did I hit my head?

He reaches a hand down and helps me up.

"Thanks," I say still feeling awkward.

"I guess you were right," he says with a cold indifference.

I look at him confused.

"You said I'd win."

I try my best to smooth the mud out of my hair but there's no fixing it at this point.

"Oh yeah, I did say that. Guess my feelings were right," I chuckle like a middle school girl. "Congrats by the way. That didn't look like an easy win at all."

I gesture to the messy track and his gear.

"Exhaustion will hit me soon, but totally worth it." His mouth quirks slightly.

"You might need a few showers too. I'm sure there's mud *everywhere.*"

He catches me staring at his pants and I about slam my palm to my forehead. When I thought I couldn't make this any more awkward I just put the icing on the cake.

Yep. He caught it. Where's the nearest mud puddle so I can submerge myself for eternity?

Fuck.

Now he's almost grinning. What an asshole.

"Anyways.... I'll leave you to it." I start to turn.

"I'll make sure I clean every. *Single. Inch.*"

I quickly walk away before my knees give out.

I'm totally screwed. Must be a concussion.

I kick the hotel door shut with my heel and drop my muddy boots just inside the entryway, careful not to destroy the already questionable carpet. The room smells faintly like industrial cleaner and cheap soap, and I'm still clutching my dirty beach towel like it's my emotional support blanket. I toss it over the back of a chair and pull my phone out, flopping onto the edge of the bed.

Lex answers the Facetime call, before I even get the chance to see myself.

She squints at the screen. "What the *hell* happened to you?"

I tilt the phone down just enough to show my mud-splattered jacket and hair that looks like I'm having a quarter life crisis.

"...I fell."

Her eyebrows shoot up. "You fell."

"Yep. Slipped in the mud."

She leans closer to the camera, unimpressed. "Absolutely not. You don't get *that* look from just falling. Start talking."

I sigh and roll onto my back, staring at the water-stained ceiling. "I might have slipped... and pulled someone down on top of me."

Her mouth drops open. Then a slow grin spreads across her face. "Oh my God. Who was it. Please tell me it was a hot guy."

I close my eyes. Defeat washes over me. "It was Axel."

She screams. Like, full-on banshee scream, the kind that makes me pull the phone away from my face.

"STOPPPP. No way. Are you serious? Was he on top of you? Could you feel his—"

"Ew! Lex—no!" I sit up, mortified. "Absolutely not. I'm not answering that."

She's still grinning like she just won the lottery. "So you *did* feel something."

"I said no!" I pause, then groan. "...Okay, maybe. I mean— his whole body was hard. That's just... muscles and riding pants. He's an athlete. It doesn't mean anything."

She cackles. "Uh-huh. Sure."

"I'm hanging up," I warn, already standing and grabbing my towel.

"Wait...did you like it?"

I hesitate for half a second too long.

"...It felt good being underneath him, but I did hit my head," I mutter. "There. I said it. I'm done. Goodbye."

She squeals as I end the call and toss my phone onto the bed, pissed at myself.

I head into the bathroom and turn the shower on full blast,

steam filling the small space almost instantly. As I peel off my muddy clothes, my thoughts go immediately somewhere I don't want them to go.

Did I feel his dick?

No. I definitely would've remembered that. I remember his weight. His arms braced on either side of my head. Those stupid eyes locking onto mine like he knew exactly what he was doing. Like he wasn't thinking about how inappropriate it was at all.

As if he'd even be hard with a *Carson* beneath him.

God, I really am losing it.

I step under the scalding water and let out a long breath, tilting my head back as the mud finally starts to rinse away.

Hot showers are supposed to fix everything, right?

Except they don't erase words. And no matter how much soap I use, Axel's voice slips right back in—

I groan and press my forehead against the tile.

Damn, I hate him.

12

Axel

"I thought you'd look a little happier today after a win like that."

Ben's already sitting across from me in the mess hall when I show up, coffee in hand, boots kicked out, relaxed. We make a point to eat breakfast together once a week, whenever the schedule allows. And whenever a certain someone doesn't fuck it up. If we didn't, the constant grind of travel, pressure, expectations... it would eat us alive. He's my mechanic, yeah, but more than that, he's the one person who keeps me from losing my damn mind.

Truth is, I need him. Not just to keep my bike running, but to keep *me* level.

He studies me over the rim of his mug, eyebrows pulling together the way they always do when something's off. He knows me too well. I should be riding the high. I went 1–1 in a brutal mud race. My points are solid. The media's eating it up. My image has never looked better, and for once I don't have to worry about captions or damage control. I was floating. Right up until a certain woman yanked me out of the sky.

How does that even happen?

One second I'm celebrating, adrenaline still buzzing through my veins, and the next I'm on top of her, the rest of the world completely wiped out. The way she grabbed my jersey like I was the only solid thing left in a storm. Her fingers curling into fabric stiff with dirt and sweat. And her eyes—Jesus. Bright, sharp, too damn alive. Like something green and untamed pulling me in whether I wanted it to or not.

I pulled away fast. At least, I *think* I did. It's hard to tell how long anything lasted when your pulse is still pounding in your ears. Was it the win? Had to be the win.

But, seeing her underneath me, soaked, muddy, and breathing hard—she looked... beautiful. I swear I could feel her heart racing against my chest, like it was trying to match mine.

"She ruined it," I shake my head keeping my eyes on my plate.

"What?" Ben lowers his cup.

"Stephanie-fucking-Carson."

I shovel a forkful of scrambled eggs into my mouth, the taste tainted.

He just shrugs, nonchalantly. "I've seen how she's helping with your socials and stuff. Looks like she knows what she's doing. And I think she's nice."

"You'd think a rattle snake is *nice*," I scoff while he remains unfazed.

I'm not surprised though. Ben always sees the good in people. Must be nice to have a reason to.

"If she knew what happened," I snap, "how would you feel then?"

He goes still for a second. Ben's the only one who knows the full story, my family, the Carsons, all of it. I don't talk about it. I barely think about it unless I have to.

"You don't know that," he says calmly. "She was a kid. Probably doesn't even remember. You can't pin that shit on her."

I snort. "She was probably groomed to manipulate people."

"Or," he says, pointing his fork at me, "maybe she deserves the benefit of the doubt. Maybe you could... oh, I don't know... talk to her?"

I shove my empty plate away and cross my arms. "Talk to her? About what? I can barely talk to *you* about it, and you were there."

He pauses as I can see his wheels turning. Then he smirks.

"Rolling around in the mud with her didn't seem to slow you down."

I glance at him. "You saw that?"

"Oh yeah," he says, way too satisfied. "I thought you two were going to make a mud pie baby for a hot second. I'm shocked nobody caught it on camera."

Shit.

I lean back in my chair. "What, you think I *like* her or something?"

Ben's grin keeps growing. "I think she gets under your skin. Which is rare."

"She pisses me off," I say immediately. "She challenges me. She doesn't back down. She's—" I stop myself. "She's annoying as hell."

"Sounds awful," he says, deadpan. "Tragic, really."

"I can't even imagine being with her," I add, firmer now. "I won't."

"I'm not saying marry her," Ben replies. "I'm saying get the full story. Figure out who *she* is. She might not even know the connection."

My original plan flashes through my mind. Pull her in, mess with her head, leave first. Easy, clean, controlled.

"I might have a way to get her to open up." I say slyly.

I don't miss the look Ben gives me.

"Don't be an asshole," he says with a sigh.

"No promises."

He just shakes his head, already knowing how this will probably end.

If she knew the truth about what happened and still lets herself fall for me, walking away will be easy.

And if she doesn't?

...Then I'll deal with that later.

I can get her underneath me again without catching feelings.

Easy.

13

Stephanie

I climb up to the observation tower to watch the riders practice. It has the best view and a bonus. It's shaded. There's a few spotters up here today including Axel's spotter, Rick. They have their headsets on relaying messages to the mechanics on what they see. It's entertaining just listening to them sometimes. Rick's deep, loud voice stands out the most.

"He's gotta move quicker on those turns Benji!"

Wait a minute.

"Did you just say Benji?" I ask.

He looks over and smiles.

"I heard about your little nickname for him and it just kind of, stuck," he shrugs. "It's a small compound."

Whoops.

I chuckle then internally cringe hoping he doesn't know my nickname as well.

"What's going on with the big bad rider today?" I ask as I peer over the railing.

Rick shakes his head as sweat stains line his white v-neck

T-shirt.

My eyes find Axel as he appears to be falling behind more and more on every turn. He starts strong as he begins a jump section but quickly looses rhythm by the end of it. On the last table top jump his back tire jerks sideways, which makes him land off centered. It doesn't make him wreck but I watch him veer off the track. Dust continues to fly as the other riders continue their practice.

Axel cuts his engine as Ben automatically grabs the bike. His hands are moving too quickly to undo the helmet strap. His pair of goggles landing in the dirt. Ben says something low, trying his best to calm him down, but to no avail. Axel storms off to a nearby canopy ignoring Ben's words and the eyes watching him.

Even from here, the energy rolling off him is unmistakable. He looks torn apart. Angry, yes, but there's something else underneath it. Something conflicted and restless that makes my stomach twist.

I would've thought he'd be untouchable this week after the win. The fans are eating him alive in the best way, and the sponsors are finally breathing easy. He should be riding that high straight into the weekend. So, what's rattling him like this?

We haven't spoken all week. Not since *that* moment. And if I'm being honest, I've been avoiding him. Part of me is scared of getting too close again, scared of what might surface if I do. What if my mother's warning wasn't just paranoia? Or worse... what if whatever I felt between us wasn't just adrenaline or bad timing?

What if it actually meant something?

"What the hell is he doing?!" Rick yells into his headset.

Screw this.

I lightly slap Rick's shoulder with the back of my hand.

"I'll talk to him," I say confidently.

"You sure?"

"I can handle him."

"Good luck, hun." Rick says warily as he gives me a much needed encouraging nod anyways.

Here goes nothing

With every step I take, my thoughts spiral faster, colliding into one another until I can't tell which worry is louder. What's really eating at him? What do I even say? And if I say the wrong thing... will he shut me out completely? I come up empty by the time the bright green tent comes into view. Marvin huffs, in what sounds like a warning, as I walk past. Even the team donkey knows to stay away.

A large water cooler sits crooked on a plastic folding table, condensation dripping onto the dirt below. A few empty chairs line the other side, untouched. The canopy *should* be crowded—riders cooling down, mechanics hovering, but no one has ventured near. Either no one wants to deal with Axel right now... or they know better. Maybe this is normal. Maybe everyone's learned to give him space when he looks like this. Everyone except for me.

He's slouched in a folding chair, a paper cup dangling from his left hand. His dark hair is a mess, like he's been dragging his fingers through it on repeat. His right leg bounces, fast and restless, shaking the dirt beneath his boot. His eyes are locked on the track, but whatever he's seeing isn't happening out there.

I sit down in a chair beside him and decide to stay silent. I begin to think he has no idea I'm here until his stern, clipped voice breaks the tension.

"What are you doing here, Kill Switch?"

He doesn't turn his head, but I catch the tick in his jaw. The tension in his shoulders. Like he's holding himself together by sheer force.

"I work here," I replay lightly. "Remember?"

The whooshing sound of his riding pants scraping against the chair darts my eyes towards him as he faces me. He lifts his left arm and tilts the empty cup towards me.

"No, I mean what are you doing *here*, here? No one else is dumb enough to come near me when I get like this, so why you?"

"It's my job," I shrug, slouching deeper into the chair like I belong here. Like my heart isn't beating too fast.

Is this my job? Not really. I didn't *have* to come down here. It's not like this is a public event, or an interview. I could have went home hours ago. The evening sun is starting to descend as I watch the other riders push through the jumps and turns. The exhausts and the voices of team members filling the silence.

Can I admit to him how I hated to see him upset when I won't admit it to myself? I'm the last person he wanted down here, I'm sure, but maybe this will give him an opportunity to open up? To finally explain why he hates my family so much? I subtly shake my head. Who am I kidding? Where would I even start? I thought men were supposed to be the emotionally constipated ones. And here I am, drowning in thoughts I can't untangle.

I should have been back at the apartment by now, but my body just can't seem to move. I text Lex to let her know I'll be home late tonight. She responds almost immediately.

Lex: I hope to GOD you have an exciting excuse!

Me: Noooooo. Work. Obviously.

Lex: *eye roll emoji

She says this like this is anything new when it comes to me and my social life.

I slide my phone away and glance back at Axel. Neither of us moves. Neither of us speaks. One by one, riders exit the track with their crews. The noise fades as the sky deepens into gold and burnt orange. We should talk, but I can be stubborn like him, too. I have time.

I'm also... strangely okay just sitting here with him.

The track stretches out before us. A once alive place, now quiet. A dirt kingdom gone still. And it's possible king sits brooding on his throne.

"Let's take a walk," the words leave my mouth before I can overthink them.

I stand, my legs slightly stiff, as I shake the arm of his chair. He looks up at me, eyes unreadable, but doesn't argue. My feet begin to lead us towards what we've been staring at for the last two hours.

"We're going to walk the track?" he asks.

"Why not?" I haven't walked one in years. It brings me back to when I was a kid and climbing a dirt pile was better than any toy out there. And with no one else around? It's almost... freeing.

We step onto the first straightaway, his heavy boots the only sound between us. A few minutes go by before he breaks the silence.

"Did you know?"

His question hits me sideways.

"What?"

"Do you know what happened twelve years ago?"

Twelve years ago... my mind starts racing. Should I know this? I feel like I should. My eyebrows scrunch together as I look over at him. His gloved hands twitch beside him, shoulders curved inward, as his heavy eyes meet mine.

"No," I say quietly. "I don't."

He exhales, long and strained, staring straight ahead.

"Talk to me, Axel," I plead.

His jaw tightens. He holds it in for a moment longer before finally turning to me.

"I had a brother." His words a punch to the gut.

My mind flashes through all the research I've done, all of his social media... nothing. I have never seen anything about there being a Milano sibling. Not a single mention. Growing up around racing you'd think I would have heard of or at least recognized something.

"What?"

Of all the things I could say, *that* is what comes out? I mentally scold myself.

He flicks a glance at me, then looks ahead. This is obviously a sore subject.

"You don't have to talk about it if you don't want to," I reach over and put my hand on his arm.

His body tenses under my touch and I quickly pull back.

"We have to talk about this," he says softly.

"We?"

I still don't understand why I'm involved? What am I missing?

"His name was Maddox. He was a few years younger than me," he lets out a strained laugh and shakes his head. "I remember his dark hair constantly being in his eyes because he refused to let mom give him a hair cut. He'd call himself Mad Madds. He was so stubborn..."

I smile sadly as we climb up the face of a jump. I don't speak until he's ready. This man beside me, is supposed to be intimidating and this should be a work related conversation, professional even. Right now, it just feels like Stephanie and Axel. Just two people trying to figure out the other.

"One night, the four of us decided to get pizza, to celebrate, after a race. Neither of us won, but our parents were still proud. It was always chaotic trying to get out of the parking lots after a race, especially when it was dark and rainy. We finally got onto the main road when..."

I get this sick feeling like I know where this is going.

"This white SUV came out of nowhere and..." his voice cracks. "I can't do this."

He turns, heading back down the jump. I slide after him.

"Axel wait!" I grab his arm to stop him. "Axel, I'm sorry that happened to you and your family."

He slowly turns to face me.

"I pulled him out, I tried cpr, I..." he rambles on, then pauses. "He was eight."

One single tear slides down, clearing a path through the dirt on his face. His once blue eyes now a stormy sea. His fists clench at his sides. My eyes begin to burn. To lose a brother... I can't even imagine what that's like.

"Oh Axel, I'm so sorry... do.. do you know who did it?" my voice shakes.

His entire body goes rigid like it's on the brink of exploding. His eyes bore into mine as his next words knock the wind out of me.

"Yeah I know who did it," he says sternly.

My heart starts to race. Why is he looking at me like that?

"Who Axel?"

Another pause.

My chest about ready to combust.

"Who?"

Pause.

"Your *mother.*"

My knees threaten to give out, my mind going in a million different directions, my eyes searching his and hoping he's joking. Pure fire is what stares back at me, after saying two words I'd never expect. Thousands of questions remain.

Have I been lied to my whole life?

"Howw.. how?" I stutter.

"So, you didn't know anything about this?" He points at me. "Last chance to come clean."

Twelve years ago

Despite the life altering news, I attempt the mental math. So, I would have been ten at the time and Rad would have been twelve. He obviously was racing at that age. We'd go to one every weekend, *of course.* We'd ride in the motor home while my mom always drove her *white* SUV until...

She hit a deer.

"Fuck!"

I start pacing, back and forth, like if I keep moving I won't completely shatter. My breath comes too fast, scraping out of my chest in uneven pulls. Dirt clings to my shoes, coats my palms, smears into my clothes like it's branding me with the truth. There's no part of me untouched by this moment.

So all this time... my mother has been a fucking murderer?

The thought lands heavy and sickening. My stomach twists as another one follows close behind. Am I that much of an idiot?

Does Rad know?

The question claws it's way through me. Has he always known? Am I the only one who was kept ignorant, protected, and lied to? No wonder Axel hates us. No wonder his eyes burn when he looks at my last name. We didn't just ruin his childhood, we erased his brother and walked away clean.

I stop pacing and force myself to face him. I need him to see it, to see the tears streaking down my face. To look at the way my hands are shaking. I need him to know this truth matters. He lost a member of his family.

All my mother lost was a car... and maybe some smeared mascara from an airbag.

"Axel," I whisper, my voice breaking under the weight of it. "Believe me when I say I truly didn't know. All I... all I remember is my parents telling me my mom hit a deer."

The words barely leave my mouth before his rage explodes.

"My brother was no fucking deer!" his voice booms. "You know how ridiculous that sounds?! How fucked up that is?"

The force of it rattles through me, but I don't step back. I don't flinch. Somehow, I know he won't hurt me, not physically. The pain in his voice is too real, too raw for that.

"I know, Axel," I cry, tears spilling faster now. "I know. I'm so—"

"They covered it all up!" he roars, the sound tearing straight through the quiet track. "Blamed it on road conditions. The court ruled it an accident and she walked away like nothing happened. They *had* to have paid someone off.." he scoffs. "Anything to protect their perfect fucking image!"

His hands clench into fists, his whole body vibrating with years of bottled fury.

"She wouldn't even look at us," he continues, voice cracking. "Didn't come to the funeral. Had their minions do all the work. Like Maddox never existed," his breath stutters. "And my parents? They didn't have the money to fight back. They spent everything they had on racing. On us. They never saved any for themselves. Especially that piece of shit truck they had."

He swallows hard, eyes glassy but still burning.

"After that night, they fell apart. Racing reminded them of him, of that night, of everything they lost," his voice drops, rough and unforgiving. "They wanted nothing to do with it anymore. And that included me, because I didn't want to quit. Because Maddox would've kicked my ass if I had."

A strained laugh escapes him, sharp with grief. "His stubborn little ass would've told me to go win."

My chest aches as I watch him.

"So I did everything myself," he says. "I finished school, hustled for money, and bought my own bikes, my own gear. Everything." He looks away. "Ben's the only one who ever stuck around. The only one who believed in me."

So this is what Ben meant.

I should be scared of him right now. Years of pain spilling out all at once, emotions cracking open like a fault line, but I'm not scared. I'm devastated.

And I do what any crazy woman would do.

I step into him.

My cheek presses hard against his chest as I wrap my arms around his waist, holding on for dear life. I become an anchor, worried if I'd let go, he'd disappear. His body goes rigid for half a second before he falls apart. He folds into me, forehead dropping to my shoulder as his whole body shakes, crumpling beneath my grip. It's silent at first, then not.

I tighten my grasp, anchoring him, feeling his grief pulse through me. There are no words that could fix this. No apology big enough to touch it, not even close. My heart feels like it's ripped in half. But, right now that's not important.

So I stay.

I hold him tighter, knowing this moment has rewritten everything.

I'll deal with my family later.

14

Axel

She's... hugging me.

It's not stiff or awkward. It's not the kind you give someone, because you don't know what else to do. She's really holding me.

Her family lied to her for twelve years. I just shattered her reality, screamed at her, unraveled like a goddamn ticking time bomb, and instead of pulling away, she wraps her arms around me like I'm the one who needs saving.

Yeah. The head injuries finally did it. I've officially lost my mind.

I don't know if I should run as far away from this woman as possible or marry her before she comes to her senses. My chest feels too tight, my thoughts are too loud. I've spent years hating the Carsons, resenting them. I used them as a stand-in for every ounce of rage I couldn't aim at the people who actually deserved it. And apparently, that included the woman in front of me.

And she didn't even know.

I always told myself there was a chance this was the truth. A small one. A stupid, hopeful one I buried fast. But, I never really believed it. Believing it would've meant facing the possibility that all this anger... was misplaced. That I was wrong for treating her this way.

Her arms tighten around my waist, small but fierce, like she's afraid to let go. Her cheek presses harder against my chest and it knocks the air straight out of me. She feels solid, warm, and real. Like an anchor slammed into the dirt beneath my feet. I didn't know how badly I needed that.

For the first time since the accident, since the night everything broke, I stop thinking. I stop replaying the headlights, the rain, the scream I'll never forget. I stop bracing for the hit that never really stopped coming.

I just feel.

I always thought locking my brother away in the deepest part of myself was survival. That if I didn't talk about him, didn't say his name out loud, he couldn't be taken from me again. Maybe that was selfish. Maybe it was cowardly. But he was my brother. No one else got a say in how I grieved him. They had no right.

I force myself back to the present, back to the woman holding me together with nothing but instinct and kindness. My hands slide up to her shoulders, hesitant, unsure. Like if I move too fast I'll break the moment, or her.

She slowly looks up at me. Her fingers are still curled into the back of my jersey, gripping like she needs proof I'm actually here. When she lets go, the absence hits immediately. My chest feels exposed.

Cold.

My hands trail down her arms as our eyes lock, and the hurt in her expression punches straight through me. I've seen pain before. Hell, I lived in it. But seeing it on her face, knowing I put it there, makes my stomach twist. I never want to see her look like that again.

A tear slips free and tracks down her cheek. My gloved hand moves before my brain catches up, brushing it away. Too gentle for a guy like me. She returns the favor by reaching up and wiping my cheek as well. A reminder of something I've never done in front of a woman. Cry. It's too intimate. Too much. Neither of us moves.

The world goes quiet, like it's holding its breath with us. Her lips part slightly. My pulse roars in my ears. We drift closer without permission, drawn in by something heavier than logic. Her breaths are short now, shallow, and I swear I can feel each one against my skin.

Then—

An engine explodes to life.

We jump apart like we've been electrocuted, the spell snapping violently as a dozer crawls toward us.

Of course.

Of *fucking* course.

Track maintenance. The same time, every day. How the hell did I forget?

"Let's go."

My voice comes out rough as I grab her hand and pull her toward the parking lot. I don't trust myself to stop, to think, to want. As much as I want to stay in that moment, to see what would've happened, this isn't right. Not tonight. Not with everything cracked wide open. We aren't thinking straight, our emotions getting the best of us.

And she has her own wreckage to sort through now.

She leads me to her red Honda Civic, dust still clinging to

the tires. I walk her to the driver's side and step in front of the door when she reaches for the handle.

"Hey... um. Thanks," I say stumbling over my words.

Pathetic. That's the best I've got?

My free hand rubs the back of my neck as I stare anywhere but her eyes.

"No," she says softly. "Thank you. For telling me."

She straightens, resolve burning behind her gaze. Fire. Pure, unfiltered fire. It drags at something deep in my chest, something dangerous.

She's nothing like anyone I've ever met.

And I really, really need to walk away before she notices what's happening in my riding pants.

She must sense it, because her eyes flick down for half a second before she slips into the driver's seat. I lace my fingers behind my head and watch her pull away, the car disappearing in a cloud of dust.

Holy shit.

I need my therapist.

The workshop lights are still on, no surprise there. If loyalty were a job requirement, he'd own the place. I drop into one of the chairs like this room is my personal confession booth.

"Hope you didn't wait up for me," I mutter, dragging a hand down my face.

Ben turns, smirk already in place. "Of course not. I knew Steph had it handled."

"Ha. Ha. You know, you really shouldn't have left me alone with her."

"Why?" he asks. "What happened?"

"She didn't know," I say quietly. "And then everything I've kept buried for years just... came out. And she *hugged* me.

Fuck."

I duck my head and start stripping off my gloves, half-hoping the memory of her touch comes with them. Ben doesn't say anything, just hands me a wrench.

I roll closer to the bike and start checking bolts, spokes, anything to keep my hands busy. He sits on his small rolling toolbox, watching me while *It Ends Tonight* by The All-American Rejects, hums low in the background.

I huff a laugh.

Well that kinda fits.

"Well?" he finally asks. "How do you feel?"

"I don't know," I say after a beat. "Good, I think."

I feel lighter. Like something I've been dragging behind me finally loosened its grip.

Stephanie, though?

That's foreign territory. Something forbidden and confusing as hell.

"Did the hug turn into something more?" he asks with a touch of curiosity.

"Nope. Nothing more," I say flatly without looking at him.

Thanks to the fucking bull dozer, but I'm not telling him that. I'd never hear the end of it.

15

Stephanie

"What the fuck do I do now?!"

The words bounce off the windshield and die somewhere between the dashboard and my chest. I slam my palms against the steering wheel, my breath coming fast, shallow, like my lungs forgot how to work properly.

Who do I even talk to first?

Do I go back to the apartment like nothing just imploded? Do I drive straight to my parents' house and demand answers at night like some unhinged Lifetime movie? Do I scream? Cry? Throw up? All of the above? The car answers for me.

I don't even realize where I'm headed until the familiar gates loom in front of me. Rad's neighborhood. Of course. Because when everything goes to shit, I always end up here. Even after all these years.

Muscle memory.

I punch in the gate code with fingers that won't stop shaking and roll through, the tires crunching softly against the pristine pavement. His house sits at the end of the long driveway like it always has. It has it's stone façade and sharp lines. The type that looks expensive without trying too hard. Three thousand square feet of success and expectation.

Behind it, the home track stretches out under floodlights, ruts smoothed, jumps sculpted perfectly. But it all looks unused tonight. That alone makes my stomach twist. Rad rides when he's pissed. He rides when he's restless. He rides when he can't sleep. The fact that the track is untouched feels wrong. At least the lights are on inside.

There aren't any other cars parked out front. There's no friends, no girls, and no party. Either he's trying to be good tonight or he's already past the point of wanting company. Neither option makes me feel better.

I consider calling him or warning him. At least give him a chance to prepare, but I'm already here. And frankly, I already know how that would go. I'd either completely lose it or at least lose my temper. And I don't want either of those options. I want to see his face when I ask him. I want to watch him decide whether he wants to lie to me. I need to see him.

My heart is trying to break out of my ribcage by the time I ring the doorbell. Seconds tick by. Too many. Just as I'm about to ring it again, the door opens. Rad stands there barefoot, wearing gym shorts and no shirt, his hair damp like he just got out of the shower. A grin starts to spread across his face when he sees me.

"Steph—what the—"

It dies instantly.

His eyes sweep over me, taking in the dirt still smudged on my shoes, the dried tear tracks I clearly didn't wipe well enough, *or Axel for that matter*, or the way I'm vibrating like I drank six espressos.

"What's wrong?" he asks, already stepping aside.

"Can we talk?"

The words come out thin. Fragile. Like if I push them any harder, I'll shatter.

"Yeah," he says immediately. "Yeah, of course. Come in."

The door shuts behind me with a soft click that feels way too final.

His living room looks like a magazine spread. It has the classic white sectional, sleek black accents, open floor plan that screams *I made it.* He bought the place a few years ago, riding high on sponsor money and title winnings, finally breaking free from our parents' roof. Of course, he picked something close to Honda headquarters. And with enough land to have a track with a custom layout.

I drop onto the far end of the sectional and immediately regret it. Why do people buy white couches? Do they hate themselves? I've never understood it.

Rad sinks into the recliner across from me, leaning forward with his elbows on his knees.

"It's late," he says gently. "Did something happen at work?"

I don't answer that. Nope. I dive head first with no life jacket.

"Did Mom *actually* hit a deer twelve years ago?"

The air leaves the room as Rad freezes. It's not just subtly or gracefully. He stops completely, like I just pulled the plug on him. His eyes snap up to mine for half a second, long enough for me to have my answer, before he looks away.

He tucks his chin down, leans back, and starts picking at the armrest. A nervous habit he's had since we were kids. His hand drifts to the end table, closing around a beer bottle I hadn't noticed before. The label's already half peeled off. Right as the glass meets his lips, he says it.

"No."

Son. Of. A. Bitch.

Everything inside me detonates. I'm on my feet instantly, pacing back and forth like a caged animal. The second time today, but a different floor. This one is clean and untouched but the effect is all the same.

Traitor.

I rake my hands through my hair and spin back toward him.

"You're kidding me," I say. "You have got to be fucking kidding me."

Rad stays quiet.

That silence feels like betrayal all on its own. Rad watches me with that same helpless look he's had since we were little, like he's bracing for impact, but has no idea how to stop it.

"Why?" my voice cracks despite my best efforts. "Why am I the only one who didn't know? Isn't there some kind of sibling code? A rule? Or did you all just decide I was too stupid or young to handle it?"

"That's not fair."

"Then explain it."

He exhales sharply, scrubbing a hand down his face.

"I wanted to tell you."

"Then why didn't you?"

"You were ten," he says, his voice softer now. "I wanted at least one of us to grow up without the family trauma. Without the guilt. Without the shit that comes with knowing."

He lets out a humorless laugh.

"Guess I failed at that too."

I stop pacing.

"How did you even find out?" I ask.

Rad stares at the beer bottle like it might answer for him.

"I only knew, because I overheard them."

My pacing slows.

"Overheard them how?"

"I couldn't sleep," he says, lifting the beer again but not drinking. "I used to sneak into the garage at night when my mind would be a little too loud. It was quiet there. That night, I was still wired from the race and couldn't sleep. When I got close to the door, I heard them arguing."

His jaw tightens.

"They weren't even whispering."

I feel sick.

"They were arguing about lawyers, money... about making it all disappear," he pauses.

"I should've done something," he continues, his voice raising slightly. "I should've barged in. Yelled. Made them do the right thing. *Anything*. But I didn't."

He finally drinks, longer this time.

"I've been trying to forget it ever since."

My math was right.

He was twelve. A kid not much older than me.

I stop pacing and really look at him. I look at the way his shoulders slump, how the beer bottle never leaves his hand, how exhaustion sits behind his eyes no amount of wins can erase. He's held this in for far too long.

Can I blame him?

Would I have been brave at twelve? I want to say yes. I want to believe that version of myself exists. But our parents were terrifying when they wanted to be. Dad had the money. Mom had the brains.

The perfect combination.

If they could get out of something like this... what else have they escaped?

"You were twelve, Rad," I say quietly.

His shoulders shift like I just took a weight off them.

"So, Axel told you," he says after a moment.

"Yeah," I answer, sitting back down, but on the edge this time. "No wonder he hates anyone with the name Carson."

Rad exhales slowly.

"I tried using the rivalry," he admits. "Thought if we kept it about racing, it would... burn off some of it," he huffs a bitter laugh. "Turns out that's not how trauma works."

No shit.

This explains *everything*. The tension. The hatred. The way Axel looks at us like we're ghosts he can't expel from this realm.

"What do we do now?" I ask.

The question hangs between us, heavy and unanswered.

It's too late to confront our parents tonight. And honestly? I don't trust myself not to burn everything down if I do.

Finally, he says, "I don't know. But I know we can't keep pretending it didn't happen."

For once, neither of us argues. Rad and I look at each other, silently agreeing on one thing, we'll fix this. Somehow. Because we have to.

I hug him before I leave, squeezing tighter than usual. I don't miss the way his grip lingers, or how his hand drifts back to the beer bottle the second I pull away.

I notice, but I say nothing. Some fights have to wait.

***

The Foxhole parking lot the next morning feels... complicated.

I'm relieved to be here. It's a safe distraction. But, I'm

absolutely dreading the high possibility of seeing Axel. What do you even say to someone after *that*? Good morning? How's the track? Sorry my family destroyed yours, should we finish that almost kiss?

Fucking ridiculous.

I chug my coffee like it will fix all of my problems and thank the lord that Lex was awake when I got home last night. She listened. She let me spiral and rode the emotional roller coaster with me. She only made *one* inappropriate comment about the almost-kiss, which honestly deserves a medal. It was the therapy I needed to get through the night.

It's mid-morning. I grab my stuff and head towards the bunkhouse building, my stomach finally reminding me that I haven't eaten since yesterday morning.

My office, the mess hall.

Engines roar nearby, race fuel hanging thick in the air, but I don't look. I *refuse* to look. I have work to do. I have to focus on these things called goals, you know, my *career*. I say these things like I have to remind myself or something.

I make it to my favorite table by the windows, open my laptop, and attack my plate. My tunnel vision is so bad that I never noticed I wasn't the only one at the table. I'm halfway through my full plate when someone clears their throat.

"Hungry?"

I glance up to find Benji across from me, trying and failing, not to laugh.

"A little," I say as my cheeks heat slightly.

He's sweaty and flushed, clearly already working. I glance at the clock. He shouldn't even be in here.

"What's up?" I ask.

His smile fades as he leans forward.

"I talked to Axel."

My stomach drops. So that's another thing we share—confiding in our best friends when everything else feels too heavy.

"Oh," is all I manage to say.

"He looked different last night," Ben says quietly.

"He did?"

"Yeah, in a good way." He gives a small smile.

"Oh... I'm glad."

I shift in my seat, as there are no words to describe it.

"Thank you," he adds quietly.

"I didn't do anything," I say, staring at my keyboard.

"You did," he counters. "You just don't see it yet."

He stands and taps the table, leaving me there, speechless. And for the first time since last night, I wonder...

How the hell do I move forward from this?

16

Axel

"Fuck, it's hot out."

But really, what else is new. It's California... in the summer. The sun isn't just sitting overhead, it's pressing, baking the track until the dirt turns to powder. My bike is practically boiling at this point. I feel like I'm on fire, and not just from the heat.

Ben tosses me a water before I head back out for a couple more laps. Everything is going smoother today like something finally clicked. My lines are cleaner, I've even cut my lap times down, which surprised the whole team. I pass Watson, who looks wrecked, shoulders sagging as he leans against his bike. AJ, another teammate in the 450 class, is still hammering a double jump over and over again, obsessed with perfecting his form as always.

I finish my lap and coast back toward Ben who looks just as overheated as I am. His shirt clinging to him as sweat lines his forehead.

"What time is it?" I ask ripping my goggles off. "It's too fucking hot out here, man."

He checks his watch and shrugs.

"Close enough, fuck it. Even Marvin hasn't stepped foot into the sun today."

We both glance over to where the gray donkey is sprawled out under a canopy, perfectly content, a water bowl sitting beside him like he's on vacation.

Smart bastard.

I swing my leg over the bike, ready to call it, when something clicks.

"Hey, where did you disappear to earlier?"

Ben hesitates just long enough for me to notice.

"Mess hall," he says casually, eyes fixed anywhere but me.

"During practice?" I arch a brow. "That's basically a crime for you."

"I needed to take care of something."

"Whatever, man," I say, letting it go. "Just curious."

He reaches for the handlebars to take the bike back to the workshop but my attention drifts past him, towards the parking lot. And there she is.

Kill Switch.

The woman who's somehow managed to flip my world upside down in under forty-eight hours. She proceeds to walk farther into the lot, keys in hand, and something reckless sparks in my chest.

"Hey," I say quickly. "I'll take the bike back later."

Ben tracks my line of sight, then steps away with a knowing smirk.

"Make sure you clean the bike off when you're done."

"Yes, Dad," I say mockingly, giving him a salute, as I take off.

I stand up, my feet planted on the pegs as I weave through

the parked cars. My bike gravitates towards a particular blonde that just managed to climb into her car. I stop dead in front of the hood and twist the throttle. She jumps, then glares at me through the windshield, her hands locked on the steering wheel.

Slowly, she opens her door, her hesitation evident.

"What the *hell* are you doing, Milano?"

I pull my goggles off so she can see my face.

"Take a ride with me!" I raise my voice over the engine, her eyes widening.

"Right now?!"

"Yeah, you busy?" I grin.

"No, I was just..." her words fading as she looks around.

"What? It's not like you haven't ridden before," I say.

"Yeah, but not with you. And it's too hot out." She crosses her arms to act like she's unimpressed, but I see right through it.

"Climb on, Kill Switch."

She rolls her eyes at me, but moves closer. I scoot forward, making room. Our eyes lock as she reaches for my shoulder. Her fingers hesitate, just a fraction, before settling there. Like she's aware of how much damage a single touch could do. The moment her body presses against my back, a jolt racks up my spine.

Fuck.

This was a terrible idea. Or the best one I've had in years. Hard to tell.

Being this close to her felt more dangerous than any triple I've ever cleared, because I knew exactly what I wanted to do and exactly why I couldn't.

Her voice cuts through my thoughts.

"Sweating a little today?" She leans back a fraction. "And where exactly are we going?!"

I smile beneath my helmet as I peer back at her.

"My secret spot."

"Where's—"

I kick it into gear and take off. Her arms wrap around my waist instinctively, and I'm hit with how *right* it feels, how natural. Two days ago, I couldn't stand her. Now she's pressed against me like she belongs there.

Maybe I should get my head checked again.

We loop back towards the track, but instead of entering the straightaway I veer off of it and aim straight up the hill. The climb gets steeper, rougher. Her grip tightens the higher we go. She knows bikes. I can feel it. But, riding with someone is different. Losing control is different. I hope I'm one of the few she's trusted like this. That thought makes me smile.

We crest the hill and I can feel the moment she relaxes. The subtle shift of her weight, the way she settles against me like she's decided she's safe. I weave through trees until the view opens up, my favorite place on the property.

The engine cuts, and the sudden quiet feels loud. Too loud.

Stephanie swings her leg over, her hand landing on my shoulder again, lighter this time, like she's testing something. Or me. My bike ticks as it cools, metal popping softly, but I barely hear it. All I can focus on is the space she's just left behind. The absence of her warmth hits harder than I expect.

"You could've at least let me borrow a helmet before charging straight up a damn hill!"

She smacks my arm and I laugh.

How did I know she'd give me shit for that?

Her irritation vanishes the second she sees the view. Her

green eyes light up, lips parting as she steps forward slowly, taking it all in.

I should be getting off this bike. I should be looking at the valley stretched out below us. The miles of California land soaking in the sun.

But... I'm looking at her.

And then she turns back and smiles at me. A true smile.

I'm fucked. Completely.

"It's beautiful," she breathes. "I had no idea this was so close to the track."

"Yeah," I manage after clearing my throat. "I like it."

That's an understatement.

I finally swing my leg over the bike and lean it up against the nearest tree. I set my helmet on the handlebar before I join her. I stand close, but not touching. The space between us feels deliberate, fragile, like if either of us moves the wrong way, something will snap. We stand there in silence. The kind that isn't awkward but heavy. Loaded. She breaks it first.

"How are you?"

The question lands deeper than it should. I look down at my feet before looking back at the valley.

"I'm okay," I say quietly. "Thanks to you."

She scoffs softly, cheeks flushing.

"I didn't do anything."

I shake my head. "You did."

She doesn't argue this time.

"How are *you* doing?" I say back to her.

She immediately drops her gaze, nudging a loose rock with the toe of her sneaker.

"To put it simply?" she says. "I'm pissed, hurt, sad. Avoiding my parents because I don't even know where to start or what to say to them," she swallows. "I talked to Rad after I left here last night."

Something tightens in my chest, but I don't react. I don't want her to think she has to choose her words around me. She looks up searching my face. Like she's waiting for anger, for judgment. I don't give either.

"That makes sense," I say quietly.

Her shoulders sag, relief flickering across her face before the rest pours out.

"He told me everything he knew," she says, letting out a strained laugh. "Said he didn't tell me so at least one of us could get away without a fucked up past. Can you believe that?"

Her hands lift, gesturing wildly now, emotion bleeding through the cracks.

"And I didn't realize it until last night, but I think he's drinking too much. Like... not just socially. He looked wrecked, Axel. He's blaming himself for everything."

Her voice breaks.

"How am I supposed to fix that? And my mom-" She stops, jaw clenching. "What the hell am I supposed to do with that?"

Tears finally spill over, streaking down her cheeks. She drags a hand through the strands of hair that have fallen from her pony tail.

"Goddddd-" she snaps at herself. "You don't deserve this. The last thing you need is a Carson unloading her shit on you."

She turns away, pacing a few steps towards the trees like she might leave. Something in me snaps. Not anger, instinct.

I cross the distance in two strides and pull her into me. She freezes at first, breath hitching, body stiff like she's deciding whether to let it happen. Or she remembered how bad I probably smell. Who knows. But then, she melts. Her forehead presses into my chest, arms sliding around my waist. Her sobs are quiet, controlled, but they wreck me anyway. I hold her tighter than I should.

"Now we're even," I murmur into her hair that smells like lavender with a hint of dust and sweat.

She lets out a shaky laugh then she *really* laughs. Full on belly laughs. I'm almost concerned for her mental state before she pulls away from me. Her face is blotchy, mascara smudged, eyes bright and wet and I can't help, but laugh with her.

I should kiss her.

The thought hits hard and fast and I hate myself for it. Not because I don't want to, but because I want to, *too* much.

So I don't.

"We're so fucked up," she manages to get out.

"You definitely are," I snort.

Her jaw drops as she shoves me hard enough to make me stumble back a step.

"Excuse you!"

I grin, and for the first time in a long time, it feels easy.

She darts toward the bike. "Don't make me take this bike back and leave you here!"

I catch her easily, hands landing on her waist as I lift her just enough to stop her escape. She laughs, twisting half-heartedly, her back pressing into me. Her laughter fades.

The air shifts.

I lean in, voice low, barely brushing her ear.

"You know... no one would hear you up here."

She stills completely.

"It is my secret spot for a reason."

Her breath quickens. I can feel it. Feel her heartbeat where she's pressed against me. For one split second, I think she might turn around. That she might close the distance herself. She doesn't.

Neither do I.

I step back first, breaking it.

"Let's go," I say, before I do something I won't be able to undo. She looks stunned, but then her mouth curves into something knowing as she climbs onto the bike behind me. Her hands settle lower this time, too low. Intentional. Teasing.

I grit my teeth and start the engine.

She knows exactly what she's doing and it's infuriating.

The ride back is torture. By the time we reach her car, I'm wound tight.

This fucking woman

She dismounts slowly, one hand sliding down my hip as she steps away. Her fingers graze my thigh, just barely.

"Thanks for the ride," she says sweetly, eyes gleaming.

I nod once, because if I open my mouth, I'll say something I shouldn't. She drives off in a cloud of dust. I stare after her longer than I should. I don't know how or when things changed but they did. And I'm not too sure if I'm happy about it.

Back in the workshop, I scrub the bike harder than necessary, cursing under my breath.

"Go figure," I mutter. "I wore my *blue* kit today."

Wanting her, I've realized, is easy. Not taking her? That's the hard part.

I shake my head. Who knew a Carson would be this kind of trouble.

17

Stephanie

"Don't be stupid. Don't be stupid," I mumble under my breath like a prayer as Axel steps up for his post-race interview. He got second overall. Again.. With Rad placing first... *again.* Second week in a row.

The crowd presses around the stage, vibrating and loud, their excitement a stark contrast to Axel's rigid posture. He's trying to look indifferent, but I can already tell, he's pissed. His dark hair is damp with sweat, strands going every which way, a complete mess. Honestly? Fair. But he just needs to hold it together for five minutes. That's it. Smile, nod, and don't burn any bridges.

Easy.

I stand off to the side of the stage with the rest of the staff, fingers crossed so hard they might cramp. They start with AJ, who looks ecstatic to just be on the podium. His grin is wide and genuine, soaking up every second, like he can't believe he made it up there. Just to have two from Team Green in the top three is fantastic. The staff is very proud.

Axel inhales deeply beside him, jaw tightening as if he's

bracing for something more than a couple questions. I tried giving him more advice on interview responses before the race today, but you never know if he actually listened.

"Axel! Nice motos today!" Charlotte says brightly. "Fighting through the pack after tipping the bike over at the start of the second moto was no easy task. How do you feel after taking second overall?"

The crowd, and me included, are on the edge of our seats waiting for his response. Axel's right hand rests on his hip, his left hand holding a Red Bull can, and a clean pair of goggles rests around his neck.

"Not easy at all, Charlotte," he says evenly. "But, I was able to push through and make podium today. I've been working hard and I feel good about this season."

Polite, professional and no explosions. I call that a win.

"Thank you Axel," she says as the crowd cheers. "And now let's talk to the one that has dominated this season and has won the overall once again, Rad Carson."

Axel's head dips slightly as Rad steps forward, all confidence and camera ready charm. The crowd erupts as Rad gives them his Hollywood smile. He glances at Axel for half a second, and I catch the change in his eyes. He snaps his public mask back in place, before answering the reporter's questions.

Rad finishes up and then, because the universe hates me, his gaze lands on mine. He waves and everything after that happens in slow motion. Fans start turning, then the cameraman, then the reporters and, finally... Axel.

If looks could kill, I'd already be in the ground. Is he mad about the cameras? Rad? Me existing within a five-foot radius of him? I thought things were turning around.

I paste on a smile like my life depends on it. The kind that says *Yes, I belong here* and *Please don't perceive me too closely.*

No one comes over. I blink in surprise.

You're kidding me.

The reporter jumps over to Axel before he can bail. "Axel! One last question if you don't mind?" he nods once.

"How does it feel to have a Carson on Team Kawasaki? Especially after this race?"

The whispering starts instantly. I swear the temperature drops ten degrees. My stomach knots as sweat beads my hairline. If he loses it right now, I won't blame him. I'll jump in if I have to. I'll take the hit.

I meet his eyes and give him a small nod, an unspoken *I get it.* He pauses and turns back to the reporter.

"You mean Stephanie?" he says casually. "She's been a great addition to the team. I keep trying to get her to give me tips on how to beat her brother, but she won't budge."

The crowd explodes as Axel winks at me. He fucking *winks* at me. Talk about whiplash. Rad bursts out laughing as he slaps him on the back, the tension snapping like a rubber band. I just stand there, stunned. He could've thrown me under the bus, said anything. But, he didn't.

What the fuck just happened?

"Jim and Kevin might give me a raise after this interview," I mumble and laugh in disbelief.

The Red Bull girls step up for photos, trophies raised, and smiles flashing. And guess who's standing right next to Axel? Yep. Ding, ding, ding. Non other than, Bitch-face-Bethany. Her fake tits on display, ass angled. She even pretends to drop something, bending over like its a performance.

I scowl.

Axel subtly steps away, glares at her, and it makes me want

to flash my very real, very earned tits in solidarity.

The stage clears and press wraps up. I jot down notes, nod politely, and finally head towards my rental car. The Denver air is cool and quiet now. The crowd starts thinning as I make my way through the parking lot, the adrenaline finally bleeding out of my system. My ears are still ringing, boots crunching over gravel and discarded beer cans, the smell of exhaust and dirt clinging to my clothes. I don't make it very far when I hear loud steps running up behind me.

"Hey!"

I turn around to find Axel now in a T-shirt and shorts. His black snapback covers most of his wavy hair and I look down to see socks with slides. Criminal behavior, honestly. How he managed to not trip is beyond me. His tattoos are on full display and he looks... normal. Relaxed. Drool worthy. Rude.

"Can I walk you to your car?" he says casually.

"With those shoes?"

"Forget I offered," he teases pretending to walk away.

"Fineee," I smile up at him as he turns and matches my pace.

We walk in silence for a few seconds before I congratulate him. Making top three still calls for celebration.

"Thanks."

"And where the hell did the charming Axel come from?! I think you got the most autographs after that one."

"Maybe I took a play out of Rad's book?" he smirks as I playfully smack him.

We walk in comfortable silence for a few more beats, halfway to my car when it hits me.

That feeling.

The one that starts at the base of my spine and crawls

upward, cold and familiar.

I slow, my steps faltering.

No.

Please, no.

"Stephanie?!"

The voice slices through the noise, sharp, clipped, unmistakable. My stomach drops so hard I swear I feel it slam into my ribs. I turn slowly, already knowing what I'm going to see.

My mother strides toward us, heels sinking into the gravel like she doesn't even notice. Her hair is perfectly styled, makeup flawless, expression tight with irritation rather than surprise. It's as if she's inconvenienced by my existence instead of shocked to see me here. She looks painfully out of place among the chaos, like a press photo cutout dropped into real life.

I feel it instantly. Axel's entire body goes taut, shoulders locking, jaw tightening as his eyes flick from her face to mine. He knows. He knows exactly who she is.

"Stephanie," she says again, already reaching for me. "We need to talk. Now."

Her fingers clamp around my arm. The touch is like a match to gasoline.

I jerk away, heat rushing to my face. "Don't touch me."

Her brows knit together, offended. "Excuse me?"

Years ago, that look would've shut me up. Would've made me fold.

Not tonight.

"Why? So you can kill him too?!"

Her face drains of color.

"Lower your voice," she hisses, glancing around. "You're causing a scene."

I laugh, sharp and humorless.

"A scene? That's rich, coming from you."

Axel shifts closer, his presence solid and grounding at my side. I don't look at him, but I feel him, steady, protective, barely contained.

My mother's gaze flicks to him, recognition dawning too late.

"Oh," she says slowly. "I see."

She squares her shoulders, chin lifting. "This is a private family matter."

I snap.

"Family?" my voice cracks, loud enough that a few heads turn. I don't care. "You don't get to use that word. Not after what you did."

Her lips part. "Stephanie—"

"I know the truth," I cut in. The words taste like blood. "All of it."

For the first time, real fear flashes across her face.

She steps closer again, voice dropping into that familiar, controlling whisper. "You don't know what you're talking about. This is not the place—"

"Is this where you deny it again?" I spit. "Where you pretend you hit a deer instead of a person? Or do you save that lie for later?"

Her eyes dart wildly now, scanning the lot, the team trailers, the lingering fans. Panic seeps through the cracks of her polished exterior.

Axel moves before I even realize it. His hand slides into mine, firm and deliberate, thumb pressing into my palm like an anchor. He steps half a pace in front of me—not aggressive, not threatening. Just unmovable.

"Have a nice night, Mrs. Carson," he says calmly.

The way he says her name, cool, distant, final, makes my chest ache.

She looks between us, lips trembling. She pauses, calculating and cornered.

"This isn't over," she says tightly.

I meet her gaze, steady despite the burn in my eyes. "It is for me."

Axel squeezes my hand once and gently pulls me away. I don't look back.

Not when she calls my name. Not when she gasps in frustration. Not even when my heart feels like it might split open.

He continues to hold my hand as a tear begins to fall down my cheek. Finally reaching the car, I unlock the drivers side door, opening it but changing my mind and slamming it back shut.

"Dammit! It's so frustrating," I snap. "All she was worried about was getting caught. Unbelievable!" I spin around and cross my arms over my chest, my back grazing the door. Axel looks at me, complete understanding in his eyes.

"I know," he says softly.

"How are you so calm?"

"Her time will come. Don't worry," he reassures me while he places his hands over mine. My heart instantly starts beating faster while my stomach flutters. The dim lamp posts making his eyes look like two dark storm clouds.

"We'll figure it out together."

Together.

His left hand comes to meet my face as his thumb swipes my cheek. I pull away before I do something stupid.

I should go.

I smile up at him weakly and reluctantly pull my hand away. The loss of contact leaves an instant emptiness. It's quick, sharp, and unsettling. Something I'll have to unpack later. I open my car door and pause before climbing in. His brows knit together like he wants to say something, anything, but the words never come.

"Thank you for walking me to my car," I say softly. "I'll, uh... see you at work?"

His shoulders straighten just a fraction as he nods. "Yeah. I'll see you then."

I don't trust myself to linger, so I start the car and pull away before I completely lose it and ask him to stay at the hotel with me. God. Can you imagine?

I scan my room key and step into my small hotel room, the door clicking shut behind me. I drop my bag and flop face-first onto the queen-size bed, screaming into the pillow. Muffled, dramatic, and totally necessary. When I finally roll onto my back and stare at the ceiling, I feel a little better.

My phone buzzes in my pocket. I grab it thinking it's Lex.

Mr. Milano: Make it to your room?

Me: Yeah I did

Mr. Milano: Is the bed warm enough for you?

I freeze. Is that... no it can't be. Is that a flirt text?! Is this actually happening right now?! Wow. I am overthinking this wayyy too much. I immediately screenshot the conversation and send it to Lex.

*Me: *image*

Lex: OMGGGGG!!!

He wantssss to warm up that bed for you girl!!

Me: You think?!

Lex: YES. Time to break out the pickup lines, my friend.
Maybe he'll take you on another ride ;) Let me know if you need help since it's been awhile! jkjk love youuuu

Me: HA HA
**middle finger emoji*

I switch back to the thread with Axel.

Me: Wouldn't you like to know

I bite my thumb nervously while I wait like I'm seventeen again. The three dots appear, disappear, and appear again. My heart does an embarrassing little flip when his reply finally comes through.

Mr. Milano: All I know is that mine's pretty cold tonight...

Being the asshole that I am, I respond with a little attitude.

Me: I bet bitch would help you out
*I mean *Bethany*
Damn autocorrect

*Mr. Milano: *laughing emoji*
She tried convincing me but I told her I was staying with you tonight.
She wasn't real happy.

Excuse me—what?! What do I even say to that? *Wish you were?*
No. Absolutely not. Bad idea.

I have to remind myself that I *work* with him. I already have the Carson name attached to me. I can't risk anything else making me look reckless or unprofessional. As much as my body is screaming at me to just go for it, I type something safe.

Me: Yeah, could you imagine?

Mr. Milano: I'd imagine you wouldn't let me get much sleep

Me: Why's that?

Mr. Milano: You wouldn't be able to keep your hands off me

Me: You sound pretty confident about that

Mr. Milano: Very

Me: You should put that confidence into winning races

Too harsh? God. Self sabotage at it's finest.

I toss my phone onto the bathroom counter and turn the shower on. Steam quickly fills the small space as I strip down, my eyes flicking back to my phone at least a million times.

Nothing. No response.

I chased him off. Good. This is a good thing.

So, why does it bother me that I want him to answer. To fire back. To challenge me again.

I scrub shampoo into my hair harder than necessary, annoyed with myself. I haven't been interested in dating lately, because nothing ever feels right. I don't have time for someone who's going to waste it. Long distance would be pointless. I'd rather travel with the team with no strings attached. And most importantly, I'm trying to carve my own path, build my career. I need someone who meets my level, someone who makes me better.

Especially someone who doesn't work with me. I refuse to be the stereotype. A woman working in motorsports sleeping with a rider is a headline I won't be apart of.

And yet... if I didn't work with him, maybe I'd get a little taste of what's underneath all that gear? At least once? I don't know...

A sigh escapes me.

Hopefully I scared him off enough that I don't have to worry about it.

Axel

I stare at her last message as it stings more than I'd like to admit.

She's not wrong. I *should* be winning races. But this isn't going to be some "if I win, I get you" bullshit. Fuck that. If she wants me, she can come and get me.

I can tell she's holding back. Fighting it. I can see it in her eyes.

At first, I pegged her as the kind of woman who only keeps "the best" man beside her. But the more I've gotten to know her these past couple of weeks, the more I realize the Carson façade isn't who she really is. Not that I'm looking for anything long-term, but if I could see how her ass looks bouncing on my dick? Now, that's something I can get behind. Literally.

And yeah... it would be one hell of a kicker to her mother. Poetic justice, really. Stephanie might even enjoy it, even if we have to work together afterward. It's not like she'll be personally assigned to me forever.

Probably just this season.

I decide not to answer her. Let it simmer and let her wonder.

Challenge accepted sweetheart.

There's no race next weekend, which means a mini vacation. Most riders and staff, Ben included, go home and visit family. Those of us who stay, still practice, of course, but we've got more freedom.

And I already know exactly how I'm going to keep myself busy.

18

Axel

Waking up this morning, I'm surprised to find myself out of bed as soon as my alarm goes off. I'm never this eager to leave my bed on an off day. But here I am, brushing my teeth, looking in the mirror, wondering if hell froze over.

I put on my riding gear and head down to the mess hall for a quick breakfast. The tables are mostly empty except for a few stragglers. I choose a seat by the window without really thinking about it. The view stretches out over the quiet track, soft clouds hanging low in the sky. I snap a picture and hit send to set my plan in motion.

*Me: *image*

*Meet me at the track this morning. Wear pants and tennis shoes or if you still have a riding kit *winky face*

I finish my breakfast burrito faster than usual, heart beating a little harder than it should. Outside, the morning sun hits me full in the face, and I nearly walk straight into a furry brick wall.

Heeeehawwww

"Hey Marvin," I say rubbing his nose. "Wish me luck today."

He huffs, as if he knows what I'm up to. I give him a snack, pat his neck, and shake my head.

"I know buddy, I know."

The workshop doors creak open as I step inside, my boots echoing louder than usual. It takes me way longer to wrangle the bike, stand, and gear all at once. Ben would be laughing his ass off if he could see this. Especially when I fight with the stupid water cooler. No wonder why he calls me a spoiled brat.

By the time I get everything set up at the track, the place is completely empty. There's cloud cover and cool air.

Perfect

I check my phone one last time before tossing it on the camp chair under the tent.

No reply

I look over at the two bikes on their matching stands with my hands on my hips.

"Well this will be awkward if she doesn't show," I mutter.

Especially, if I have to explain why I have a 250 out here alongside my 450 bike. It's not that I doubt her ability, I just feel like, size wise, the 250 would be easier for her to handle. It's still powerful though. Between your legs it can do some serious damage. My mind immediately goes somewhere it shouldn't.

"Would you ride with me, Marvin?" I ask.

"Hee-Haw!" the donkey says as he's standing in the shade watching me.

"I take that as a yes?"

"Am I interrupting something?"

Shit.

I turn around as the world fades away. Stephanie stands there, sporting a light blue tank top and spandex type shorts. A duffle bag hangs over her right shoulder while her bare toes wiggle in her crocs". My eyes finally slide up to see that her long golden hair is braided down her back while an eyebrow quirks at me.

"Would you like to ride with me today?" I manage.

She smiles and looks around.

"Oh, is that what we're doing?"

"Yeah, I know it's hard to tell," I say as I gesture to the bikes in front of us. She laughs, eyes glittering. They dim seconds later.

"Are we even allowed to do this?" she asks.

"Probably not," I shrug. "But no one is here. Fuck it."

She's hesitant, but lets it go, as she looks around.

"I assume you're letting me ride your 450 today, right?"

She begins to walk up to it and place her hand on the seat like it's a prized horse.

"Absolutely not," I say as I shoo her hand away. "I can't risk you messing with my moneymaker."

She throws her head back, laughing.

"Fine. The 250 will have to do."

She drops her bag under the tent and—fuck me—her ass is suddenly my entire field of vision. When she straightens, I notice the riding kit inside.

Is she going to get dressed right here?

Since I'm a total asshole who is already dressed and ready to go, I decide to walk over to the tent. I plop down in an empty camp chair right in front of her. All I'm missing is the popcorn and the 3D glasses, as I cross my arms and get ready for the show. Her body freezes as her eyes stare at my boots.

"Creep much?"

"Don't worry," I say dryly. "I won't look." My eyes do not move.

She shakes her head but sits, pulling on her riding socks slowly. Painfully slow. One smooth leg disappears at a time. Then she stands, tugging her riding pants over her shorts, giving her ass a little wiggle that makes my jaw clench. A reverse strip tease that I'm apparently into. It makes no sense whatsoever.

She leaves the pants unfastened as she snaps her riding boots on, white, scuffed and clearly used. I respect that. Three buckles each with no hesitation. Then she looks up. Not playful, or teasing. She's focused, intense. It knocks the air out of me.

She pulls her tank top over her head and grabs her jersey. Her sports bra does little to help my situation. My body reacts before my brain can catch up.

Too soon, she's fully geared. Too goddamn soon. We're both breathing harder than normal. We haven't even started yet. Something about that moment wasn't just about skin or how it was covered. It was... something else. It was deeper, heavier.

My mind is reeling as I lift the 250 off of the stand and hold it up for her. She swings a leg over smoothly, helmet snugly in place. Purple and white to match the rest of the kit. Cute and dangerous.

I wonder if she wears matching bras and panties as well?

I then lift my bike off the stand and hold it up using my hip while I pull my own black helmet on. Am I trying to show how powerful my hips are? Maybe. Will she notice my arms flexing? Probably not, but worth a shot.

Luckily, she speaks first because words still aren't working for me at the moment.

"Would you like any pointers before we get started?" she says with way too much arrogance.

"Pointers?" I laugh. "Fuck it. Let's hear it."

"Elbows up in the turns," she says easily. "You lose form when you focus on passing. It's been costing you."

...Well shit.

"Been watching me have you?" I ask.

She starts the bike, gloves on.

"Yeah. Watching you lose."

She takes off and leaves me in a trail of dust, her laughter echoing on the track.

"Fucking savage..." I shake my head but can't help but smile.

I join her.

We create a dance-like rhythm between us. I pass her on one side of the track and then I let her pass me on the next. For once I'm not thinking about the next race. I'm not trying to beat my best lap time. I'm actually having... fun. I should ride with a woman more often. It makes things a lot more interesting.

She's good. Really good. Her form is solid. When she stands, weight perfect, legs gripping the bike, I get an idea.

I wait until she cruises down a straight away before I speed towards her. When I get along side her, I keep my right hand steady on the throttle. I use my left hand to reach over and smack her right on the ass. She jumps a little as I place my hand back on the grip. She looks over at me and shakes her head. With the helmet and googles, I can't tell if she's smiling or if she's annoyed. Either way, worth it.

I laugh and fly over a jump, adrenaline roaring. Who would have thought a woman would make me realize that riding can feel like it used to feel? Before all the pressure? A woman that I've never even kissed yet for fucks sake.

I finish a lap and ride over to the tent. I place the bike on the stand and grab some water. "I need to cool my ass down," I say to myself as Stephanie pulls up behind me. I set my water down so I can put the bike on the stand for her.

"Thanks," she says while taking her gloves and helmet off. She returns the sentiment by handing me my water before she grabs her own. She takes a sip of water as she pushes a stray hair out of her face. She's flushed and glowing, sweat at her hairline.

If you're not in the moto world, it's hard to understand how much of a workout riding a dirt bike really is. If you ride one correctly then you'll use your entire body. It's a lot of work using your legs to grip the bike, while your arms grip the clutch, throttle, and the front break. Keep in mind that your feet also have to shift and activate the rear break. So, as much as the body has to focus, the mind has to also.

"Thank you," her faces beams at me. "This is fun."

"I needed it." I gaze out towards the track.

"You need to take a break sometimes and just enjoy it. Says someone who never takes breaks," she scoffs beside me.

"This is the perfect date for us then," I tease.

"Oh, no. This is NOT a date," she says quickly as she waves me off.

Got her.

"Why not?"

"I don't date riders." She shakes her head.

I burst out laughing. "Is that so?"

"What's so funny about that?" She questions, crossing her arms.

"Because, it's ridiculous."

"Well, it's my rule," she says more confidently.

"Your rule? Then why does your body beg for mine?" I say seductively, catching her off guard.

She glances down and I see her swallow.

Busted.

"I don't know what you're talking about," she says firmly as she sits in one of the chairs.

I join her although I know she's full of shit. There's no denying it. The way her thighs move together when I look at her for a second too long. The way her breath catches when we stand too close together. I bet if I checked her right now...

"We do have the place to ourselves.. for the most part." I wink and lean forward a little, resting my elbows on my knees.

She raises an eyebrow at me, but doesn't bite. She redirects the conversation instead.

"Why are you here this week? Everyone usually visits family on their weeks off."

Shit. What do I say? That I'm basically alone? Ben's the only one I have. His family has always been welcoming and they're good people, but it just isn't the same as your own. I don't want to be the charity case that they feel obligated to invite. So, I stay here... always.

"My parents don't talk to me, remember?"

I rub my hands together, anxiously.

"You don't have anyone else?"

"Just Ben, but I want him to enjoy his family without me dragging him down." I glance down at the dirt at our feet.

"If it makes you feel better, I don't go home much either."

She gives me a small smile.

For some reason it doesn't make me feel any better. How much of great childhood did she actually have? If Rad's an alcoholic then probably not the best. I never thought I'd actually feel bad for them.

This is a direction in the conversation that I wasn't expecting to go. I do what I do best and deflect it back.

"So, tell me why you don't date riders?"

"Because they're assholes," she chuckles and gestures to me.

"Assholes, huh? I'm shocked." I place a hand over my heart dramatically.

"Yes! Total players and they're terrible in bed." She cringes and waves her hand around before she starts laughing. She's full on amused now. I shake my head.

"You have no idea."

"Doubtful."

Ohhh she's asking for it. I place my hands on the edge of the chair and push myself up. I stand in front of her. My shins butt up against her bent knees. My right hand brushes against her cheek and slowly moves to the back of her head. I gently squeeze the back her neck, my thumb grazing her jaw as my voice drops.

"The way I'd make you come for the first time. How *sweet* you'd taste. How your pussy would tighten around my cock afterwards. How it'd take over your mind. Your *body.* It'd change your mind. *Trust me.*"

Her mouth opens slightly as her eyes shimmer with desire. Hook. Line. Sinker.

And I walk away.

1...2...

"Excuse me?!"

"You heard me." I don't even look back when I answer her.

I reach for the 250 and wait for her. Her boots clunk behind me and I smile to myself. Her hand touches the handlebar and I remain there until she gets on the bike.

"Thanks," she says sarcastically.

I smile slyly at her. I turn to walk over to my bike when I feel a sting... on my ass.

She fucking smacked me.

I look back at her, completely surprised. She can't contain her laughter as she shrugs her shoulders.

"Payback's a bitch."

"Ha-Ha, real funny Kill Switch," I say as I climb on my bike. *This woman will be the death of me.*

We continue our dance on the track challenging each other and, it's just plain, easy.

"Do you need help putting the bikes away?" she asks as we finish up.

"No, that's okay. I got it." I say even though I wouldn't mind her staying here longer. But, I know she has dinner plans with her friend. I'll be busy with the tedious tasks of cleaning the bikes and doing the post ride maintenance. It will be good for me. What else do I have to do today besides get rid of this all-day hard on?

She tucks a blonde strand behind her ear and gives me a genuine smile.

"Thank you for today. It really was nice."

"Break your rule so it can be a nice first date." I smile and tip my chin up at her. She starts to walk away.

"Nice try *Mr. Milano!*" She throws over her shoulder as she struts to her car.

"Oh, I've not given up yet," I say to myself as her dust trail remains.

Not at all.

19

Stephanie

"I thought you got kidnapped or something!"

I barely make it into the booth before Lex is already halfway out of her seat, red curls bouncing as she scans me like I might be missing a limb. I toss my purse in first and slide in across from her, exhaling hard.

"No kidnapping," I say. "Unless you count emotional turbulence."

"That sounds illegal." She squints.

"It should be."

She laughs and pushes a glass of water toward me like she's seen this exact version of me before. Which, annoyingly, she has. I take a long drink, suddenly realizing how dry my throat is.

"Little thirsty?" she asks, smirking.

"A little?" I deadpan. "I feel like I just ran a marathon while being aggressively flirted with."

Her eyes light up.

"Oh it was *that* kind of day."

I roll my eyes, but I can't stop the smile that sneaks out. We look down at the menus even though it's pointless. We are at her favorite Italian restaurant, Luna's Di'napoli. She is here so much she could make the dishes herself at this point. She leans forward, elbows on the table.

"Start talking."

So I do.

I tell her about the empty track. The bikes. The way Axel looked standing there like he'd been waiting for me his whole life. I try to gloss over the part where he watched me get dressed, but Lex clocks it immediately.

"He sat down and watched?" she interrupts.

"I mean… sat is generous. It was more… looming."

She presses a hand to her chest. "Disgusting. I love him."

By the time I get to the riding, she's nodding along even though she has no idea what half the words mean. I describe the rhythm, the way it didn't feel like competing, just existing in the same space. How easy it was. Then I hesitate.

Lex notices, of course she does.

"What?" she asks softly. "What did he say?"

I lower my voice instinctively, even though the restaurant is loud.

"He said.." I clear my throat and tell her.

Her fork freezes in mid air.

"He said what now?!" I look around to see if anyone heard.

"Lex—"

She slams her hand on the table. "NO. Do not 'Lex' me. Repeat it."

So I do.

She leans back slowly, fans herself with the drink menu and, mutters, "Hot damn."

I snort despite myself. "That's what I'm saying! Instant

puddle, followed by instant panic."

"Of course it was," she says. "Because you're allergic to enjoying things."

"I am not."

"You absolutely are. You were probably like, *wow*, that was *hot*, and then immediately thought about HR violations and your mother."

I groan. "Why would you say that out loud?"

"Because it's true," she grins.

I twirl my fork through my pasta without eating it, the earlier excitement settling into something heavier, quieter.

"He felt... different today," I admit. "Not just flirting. It was like he was actually there. Not looking at me like I'm just... my last name."

Lex softens instantly. "That matters."

"It does," I say. "And that scares the hell out of me."

She studies me for a moment. "You like him."

"I—" I stop. Sigh. "I might."

Her smile turns gentle. "Steph."

"I know, I know. I sound like a high schooler with a crush. I hate it."

"You don't hate it," she says. "You hate that you can't control it."

...Rude. Accurate. But *rude*.

"But I still hold by my rule," I say. "I even told him about it. No dating riders. We work together and it's messy. I don't want that."

"And yet," she points out, "you spent your day riding alone with him on his week off."

I open my mouth. Close it.

Damn it.

"He asked if it was a date," I add quietly.

"And?"

"I said no."

Lex tilts her head. "Did you mean it?"

I think about his hands steadying the bike. The way he looked at me like I wasn't fragile or off-limits. The way he walked away instead of pushing.

"I don't know," I admit. "But I don't think he's playing me. Not after we cleared the air."

"Exactly," she says. "If he was, he wouldn't bother with the slow burn. He'd already be in your bed."

I choke on my water. "LEX."

She laughs. "I'm just saying. He's trying and you're letting him."

I stare down at my plate, then finally take a bite.

"Maybe," I say slowly, "I'm just tired of running."

She reaches across the table and squeezes my hand. "Then don't. I'm not saying to rush it. See where it goes. You don't have to decide anything tonight. I know it's complicated."

I smile, warmth spreading through my chest.

"Also," she adds, eyes gleaming again, "If you don't at least kiss him soon, I might do it for you."

I laugh. "You would not."

"Try me."

We laugh.

20

Stephanie

"You ready?"

Axel sits at the folding table just off the edge of the track, dressed in a plain black pocket T-shirt and a black snapback pulled low over his brow. The black cross at his neck rests perfectly against his chest, catching the light every time he shifts. He gives me a short nod while I triple-check the setup like my life depends on it.

My laptop is propped open in front of him, webcam angled just right. A canopy shades us from the brutal California sun, the fabric snapping faintly in the breeze and doing its job—no glare, no squinting, no excuses. The distant sound of engines revving, hums through the air, muffled but constant, like a heartbeat beneath everything.

I move just off camera and pull out my notebook, telling myself, *commanding* myself, to focus on notes instead of doodling *I heart Axel* like an idiot. And I hate him for it. I shake my head hard, trying to physically dislodge the thoughts clinging to my brain, and look back up at him.

Big mistake.

His tattoos are showing, ink tracing muscle and skin in a way that makes it slightly difficult to breathe. My mind betrays me immediately, replaying flashes from our *not-a-date*. Damn him for being attractive in moto gear. Damn him even more for being devastatingly hot in normal clothes. What an asshole.

"Okay," I say, slipping into professional mode like it's armor. "Let's go over everything one more time. You'll be a guest on the *Danny Talks Moto* podcast. If you somehow missed it—his name's Danny." My serious expression falters for half a second. "Anyways. He's got over a million followers and he's known for asking the dirty, detailed questions. Do you want to review anything before we start?"

He picks up the Bluetooth microphone and clips it on his shirt, sliding his black chain out of the way.

"I know who he is. By the way... If I ace this interview will you go on an actual date with me?" He raises his eyebrows at me. Although my heart stops for a second, I tell him what he doesn't want to hear.

"No."

I cross my arms and legs and slightly bounce my foot as it's hovering above the dirt. His blue eyes stare at me while he slowly leans over the laptop. I internally brace myself for what he has to say.

"I bet your pussy already regrets that decision." His gaze flicks down to my shorts as his lips form a sly smile. My cheeks redden. My mind can't even form a response before I hear Danny's voice coming from the laptop.

"Good evening moto fans! I'm Danny and this is the Danny Loves Moto podcast! Our guest today is none other than Axel Milano. One of team Kawasaki's pro motocross riders! Axel, how are things going this season?"

"Thanks for having me Danny, glad to be here. I feel this season is going well so far. Obviously I'd like to be leading in points, but I'm still able to compete so I can't complain."

Not bad. He gives a small smile.

"Axel, people talk a lot about your raw speed, but lately there's been chatter about your *mental game.* Some say when things don't go your way, it shows. Fair or unfair?"

"I think passion gets mislabeled as instability. I care about winning. If that makes people uncomfortable, that's not really my problem."

My jaw tightens as I scribble *Watch Tone,* in my notebook.

"Would you ever consider working with a sports psychologist or performance coach? Some riders swear by it," Danny asks.

"I already talk to people who keep me grounded. I don't need someone telling me to breathe into a paper bag," Axel responds.

Oh my God, you cannot say that.

Jim would be pinching his nose in frustration right now.

"Let's be honest—If Rad Carson wasn't in the series right now, would your season look different?"

Diving right in there I see.

"Probably. But racing without someone pushing you doesn't make you better. Rad makes me better, even when he pisses me off."

That wasn't horrible, surprisingly. He adds a couple standard questions before he really goes for it.

"You mentioned earlier that having Stephanie Carson around adds another layer. From a performance standpoint, has that been a distraction, or a benefit?"

"She's sharp. Calls things out that most people wouldn't.

That kind of honesty makes you think, evaluate yourself—even if you don't want to hear it."

Was that a... complement? My mind is reeling even as Danny continues.

"Fans see you as intense, intimidating. What do they get wrong about you?"

"I'm actually pretty simple. Ride, train, work on bikes, stay out of bullshit."

"Stay out of bullshit? That might be the first time that's been said about you," Danny says grinning.

I snort unable to help myself. Axel gives me a warning look from over the laptop.

"The women's-only class you hosted, some people called it overdue, others called it a publicity move. What do you say to that?"

"Anyone who thinks empowering people is a PR stunt hasn't watched someone conquer fear for the first time. Seeing their faces light up when they accomplished a step was amazing in itself. And I personally feel that this sport can be loved by all. It can even be a great bonding tool for couples. There's something about enjoying your favorite hobby with not just yourself but with your partner as well."

"Are you saying that you might do couples classes?" Danny asks.

Axel quickly locks eyes with me as he smiles at the camera.

"I'll have to speak to the PR manager but I'm sure that can be arranged."

I start writing down notes, my mind already brainstorming. It's honestly a great idea, even if the idea came from a not so professional occasion. Why does it make me...proud?

"Hypothetically, if a rider and a team staffer *were* to cross that professional line, do you think it would hurt performance or help it?"

"I think chemistry, on or off the bike, always matters. How you handle it is the real test," Axel says as he gives a dangerous grin.

My blood boils.

This is *not* hypothetical and he knows it. Rumors like that could end careers before they'd even begin.

"Last one. What should fans expect from you for the rest of the season?"

Axel doesn't answer right away. He shifts in his chair, forearms resting on the table, fingers loosely laced. The easy grin he's worn most of the interview fades into something more focused. Intentional. His eyes flick, just once, past the camera, landing on me. Then back to Danny.

"Honestly? Less restraint. I spent a long time riding not to lose instead of riding to win. Playing it safe. Holding back because it was easier to keep people comfortable that way." He shrugs, like he's already done apologizing for it. "That's not why I got on a bike in the first place."

"So what changes?" Danny asks.

Axel's jaw tightens. Not angry but resolved.

"More intention. Every gate drop, every pass, every decision on and off the track." He pauses. "I'm done reacting. I'm choosing."

Another glance in my direction. Slower this time, deliberate.

"If that makes some people uncomfortable? Good. Comfort doesn't win championships."

Danny lets out a low whistle. "Sounds like a warning."

Axel smirks, the familiar edge returning.

"Call it a promise."

My pen stills mid-sentence. My stomach flips in a way I absolutely refuse to analyze. That wasn't just for the fans and that wasn't just about racing.

And the worst part?

I don't know if he's talking about the track... or *me*.

"You should be on your knees after that one."

I snap back to reality.

The nerve of this guy.

I click my pen, setting it down to meet his eyes. The laptop is shut as he unclips the microphone and sets it on the table.

"I'm afraid that's not in my job description," I say smugly.

"What about in your free time?" He quirks an eyebrow at me while he intertwines his fingers, his elbows on the armrests.

"Keep dreaming, Milano." I stand and start gathering my things. As I reach for my laptop Axel stands as well. I'm now staring at his chest as he towers over me, his voice dropping an octave.

"Still trying to resist me, Kill Switch?"

I slowly straighten and gaze up at him.

"You're really full of yourself aren't you?"

He chuckles as his hand tucks my hair behind my ear.

"Just think... the more you resist, the sweeter it'll feel when you finally give in."

He licks his bottom lip and I pray he doesn't hear me swallow. He smiles, knowing he's got me right where he wants me and then he... walks away.

Fucking asshole.

My mind screams no, when my whole body begs me to say yes.

***

I take a deep breath outside Jim's office, dragging my palms down my shorts even though they're already damp. The podcast aired which means, statistically, I'm about to be fired. Kevin asked me to come in first thing this morning, which feels intentional. Efficient. Like ripping off a Band-Aid before the sting has time to register.

At least they didn't wait until the end of the day for my public execution.

"Stephanie, please take a seat."

Jim's already behind his desk, clicking through something on his computer like this is just another Tuesday. Kevin leans against the wall, arms crossed, posture loose. Too loose. They don't look tense which, somehow makes me more nervous. Jim doesn't waste time.

"We wanted to check in with you and see how things are going."

Check in. Corporate for *evaluate*.

"The heat from Axel's incident has calmed down signif icantly," he continues, eyes flicking briefly to the screen. "Engagement is up. His fan base has actually grown."

My lungs finally remember how to work.

"So—good job."

The breath I let out feels shaky, like it's been trapped in my chest for days.

"Thank you," I say, forcing a smile that doesn't fully reach my eyes.

Kevin straightens a bit. "And the women's-only class. You did great work there. We're making it a monthly thing. We'd like you to keep organizing it."

Wait.

So I'm not fired?

Relief crashes through me, followed immediately by irritation. I hate that I was bracing for the worst when all I did was my job. I hesitate, then decide not to shrink.

"It'd be my pleasure," I say. "And I wanted to run another idea by you. Axel mentioned on the *Danny Loves Moto* podcast the possibility of a couples-only class. I actually think it could be a really strong outreach program."

Jim and Kevin exchange a look. The kind that happens when two men silently weigh risk versus optics.

Kevin nods first. "Not bad."

Jim chuckles. *Actually* chuckles. "Who is this kid?" He shakes his head. "Who knew he had it in him."

Then Jim's expression shifts—just enough for my stomach to drop.

"Now," he says carefully, "We didn't watch the interview ourselves. But we did hear about the... rivalry angle. Rad and Axel," he pauses. "And the *perception* of something going on between you two."

There it is.

The thing I haven't done. The thing that apparently matters more than the work I *have* done.

"Oh—nothing is going on," I blurt, heat flooding my face.

Jim lifts a hand, stopping me mid-sentence.

"This isn't an accusation," he says. "It's a caution."

Kevin exhales, like he doesn't love this part either. "We all know how Axel can be. He's got a reputation. Charismatic. A little reckless."

A *player*, they mean. But somehow that label sticks to him like a badge of honor.

Jim folds his hands. "And you, unfortunately, you're held to a different standard."

The words land harder than if he'd raised his voice.

"People don't see a PR specialist doing her job," he continues. "They see a woman standing next to a rider and start filling in blanks that aren't theirs to fill."

I bite the inside of my cheek as I start fidgeting with my ring.

Kevin shifts, clearly uncomfortable. "We've noticed Axel's attitude improving. The class ideas, the interviews—he's been easier to manage."

Jim shoots him a look like he's gone off script.

"I'm just saying," Kevin adds quickly, hands lifting in surrender. "Her presence has been good for him."

Good for *him*. Risky for *me*.

Jim refocuses on me. "We're not forbidding relationships. That's not what this is."

But it might as well be.

"We're protective of our staff," he says. "And rumors, especially involving a Carson, can spiral fast."

Of course they can.

Because history sticks to *my* last name, not his.

"I understand," I say, even though my jaw aches from clenching it.

Kevin offers a sympathetic look as I stand. "You're doing good work, Stephanie. Just... be mindful."

Mindful.

Of standing too close.

Of smiling too much.

Of being seen.

What a dream come true.

"Well," I mutter once I'm in the hallway, "that was a shit

storm and a half."

Thank God I haven't kissed the damn guy. I'm already getting heat for existing in his vicinity.

It's bullshit to be honest.

A man can flirt, joke, stir rumors, and it's considered personality. A woman does the same, or less, and suddenly she's a liability. I just want to do my job without having to constantly prove that my presence isn't a distraction. Especially in a sport where distraction can get someone killed.

"I'll just avoid him," I say under my breath, wiping sweat from my forehead. "Easy peasy."

The mess hall is packed with the morning rush, so I settle for coffee that's mostly creamer. I stare out the window while I sip it, watching the track wake up. Engines hum in the distance, vibrating through the walls like a heartbeat.

Buzz.

I sigh. "Of course."

"Hello?"

"Are you sleeping with him?!" My mother's voice is sharp enough that I pull the phone away from my ear.

"Do you have to yell?"

Her scoff is instant. I can picture the manicured foot tapping, the perfectly controlled outrage.

"Well?!"

"What if I am?" I fire back.

Silence. Then fury.

I don't wait for it.

I don't even care that's it's a lie. I hang up before she can respond.

I stare into my empty cup, already knowing one coffee won't cut it today.

"Going for round two?"

I look up to find Ben smiling at me.

"Oh—hi, Benji." I manage a half-smile.

"You okay?" he asks, genuinely.

"Yeah," I lie. "Nothing I can't handle."

He studies me but lets it go. As he turns to leave, I catch his arm.

"Hey—can you do me a favor?"

"Always."

"Can you tell Axel I'll be working from home the next couple days?" I hesitate. "And that I'll see him on press day."

Ben nods, no questions asked. "Of course."

As he walks away, I wrap my hands around my coffee cup and exhale.

Because apparently in Motorsports, being good at your job isn't always enough.

Sometimes you have to survive the optics too.

21

Stephanie

"**R**EDBUDDDDD!"

The fans scream it like a war cry, drowning out even the engines. Red, white, and blue explode everywhere—bandanas, tank tops, face paint, American flags snapping violently in the hot Michigan air. Horns blare nonstop.

This track is already known for being feral on a normal weekend, but Fourth of July? It's a completely different beast. I've already seen far too many shirtless beer bellies and it's not even noon.

My high ponytail is doing absolutely nothing to help the sweat pooling down the back of my neck. The sun is relentless. There's no clouds, no mercy, so my blue-tinted sunglasses are non-negotiable. My usual staff polo has been swapped for the limited-edition Fourth of July one, already sticking to me in places I'd rather not think about. Qualifying hasn't even started and I feel like I've lost ten pounds in sweat alone.

I jog over to Casey, our photographer, to see what he's captured so far. His curly red hair is already damp, curls plastered to his forehead. Okay. Good. At least I'm not the only one melting. He lowers his camera when he sees me coming.

"Alright, let's see 'em," I say, slightly out of breath, hands braced on my hips. It's early, but Casey somehow always manages to catch magic when everyone else is still warming up.

"Hey, Steph. I've only got a couple decent ones so far."

I snort. "You're so modest. They're always good."

His cheeks redden instantly, and he gives me a shy smile before leaning over to scroll through the shots. As expected—they're unreal.

The first is Watson Mays floating through the air, bike pitched sideways in a perfect whip, dirt suspended behind him like it's frozen in time. The second is AJ hammering the opening straightaway, body low and aggressive, roost firing behind him in a violent spray that practically jumps off the screen.

Then there's Axel.

It's a close-up. He's sitting at the starting gate, helmet off, goggles dangling loosely in his hands. His jaw is set, eyes locked forward—sharp, focused, almost electric. There's something in his expression that makes my breath hitch.

Determination. Hunger. Fire.

It's... beautiful.

"Wow, Casey," I say softly. "These are incredible. Send them to me ASAP."

He nods and jogs toward the media rig. Moments later my phone buzzes with the uploads and I let the staff know, so they can post the teams photos. I post the ones of Axel within minutes to his account, standard race-day captions, hashtags already lighting up.

Check. Another task done.

I flip through my pocket-sized notebook until I find a clean page. There's something grounding about pen and paper—no notifications, no noise. I climb the nearest hill overlooking the starting gate and watch a few launches, jotting down who looks sharp, who's missing timing, who's tentative. Starts win races at RedBud. Everyone knows it. Doesn't hurt to tell Axel what I've learned as well.

I keep moving during qualifying, bouncing from corner to corner, heat radiating off the dirt as bikes rip past, inches away. It's the midpoint of the Pro Motocross season, and the tension is thick enough to choke on. Rad still holds the points lead, Axel snapping at his heels.

In the first moto, Zane Ryker grabs the holeshot and the crowd loses their minds, chanting his name. The veteran hangs on for a few laps before Rad slices past him clean and decisive. Axel starts fifth, wastes no time, and charges forward—methodical, aggressive, finishing third.

The top three gather near the stage for post-moto interviews. Rad jogs up first, grinning like he owns the stage. The crowd eats it up, when he flashes a wink at a woman in the front row.

I glance at Axel beside me. He rolls his eyes.

"Please don't say anything stupid," I murmur.

He chuckles and nudges me with his elbow. "Maybe I'll say *just* the right amount of wrong. So, you have to keep working with me."

I look up at him. "I thought you wanted me to leave?"

His expression shifts—eyebrows knitting, something vulnerable slipping through.

"I did."

The lump in my throat comes fast and unwelcome.

I don't want to leave.

The late afternoon sun hangs low and vicious, turning the track into a furnace. The dirt has gone dry and powdery, breaking into deep ruts that punish even the smallest mistake. You can feel the tension now. The fans are on their feet, exhausts screaming louder, riders pushing past smart and into desperate.

This is where championships crack.

Axel comes out of the gate strong in the second moto. Not perfect, but hungry. He rides angry, charging corners harder, skimming jumps most guys are casing. Every pass is aggressive but clean, the kind that makes the crowd suck in air before erupting. Rad answers back, of course. They trade tenths of seconds, shadowing each other so closely it's almost reckless.

By lap eight, Axel nearly loses the rear end in a deep rut, saves it at the last second, and keeps charging. My heart doesn't restart until he clears the next rhythm section. It cost him a second, but he quickly recovered, continuing the battle for the rest of the race.

When the checkered flag waves, the crowd roars like they've just witnessed a war. I clap with everyone else, professional smile locked in place, but my eyes stay on Axel as he rolls back to the pits—helmet still on, shoulders tight, frustration vibrating off him like heat off the dirt.

Second place overall, again.

I get Axel settled, grabbing his helmet, handing him water, etc. Then, I congratulate Rad quickly. He's glowing, already playing to the cameras, then duck out fast, and head back to the crew. My pulse is still racing when I finally stop moving.

That's when my pocket buzzes.

Once. Twice. Then nonstop.

I pull my phone out, already bracing myself. Dozens of messages from Lex. My stomach drops. The first thing she sent is a TikTok, which I'd normally ignore, but the multiple messages following it is telling me to watch it. I tap it and suddenly the world tilts sideways.

It's me.

Kissing Axel.

I'm wearing the stupid limited-edition Fourth of July polo standing next to him on his bike when I lean over and kiss him. My face being a little distorted, and something I clearly didn't actually do.

Fucking AI.

Someone is quick on the draw.

The caption is massive, bold, impossible to miss:

Stephanie Carson kisses Axel Milano??

"What the fuck?" I whisper, my throat going dry.

I scroll.

They're dating?! Isn't that Rad's sister?

Is that even allowed?

No wonder he's losing this season.

Each comment hits harder than the last.

Then I see it.

Go figure she's fucking around with the riders already.

That one detonates something inside me. That's it. That's the stereotype. That's the rot we can't escape.

Women in this sport can't exist without being reduced to who we're supposedly sleeping with. We can manage, organize, strategize, build programs from nothing, but one video, one rumor, and suddenly we're not professionals anymore.

We're distractions, problems, and scandals.

I don't date riders because I don't want *this*. I don't want my work questioned. I don't want my success tied to a man's last name or lap time.

I want respect.

Regardless if I have feelings for someone.

I check the account. There's a blank profile picture and generic username. No trail.

Coward.

The fans are starting to clear out, the track quieting as the final bikes shut down. My breathing is shallow, hands shaking—not from fear anymore, but rage. Did Axel do this?

No. He wouldn't. He's not calculated like that and they don't have their phones. And it's race day—he barely exists outside the bike.

The walk back to the team rig turns my panic into something sharper, harder. I need answers.

Axel's under the canopy when I spot him. Riding pants still on, chest bare, a towel draped around his neck. Sweat and dirt streak his skin, his body still humming with adrenaline. My sudden approach almost makes him drop his water bottle.

"What are you—"

"I need to talk to you." my voice is low, tight.

I shove my phone in his face. "Did you do this?"

His brows knit instantly. He actually looks offended.

"Why the fuck would I do that?" he snaps. "One—I don't have the goddamn time. Two—it's stupid. And three—if we were actually dating, it'd be a hell of a lot less innocent than that."

The corner of his mouth quirks. I roll my eyes despite myself.

"Was it your mom?" he adds.

I shake my head. "No. She wouldn't risk the Carson name."

He shrugs. "So what's the big deal?"

That's when it snaps.

"You don't understand," I say, turning away. "You don't have to."

He grabs my wrist, pulling me back just enough to stop me.

"It takes women years, decades, to earn respect in this sport," I say, voice shaking now. "And one rumor can burn it all down. I'm so tired of fighting this, seeing others fight this."

His grip softens, thumb brushing my arm.

Then—

"There's the happy couple!"

The voice slices through us.

I freeze.

"I hope you liked my video," Bethany adds sweetly. "It's already going viral."

Axel stiffens below me. I feel it immediately. The shift, the restrained fury. He starts to get up, but I stop him with a look.

"I've got this."

I turn to face her.

"Let me know when she moves on to the next guy, Axel!" she calls, loud enough for anyone nearby to hear.

"Hey, Bethany," I say, flashing a polite smile that feels sharp enough to cut. "Can we talk? Just us."

Her eyes flick between me and Axel. She giggles like this is a joke, like she's already won.

"Sure," she says. "Why not?"

I walk behind the rig, not breaking stride, not giving her the satisfaction of hesitation. She follows, heels sinking into the dirt. The noise from the track dulls back here, replaced by the hum of generators and the distant cheers fading into background static.

We're alone as I turn to face her.

"Why did you post that?" I ask flatly. "You know exactly what that could do to my career."

She folds her arms, head tilting. "It's not obvious?"

"No," I say. "Spell it out for me."

Her smile sharpens. "I'm trying to ruin you."

The words hit, but I don't flinch.

"I've done nothing to you," I say. My voice rises despite myself. "Nothing."

"You have everything," she snaps back. "The job, the access, the attention."

"That's not yours to take," I say. "And it's not his either."

Her laugh is brittle. "You'll never have him."

And there it is.

Axel.

All of this, over a man. That's always the case isn't it?

I step closer. Her smile widens, like she's baiting me, daring me to prove her right.

But I'm not angry because of Axel. I'm angry because she risked *everything I've built* for a rumor.

"You think this is about him?" I ask quietly. "This is about me."

She scoffs. "Please."

That's when I shove her.

It happens fast—pure instinct, adrenaline snapping tight. My hands hit her shoulders, hard. She stumbles backward, loses her footing, and goes down in a splash of mud I didn't even know was there.

She gasps, wide-eyed, shock written all over her face.

For a split second, I stand there breathing hard, chest heaving, hands shaking.

Then I crouch down in front of her.

My voice drops. I stare into her eyes not letting her escape before I plead my case.

"If you think for one second that I'm out here sleeping my way into anything," I say, pointing a finger at her chest, "you're dead wrong."

Mud streaks her arms, her hair plastered to her face.

"I fight this stereotype every single day," I continue. "I work twice as hard, say half as much, and still get reduced to rumors like yours."

She opens her mouth, but I cut her off.

"I care about my *fucking* career," I snap. "Not about some *rider*."

My throat tightens. "And for the record, I haven't even kissed him."

Her eyes flicker. Her face full of doubt and hurt.

"Don't burn my reputation," I finish, "Just because you're jealous."

Silence hangs heavy between us.

I stand, the anger still vibrating through me, but something else creeps in too—exhaustion. This isn't who I want to be. I refuse to be a mean girl like her.

I sigh. Then I hold out my hand. I humiliated her enough.

She hesitates, looking at it like it might bite her.

Finally, she takes it.

I haul her up, wiping my hand on my shorts immediately, mud and all. Not subtle. Not apologetic.

She won't meet my eyes.

"I see the way he looks at you," she says quietly.

That one hits somewhere deep. *Fuck.*

I turn back to her, softer now.

"You deserve that look, too. You'll just have to accept... that it'll be from someone else."

Her shoulders sag. She nods her head, staring at the ground. I walk away without looking back. It's not because I won. It's because I refused to let her take anything else from me.

I do know one thing. Everybody deserves that look, deserves love.

Even bitch face Bethany.

Axel

Am I—

Hard right now?

Jesus.

I lean just enough to peer around the corner of the RV, because apparently I have zero self control and can't resist a front row seat to chaos. And listen... normally, I love a good chick fight. Who doesn't? It's basically a spectator sport. But this one? This one's different.

I could've stepped in earlier. Could've let my temper do what it does best and told Bethany exactly where she could shove her fake smile and fake tits. But then Stephanie looked at me. Those big green eyes sharp, and hurt at the same time, and I knew this wasn't mine to handle, so I stayed put.

My brain scrambles, trying to make sense of it. I assumed they were fighting over me. Wouldn't have shocked me. Wouldn't have even offended me. But this isn't about me. It's about *her.*

I've never really thought about how women get picked apart

in this sport. I worry about lap times, gate picks, and points. That's it. Watching this unfold, watching how fast a rumor can light a fuse, I get it now. I don't blame her for snapping. I don't blame her for wanting to burn it all down.

"Whatcha doin?"

I damn near jump out of my skin when Ben whispers directly into my ear.

"Shhh!" I hiss back, swatting him away like he's a mosquito.

He follows my line of sight and his grin slips right off his face.

"...I care about my fucking career! Not about some rider!"

Stephanie's voice cuts through the air, raw and pissed, right before she shoves Bethany to the ground.

Ben winces. "Oof."

"Should we... uh... do something?" he asks, already halfway to stepping in.

I shake my head. "Not yet."

He looks at me. I look back.

"If it escalates," I add, "then we intervene."

Ben nods slowly. "Copy that."

We watch in stunned silence as Stephanie does the last thing either of us expects. She *helps* Bethany up.

Ben exhales. "Damn."

"Yeah," I mutter.

We exchange a look. The kind that says *this conversation is definitely happening later.* Preferably with something stronger than water.

There's a lot to unpack after today—the race, the fallout, the fight, and the fact that Stephanie just showed more backbone than half the paddock combined.

It's going to be a hard week. In more ways than one.

"I know what to do," I murmur to myself.

Ben squints at me. "That sentence concerns me."

"It should."

22

Axel

My hand grips the throttle as I round the turn, body loose, and instincts sharp. The bike surges beneath me, suspension snapping back as I clear the tabletop clean. Wind rips at my jersey, the sound of the engine drowning out everything else—thoughts, memories, names I don't want in my head. The morning sun is muted behind my tinted goggles, the world reduced to dirt, ruts, and muscle memory.

This track is home. I know every rut, every sketchy landing that'll bite you if you get lazy. I push harder than I should, because pushing is the only thing that shuts my brain up. Red Bud is still rattling around in my skull like a loose bolt. The video. The meetings. The looks. The way everything went sideways in twenty-four hours.

I take another lap. Then another. I overshoot a corner, correct it at the last second, don't give a shit. There's no trainers, no team, and no cameras. It's just me and the bike.

One more lap.

I drop into a rut, fingers dancing over the clutch and front brake. I roll on the throttle, exhaust screaming as I exit, and hammer down the straight. I'm already lining up the jump ahead, already committing—and then something's *wrong*.

My brain registers it a half-second too late. It's a still shape where nothing should be.

I chop the throttle instinctively, the engine coughing as the bike bucks beneath me. The stall nearly sends me over the bars. I skid to a stop at the base of the jump, heart slamming into my ribs.

"What the fuck—"

I look up.

Stephanie-fucking-Carson.

She's standing at the top of the jump like she's the queen at her castle. Her arms crossed, jaw tight, blonde hair whipping in the breeze like she walked straight out of a storm. Gray T-shirt with black running shorts and tennis shoes. Her glare could punch through a helmet.

"Are you fucking crazy?!" I shout, yanking my goggles up. "I could've hit you!"

"Good," she snaps back. "Maybe then you'd actually look at me."

That stops me cold.

She stalks down the face of the jump, boots—*shoes*—sliding through loose dirt like she doesn't care if she eats shit. I plant my right foot, lean forward on the bars, flexing my gloved hands to keep from doing something stupid.

She comes right up beside me, and doesn't hesitate for a second. She grabs my shoulder and swings her leg over the bike like it's muscle memory. Her body presses into my back, tits brushing my spine, arms wrapping around my waist like she's furious and desperate all at once.

I forget how to breathe.

"Take me to the secret spot," she says, low and dangerous.

No argument. No explanation.

Okay then.

I bring the bike back to life and dump the clutch harder than necessary. We rocket uphill, dirt spraying as I weave through the trees. She clings to me, helmetless, trusting me more this time. That trust burns worse than the yelling would've.

The secret spot comes into view and my chest tightens. It hasn't felt right without her, since. Not once.

I kill the engine and she's off the bike immediately. I lean the bike against the tree, and pull my helmet off, pulse still racing, but now it's not from riding.

I step up beside her, both of us staring out over the city in the distance. The same view, but completely different realities.

"I've seen the passion you have for this job," I say finally. "You're unreal at it." I glance at her. "And yeah—selfishly—I think about having you all to myself more than I should."

She stiffens.

"But you deserve respect," I continue. "More than whispers in trailers."

I pause, hoping to work up the courage to confess.

"I talked to Jim and Kevin," I finally admit. The words feel heavier saying them out loud. "They pulled me aside after RedBud."

That gets her attention.

"They warned *you?*" she asks, incredulous.

"Yes. They said they also warned *you*," I say quietly. "About me."

Her jaw tightens. "Sort of."

"They didn't threaten your job," I add quickly. "But they

made it real clear how fast rumors turn into reputations. Especially for someone trying to prove they belong."

She exhales sharply and starts pacing again like she's trying to outrun the frustration crawling up her spine.

"You know what that video did to me?" she snaps. "Bethany didn't have to touch me to fuck me over. She just had to *suggest* something."

I wince.

"She didn't say it outright," Stephanie continues, voice rising. "She just smiled, tilted her head, had AI do it's thing, and let the internet do the rest. 'Sources say.' 'People are talking.' 'Looks like someone's getting special access.' That's all it takes. Even a fake video. I don't even post or do anything on my personal social media and I've gotten so many hateful DM's already. It's literally insane."

She laughs bitterly. "I've worked my ass off to not be reduced to that."

"I know," I say. And this time, I really do.

"You went on that podcast," she adds, spinning back toward me, eyes blazing. "You talked all that shit. Smirked. Played into it like it was a joke."

I swallow. "I didn't think—"

"No," she cuts in. "You didn't *have* to."

Silence stretches between us.

"They told me to be careful," she says more quietly now. "They didn't fire me or accuse me of anything. But the warning was there. Loud and clear."

She folds her arms across her chest, armor snapping back into place.

"And then Bethany drops that video," she finishes. "And suddenly it's not just whispers in the paddock. It's public.

Permanent. Something *I* have to clean up. Even when most people with a working brain cell can see it was fake. I shouldn't have to worry about things like that."

I rake a hand through my hair, frustration curling hot in my chest—at Bethany, at the media, at myself.

"I didn't mean to drag you into it," I say. "I ran my mouth. I thought I was being clever. I was just doing what I do."

Her gaze softens just a fraction. "That's the problem. You get to be whatever you want."

That lands like a punch.

"I have to be careful," she says. "All the time."

There's a soft patch of grass just beyond the trees, worn down from years of boots and tires and quiet moments no one's supposed to see. I gesture for her to sit, and she does without arguing. That alone feels like progress.

I drop down beside her, knees bent, boots digging into the dirt like I need the ground to remind me I'm still solid. Still in control.

We don't talk.

The world stretches out in front of us—track winding in the distance, city haze shimmering under the sun. Engines echo faintly somewhere far off, like a memory instead of a threat.

Minutes pass.

Then she shifts.

It's subtle at first. A small scoot closer. Her arm brushing mine. And then her head rests against my shoulder like it always belonged there.

Fuck.

Every muscle in my body locks up.

I stare straight ahead, jaw tight, hands fisted against my thighs, because if I move—even an inch—I don't trust myself to stop. Her hair smells like shampoo and sweat and something uniquely her, and when a quiet sigh slips from her lips, it hits me right in the chest.

"Thank you," she whispers.

Two words. Soft. Earnest.

I lift my left hand before I can talk myself out of it and cup the side of her face. My thumb grazes her cheekbone, slow and careful, like I'm handling something fragile. I feel her breath hitch instantly.

That's my cue.

I drop my hand.

Because if I don't, this turns into something neither of us can walk away from. And I refuse to be the reason her career derails.

A beat passes. Then she pulls away like she's been burned.

"I have to go," she blurts, like the words hurt.

She's already on her feet, already moving toward the bike.

"Hey—" I stand and catch up easily. "What's wrong?"

She shakes her head, eyes fixed on the dirt. I reach out, fingers closing gently around her shoulder.

"What's wrong, Steph?"

She nudges a rock with the toe of her shoe like it will solve the problem for her.

"I just..." her voice cracks. She swallows. "I gotta go. Okay?"

When she finally looks up at me, her green eyes are too bright, too full. I nod because, pushing her now would be cruel.

I grab my helmet, swing on, and she's behind me before I even start the engine. Her arms are locked around my waist like she's afraid to let go or, maybe afraid of what happens if she doesn't.

I take off.

The ride down is fast and quiet, wind tearing past us, her grip tightening every time I accelerate. She presses closer, forehead against my back, and I know—*I know*—she's fighting the same war I am.

Then her hand slaps my shoulder.

"Stop!"

I veer off instinctively, cutting around a jump and killing the engine hard. She jumps off before the dust even settles.

I rip my helmet off and let it drop.

"What the fuck is wrong with you?!" My voice is rough as I shout.

She turns on me, hands tangled in her hair, chest rising and falling like she just sprinted a mile.

"You," she snaps. "You're what's wrong."

"What are you talking about?"

"I can't—" She cuts herself off, shaking her head like the words won't behave.

"Can't what?" I step closer.

Her arms drop to her sides. Her eyes lift to mine, raw and furious and overwhelmed all at once.

"I can't be around you anymore."

She shoves past me. I move without thinking.

She barely makes it a step before I'm caught up to her, trapping her back gently but firmly against the side of the jump. My arm braces above her head, dirt crumbling down her shirt. I notice, against my will, where it stops.

"Stop fighting me," I murmur. "Talk to me, Kill Switch."

She squirms, thighs brushing together, frustration rolling off her in waves.

I lower my gaze, catching the movement.

Ah.

There it is.

I lean in, voice dropping. "That's the problem, isn't it?"

She turns her head away, jaw tight.

"You want me."

Her breath stutters.

Our bodies are too close. The air between us tightens, charged, and dangerous. Every line between us is buzzing, screaming to be crossed. I let myself watch her wrestle with it, right there under my arm, her pride warring with her desire.

I dip my head until my mouth is right by her ear.

"I won't touch you," I promise quietly. "Unless you beg me to."

"Let me go, Axel. I can't—"

"Can't what?" I whisper. "Resist? Let yourself get what you want? What is it? Tell me and I'll let you go."

Her chest rises and falls as she continues to battle the war within her. Until finally, she snaps her head back toward me, eyes blazing, decision made.

"Fuck it."

She grabs my jersey and yanks me down. The kiss detonates. It's far from gentle or cautious. It's all the restraint we've been hoarding finally setting itself on fire. Our mouths crash together, breath stolen, tension snapping so hard it makes my vision blur.

I force my hands to stay put. Every instinct screams to grab, pull and most importantly, claim. When she realizes I'm not touching her, she pulls back, chest heaving, eyes dark, and determined.

"*Fucking* touch me, Axel."

It's like the gate drops. I rush forward, my left hand grabbing the back of her neck. My right hand squeezes her waist and she whimpers. My lips crash into hers as our tongues fight for first. She reaches up and grips my hair as I lean into her. The riding pants barely hiding what all she's doing to me. Her breath catches, confirming that she feels it too.

Her hands start to move between us and I lean back to see what she's doing. It's like she stares into my soul as she rips her shirt off, never breaking eye contact. Her chest rises as her perfect tits threaten to spill out of her black lace bra. My eyes devour her as her mouth quirks into a lustful smile. It's like she knew black was my favorite color.

"Fuck, you're beautiful," I say softly. I trace my fingers lightly from her shoulder to her collar bone and to the base of her throat. My glove leaves goosebumps on her skin as I move lower. It's like the start of a race and you know what they say… I have plenty of time. And I plan on winning this one.

My fingers play with the band of her shorts, teasing her, until my knuckles grind against the spot she likes the most. A soft moan escapes her lips.

"Still want me to touch you?" I ask even though the answer is obvious.

She looks up at me and nods her head lazily.

"I want you to say it," I demand, pausing to lift her chin. Zero hesitation stares back at me.

"I want you to touch me like your life fucking depends on it," she rasps back.

That's better.

The sun hangs overhead, brutal and unforgiving, yet it's nothing compared to the fire crackling between us right now. Everything narrows to her. The way she feels, the way she tastes, and I kiss her like I'd suffocate without it, like letting go isn't an option.

My hand slips inside her shorts, still not bothering to take my gloves off. She moans against my mouth as I rub her clit.

"*Fuck.* I can feel how wet you are for me," I say in a heated whisper.

I trail kisses on her neck, gradually moving down until I get to the dip in her shoulder. Her breathing picks up as my throttle hand moves faster. It doesn't take long for her eyes to begin to roll, body shaking as she shatters beneath me.

"*Ahh*, fuck Axel!" She grips my jersey, hanging on for dear life.

"That's it baby," I praise.

I kiss her forehead, gradually slowing my pace to let her ride out her orgasm as long as possible. She looks up at me once her breathing evens out, smiling like she has no idea what she's done to me, and I smile, matching it.

I lean down to kiss her while my hand grabs one of her full breasts. It's not enough. I yank down the front of her bra, gaining me access. I drag her hard peak between my teeth, causing a small whimper to escape her lips. I make sure to give both my full attention before returning to her mouth.

My pulse spikes with the realization that follows. I've always said nothing beats the sound of a four-stroke at full throttle—the vibration, the control. But, standing here with her, I know that's not true anymore. The thought rattles me enough that I have to rein it in and refocus before it takes me somewhere I'm not ready to go.

I break our kiss just enough to start edging us toward my bike that's still leaning against the side of the jump. I spin and pull her flush against me. I kiss the back of her neck allowing my hands to continue exploring her body as we inch closer.

"Ready?" I say seductively.

"What are you waiting for?" she fires back.

I slide my hand to her throat squeezing the sides slightly so she gets the message.

"You're going to regret that attitude," I whisper the promise in her ear.

"Will I?" she dares.

I shove her forward until her breasts hit the seat.

"Oh!" She squeals.

The thought of it being too much for her quickly vanishes when I notice her heels lifting off of the ground. I tilt my hips, pressing against her ass, teasing her. I'm not surprised when she pushes back, making my dick throb. The bike barely moves.

Perfect.

I hook my thumbs in her waistband, thankful for the easy access but willing to fight through anything to finally see what's underneath. Her shorts fall to her ankles and I can't help but smile at the confirmation of what I already felt.

"No underwear? You naughty girl," I tease, smacking her ass, amazed by what's in front of me. She giggles and rocks side to side in response.

As much as she deserves our first time to be in a bed, I'm not a patient man today. Obviously, she's done holding back as much as I am. And frankly? This is more us. A true connection that is dirty, rough, raw, and a dirt bike to keep us steady.

I reach down, unfastening my pants quickly, and lowering them. My dick springs free, anticipation at it's peak. My hand wraps around the shaft as I tease her entrance.

She's ready for me.

"Last chance," I warn.

She glares at me over her shoulder not giving either one of us the option to overthink this. There's no going back now.

I slowly enter her and with each inch comes with more realization. I want to throw away every metal and trophy I've ever won. None of them matter anymore. It feels better in this moment than ever being on the podium.

When I'm fully seated inside her, my vision fractures—like I've blown past every limit I've ever known. I've been with plenty of women, but none of them come close. I fear she's ruined me in a way I'll never recover from.

"Ohh, Axel," she moans, her words bouncing off the dirt.

I reach forward and grab a fist full of her hair. I yank her head back and lean over her, until I can whisper in her ear.

"Like it or not, you're mine now. You'll always be mine." I graze my teeth on her earlobe and she shutters. "You're gunna *hate* how good this will feel."

My thrusts are fast as I pound into her over and over again, her ass smacking against me. It's pure bliss as she hangs on to the bike for dear life. She yelps as I slap her perfect ass cheek, leaving a red mark. I do it again for good measure. Then I reach around to rub her clit as I continue to fuck her.

"You're going to come for me again." I growl at her and she whimpers.

Fuckkk

It's good. It's *too* good.

A minute passes and I use my free hand to fist her hair again. I lean down to let her know I'm not fucking around.

"Come for me."

"I can't-" she pleads as her muscles quiver.

"No. You *will*," I demand, increasing my speed. I begin to

feel her tighten around me. "That's it."

She lets out one last moan before bending to my will, falling apart beneath me again.Her body convulsing, the bike shaking.

"Ah, fuck!"

I can't hold back any longer. I pull out and paint my new favorite picture on her back. A release you can make a movie about.

We stay like that for a few seconds, maybe longer. Time feels suspended, stretched thin while our breathing slowly evens out. My forehead drops to her shoulder and I let myself exist there, feeling the way she's still warm, still close, still real.

Then, I step back just enough to give her space, fastening my pants as I shrug out of my jersey. The air hits my skin, grounding me. I use the fabric to gently wipe her back, careful, deliberate—like if I rush this part I'll break something fragile between us. She glances over her shoulder at me, eyes soft now, a small smile tugging at her lips like she's in on a secret only we know.

"That's a pretty expensive towel," she says, quiet, teasing.

I huff a low laugh, shaking my head. "Worth every damn penny."

I help her pull her shorts back into place, my hands lingering for half a second longer than necessary, not because I want more, but because I don't want *less*. Then I hand her, her shirt. When she turns to face me, she's close enough that I can feel her breath again. Her fingers brush my stomach, light, almost uncertain, and it hits me harder than anything else has today.

I lean in and kiss her, not desperate, not rushed. Just honest. When she pulls back, she looks at me like she's bracing for something neither of us is ready to name yet.

"So," she says, voice softer now. "What are your plans for

today?"

I glance around at the track, at the dirt, at the bike that brought us here. Then I look back at her. "This," I say simply. "And maybe cleaning up after."

Her smile grows, slow and dangerous.

I grab my helmet, tuck my jersey under my arm, and swing my leg over the bike. I look back at her, already knowing she's coming.

"Hop on, Kill Switch," I say. "Let's get out of here."

She shakes her head, but she's smiling when she climbs on behind me. And this time, when her arms wrap around my waist, it doesn't feel like tension anymore.

It feels like a beginning.

23

Stephanie

"Holy mother of God," I mumble into the back of Axel's helmet as we ride toward the workshop.

My brain is still buffering. It's fully frozen, completely offline.

Because—hypothetically—if someone were to ask how I'm doing after what just happened, I'd tell them I feel like I just stood on the podium, champagne spraying, crowd screaming, trophy raised overhead. Except the trophy is my dignity and I left it somewhere on the side of a motocross jump.

I came *twice*.

Twice.

That has never, *never*, happened to me. And believe me, I have put in the hours. Personal research was conducted. Extensive testing occurred. Results were disappointing until approximately fifteen minutes ago.

Stephanie, how do you feel after that win?

Fucking fantastic, Charlotte.

This man absolutely ruined me. Like, deep-down, cellular-level ruined. I can feel it in my bones. My soul may need a hydration break.

We stop at the washing station on the side of the workshop. He places the bike on it's stand like it weighs nothing while I'm over here checking if my legs still work. I see his jersey tossed to the side and I chuckle in disbelief. Who knew Axel Milano was the caring type. The bar was truly in hell before this.

I keep waiting for the regret to creep in. I wait for the guilt, the spiral, the what-the-hell-did-I-just-do panic, but it never comes. There's just... calm. And something warm and steady in my chest. I finally listened to my heart. I'll unpack the consequences later. Future Stephanie can deal with that mess.

Axel starts setting up the pressure washer, all focused and efficient, like he didn't just completely alter my brain chemistry.

"Hey, there's a bathroom in the workshop if you need it," he says casually, while unwrapping the hose.

"Oh, perfect." I head towards the door but pause. "Hey, where's your air box cover at? And the side panel just pops off right? So, you don't need a wrench?"

He straightens slowly, clearly not expecting that.

So I raise an eyebrow.

"Did you forget who I am?"

He exhales a laugh, shaking his head.

"Um, right. It does. Ben's station is the first one on the left. Everything should already be on the bench—except the butt plug. But I can grab—"

"I got it." I wink, as I half laugh knowing he doesn't mean really mean a butt plug. But, it's hard not to call it that when the thing is silicon rubber, cone shaped, and is shoved in the exhaust pipe.

His smile is instant, effortless, and dangerous.

I walk toward the workshop thinking—*yeah, I could get used to making him smile.*

Before I grab the door, I glance to the side and spot a pair of fuzzy ears poking out from beneath a tree.

"Oh, don't look at me like that, Marvin," I mutter.

He huffs and turns his head away.

Good thing animals can't talk. This one would absolutely be judging me.

When I come back out a few minutes later, Axel's leaning over the bike, bare hands clasped, tattoos in all their glory, cross dangling, hair a little messy like it wasn't just me that had her hands through it... distracting. Butterflies riot in my stomach. He catches me staring and smirks. I almost drop the supplies.

"I'm pretty sure I grabbed everything," I say, handing them over.

"I'm sure you did." He takes them easily, then leans down and kisses my forehead.

My knees nearly fold.

"I grabbed you a chair," he adds. "Go relax."

"You don't need help?" I ask, tilting my head.

"I might later."

The wink should be illegal.

I sit in the camp chair, trying, and failing, not to replay everything in my head. Just as I start biting my lip, a cool mist hits my shoulder.

I look up to find Axel pretending to be innocent.

"Hey!"

I bolt toward him. He lifts the nozzle just out of reach,

laughing, and it doesn't take long before we're both soaked and breathless and spinning. The nozzle clatters to the cement as his hands frame my face. Everything else disappears.

"Who would've thought I'd get you wet again so soon," he murmurs. "Oh, actually, I would def—"

"Yeah, yeah," I cut in. "Mister confidence. I get it."

I tap his chest and back away. "Now finish cleaning the bike so I can see your bachelor pad."

"Yes, my Queen." He bows mockingly, making me laugh.

I settle back into the chair, crossing my leg over the other, gripping the armrests like a kid forced to eat vegetables before dessert.

Sweat glistens on his chest as he towels the bike down, muscles flexing, tattoos shifting, cross swinging. He glances over his shoulder like he *knows* exactly what I'm thinking.

Rude.

I wander over as he's finishing up. I reach my hand between the exhaust and the back fender and lean my hip against the side. Dirt bikes are a lot heavier than they look. When both tires touch the ground and I get it rolling, Axel lifts his head and freezes.

"Did you just lift that by yourself?"

"Yep," I smirk. "Now get the door."

He jogs over, then stops me gently. "Give me the bike, Kill Switch."

"What? Don't think I can handle it?"

"You don't need to prove anything to me," he says, steady and sincere. "I know you're strong."

Oh.

"And honestly?" He grins. "Watching you push my bike was making me way too horny."

There it is.

"Do you always have to say something inappropriate after something serious?" I tilt my head at him as he shrugs his shoulders.

"Hey," he says defensively. "You love it when I'm dirty." He winks at me and if that doesn't melt my insecurities.

***

"So, this is the famous rider's apartment?"

I let my fingers skim the blank wall, surveying the place. Whites, blacks, grays, like a showroom that forgot to add personality. There's no photos, no clutter, no proof of life. I check the fridge, and shocker, it's stocked with water and condiments. *Thrilling.*

"There is a mess hall downstairs with everything I'd ever need," Axel says knowingly.

"Don't you ever want to, you know, make something your-self?" I quirk an eyebrow at him as he rubs the back of his neck.

"I tend to, uh, burn everything I try to cook," he says sheepishly.

"Ah, I see." I close the fridge door as he continues the tour.

"Don't even say it." I hold my hand up as I stand in his bedroom doorway.

"What?" he asks amused.

"This is where the magic happens," I say while doing air quotes.

"I honestly wasn't going to say that," he chuckles. "The magic never happens here."

I look up at him confused.

"I've only been with women at a hotel on race weekends. It's frowned upon to have any woman here actually," He tilts his head at the realization. "Unless they're girlfriends or wives of course."

"And me." The words spilling out before I can stop them.

We just stand there, suspended in the aftermath of everything we haven't said. Whatever this is between us feels different. Unsettling in the best way. I don't know how to explain it, but looking at him now, I think he feels it too. Or maybe I've just officially lost it.

To break the silence, I wander farther into his bedroom. It's the only space that hints a pro motocross rider actually sleeps here. A dresser sits against the wall, every inch of its surface crowded with trophies and medals. My fingers brush over a second-place trophy from the opening outdoor round, and I smile, remembering my first race on the job.

I can feel Axel's eyes on me as I take in the rest of the room. A small TV mounted on the wall. A modest closet. There's no photos, artwork, nothing personal. Even the comforter, like his signature helmet, is black.

"You weren't kidding when you said no woman's been here," I say, glancing back at him. He's sitting on the edge of the bed now.

"This place feels like a freshman dorm room."

"I know," he says, leaning back on his hands. "It's just a place to crash and technically, I don't own it so-"

"Yeah, but I figured there'd be... *something*. A *little* personality maybe."

He shrugs. "Why personalize it when I could leave at the drop of a hat?"

"Don't you have a three-year contract?"

"I do. But in this sport? Any race could be my last."

He's right. It would terrify most people, but what I see on his face isn't fear—it's acceptance. Motocross is brutal, and he knows exactly what he's risking every time he lines up to the gate.

My gaze drifts to the nightstand. Curiosity gets the better of me. I manage to slide the drawer open barely an inch before a large hand slams it shut.

"Don't open that."

His voice wavers just enough to make my stomach tighten.

"What, are you hiding? Naked pictures?" I tease, trying to lighten the moment. "Or evidence of your victims?"

"I guess you'll find out when I take your picture," he says with a wink.

I don't let it go. "Axel. Seriously."

He exhales, defeated, and looks away. "Fine. Go ahead."

I open the drawer slowly, nervous to what I might find. Inside are scattered photographs—and a small jersey. Guilt hits me instantly. I shouldn't be here. I should close it and pretend I saw nothing. But my hand drifts to the jersey anyway.

It's bright yellow, orange, and purple. The number 143 fills the back.

MILANO.

My vision blurs as realization sinks in.

Maddox.

I fold it carefully and set it back before pulling out the photo beneath it. Axel stands with his arm around a younger boy. The same blue eyes, same smile. Their parents stand behind them, hands resting proudly on their shoulders. Both boys wear medals around their necks.

"He really did need a haircut," I say softly, angling the photo toward Axel.

"Yeah," he mutters, eyes fixed on the floor.

The resemblance is unmistakable. Axel favors his mom; Maddox looks more like their dad. The happiness in the photo feels genuine and that makes it hurt more.

I return everything exactly as I found it and sit beside Axel on the bed, resting my hand on his thigh, feeling like a major asshole.

"I'm sorry," I say quietly. "I pushed."

He covers my hand with his, thumb brushing back and forth. "It's okay. It's just... hard not to keep it private."

"I'm here," I tell him, squeezing his leg. "Okay?"

He nods.

"You look like your mom, you know."

A small laugh escapes him. "Yeah. I've heard."

"How are they?"

His jaw tightens. "I haven't talked to them in years. I don't even think they know I ride for Kawasaki."

"You never know." My chest aches. "That must be hard."

"Losing Maddox broke them," he says. "They shut down. Started drinking. Fighting. Every year I thought it would get better. It didn't, so I left. Ben's parents took me in until we could travel together. I tried staying in touch, but every time I mentioned racing, they'd lose it. Eventually I stopped trying."

I lean into his side. "Is that why you live here?"

"Yes and no," he says after a pause. "I can't really afford my own place."

I sit up. "What do you mean, *can't afford?*"

He hesitates. "I've been sending most of my paychecks to my parents—and Ben's. Anonymously."

My jaw drops. "Excuse me?"

"I just wanted to make sure they were taken care of," he

says quietly. "No one knows. Please keep it that way."

I nod, stunned. One minute I thought he was hiding porn; the next I'm finding out he's paying off his family's debt. He could be living like Rad. Instead, he's choosing this.

"There's a lot more to you than I thought," I whisper.

"Why tell me?" I ask.

"I don't know," he admits, staring ahead.

I glance at his discarded jersey on the floor, guilt flickering again. But this—this matters. I want to know him. All of him.

"Are you hungry?" I ask. "I can grab food while you shower."

"Not happening."

He stands and heads for the door.

"Wait—where are you going?"

"*I'm* getting food," he says over his shoulder. "Then you're showering with me."

The door closes behind him.

I stare at the empty room.

"...Okay, then."

24

Stephanie

"Aren't you tired of wearing those?" I gesture toward his riding pants before taking a sip of my water.

"Want me to take my pants off already?" He sets his fork down, lips curving into a lazy smirk.

"I'm just saying," I reply quickly, lifting my hands in mock surrender.

"They're basically a second skin at this point," he says. "But yeah—it's a relief once they're off."

I almost tell him it's like taking your bra off after a twelve-hour day, but that would absolutely send this conversation somewhere dangerous. Instead, I laugh softly and slide my empty plate toward the center of the island.

Axel leans forward, forearms braced on the counter. There's something predatory in his gaze now. He's still shirtless, and if it's not criminal how distracting that is—

"My eyes are up here, you know."

Heat floods my cheeks.

Busted.

I hop off the stool and push it back into place.

"Since my mind is officially in the gutter, I'm going to use your shower. If you don't mind cleaning up my dishes?"

I punctuate it with a wink and make a quick escape down the hall, shutting the bathroom door behind me.

"Hey!" he calls after me, laughter in his voice.

I lean back against the door, exhaling as I face the large mirror over the sink. The bathroom matches the rest of the apartment—clean, neutral. Black fixtures. White tile. Nothing unnecessary. The tub-and-shower combo is standard, and my gaze lingers a little too long as I picture how little space there would be for two people.

I don't bother locking the door.

Steam begins to curl through the air as I turn the water on. Clothes fall to the floor one piece at a time, the day finally peeling away from me. When I step under the spray, the heat sinks into my skin and I let my head fall back, breath catching.

So much has happened today. So much has *changed* today.

I'm standing in *a man's* shower. I can't remember the last time.

A smile tugs at my mouth just as I hear the soft click of the door opening. Right on cue. I don't turn around, but I catch his shadow moving beyond the curtain. I hear cabinets open, a drawer slides shut.

"What are you doing?" I ask, keeping my voice casual even though my pulse has picked up.

"Getting towels. And... stuff," he answers.

"Oh."

That single word carries far more weight than it should.

The shower instantly feels smaller when Axel's muscular frame steps in behind me. Heat radiates off his skin, the space between us evaporating as if it never existed. I feel his breath brush the back of my neck before he slowly presses into me, unhurried, deliberate.

A soft sigh slips from me before I can stop it—pure relief at the feel of his skin against mine. His arms come around me naturally, like muscle memory, like he's done this a thousand times before. Or maybe like he's imagined it just as often.

Either way, it feels like confirmation.

That I didn't misread this.

That choosing *this*, choosing *him*, was the right call.

"Hey," he murmurs, lips grazing the side of my head.

I tilt my chin slightly, forcing some bite into my voice. "I don't remember inviting you."

"Oh," he says softly, amused. "You definitely invited me."

"You must be mistaken."

His answer isn't verbal. His lips trace a slow path from just below my ear down the sensitive line of my neck, unspooling my attitude one nerve at a time.

"Want me to leave?" he asks, a smile in his voice. I feel it brush my bare shoulder.

What did I even say?

The water does what I can't—it washes the rest of my fake resistance straight down the drain. I lean back into him, surrendering without a word. He exhales, like he's been waiting for that.

"I take that as a no."

One arm slips free and I hear the soft click of the shampoo bottle. "Hope you don't mind smelling like me," he says.

I tilt my head back instinctively as his fingers work into my hair, slow and firm, massaging my scalp until my shoulders drop and my body goes pliant beneath his hands. His scent surrounds us—clean and dark all at once. Like rain before a storm. Like something dangerous and beautiful and entirely him.

Then he turns me.

My heart stutters the second I'm facing him.

Water streams down his face, his lashes darkened, his expression unreadable until a slow smile curves his mouth. His hand comes up, warm and steady, thumb brushing along my jaw as if he's memorizing me.

He tips my chin gently, angling my face into the spray so the water rinses the last of the shampoo from my hair. I close my eyes, caught between the heat of him and the rush of the water, suspended in the moment.

"Fuck," he breathes. "You're beautiful."

I open my eyes.

The second time he's said it today, but the way he's looking at me, there's no arrogance there. No teasing. Just raw, open fire. Something honest. Something that sees straight through me.

I've never been looked at, *like that*, before.

And I know, right then, I'll never forget it.

I'm still a little dumbfounded as he starts washing me, like my body hasn't quite caught up to the reality of what's happening. He gently gathers my hair and moves it over my shoulder, giving himself access to my back. His hands glide over my skin with careful intention—slow, unhurried—before lingering just a second longer than necessary on my ass.

My breath stutters.

My entire body hums, practically trembling with the electricity crackling between us. His hands stay steady, grounded, even as the anticipation threatens to drag us somewhere reckless and fast. I keep my gaze firmly up, refusing to look down at the undeniable proof of how affected he is.

I need *some* semblance of self-control.

Right?

Soap slips down my skin, warm and slick, and the thought hits me out of nowhere, that it feels like the past is rinsing away. The old me. The careful one. The version who always kept one foot out the door.

There's no going back after today.

Before I can spiral too far into what that means, I make a decision.

"Your turn."

I grab his arm and try to maneuver us into switching places. He stiffens slightly, more surprised than resistant.

"What do you think you're doing?" His voice drops, low and curious.

The stream of water starts soaking his hair as I guide him into the space I just vacated, my pulse racing with every step.

"My turn to wash you," I say—way too eager to sound casual about it. There's absolutely no chance I'm passing this up.

He catches my wrist gently, his hand closing over mine where I'm gripping the shampoo bottle. His touch is warm.

"Hey, Switch," he says, sincere but clearly intrigued. "You don't have to wash me."

"I know," I lift my eyes to his. "But I want to."

We hold each other's gaze, something unspoken passing between us as he considers it. Then a slow, crooked smile breaks across his face, equal parts challenge and permission.

"Alright, then," he says, stepping fully into the spray. "Have at it."

And just like that, the air between us shifts again—charged, inevitable, and ready to snap.

My chest brushes against him as I reach up to wash his hair, and the sudden lack of hot water has my body reacting instantly. I suck in a quiet breath. Of course he notices. Axel notices *everything*. His gaze drops, slow and unashamed, and I swear his attention alone makes it worse.

I rise onto my tiptoes to work the shampoo into his hair, wobbling slightly.

"My eyes are up here, Milano," I say, perfectly timed with my near loss of balance.

He laughs and steadies me, hands firm on my hips. The contact sends a jolt straight through me.

"How about you don't put your tits in my face, then?" he shoots back.

"They are *not* in your face," I argue, planting my hands on his shoulders and pushing him down until he's half-squatting in front of me.

"Hey—"

"This," I interrupt, pulling his head straight into the spot between my breasts, "is in your face."

I squeeze, trapping him there, and immediately lose it, laughing so hard my sides ache. It's ridiculous, completely unhinged, and somehow perfect.

"I could die happy now," he says, completely muffled.

That just makes me laugh harder.

I free him and pull him back upright, and see he's laughing too. His forehead resting against mine for a second before he leans down and kisses me, soft, unhurried, like he's savoring it.

"I've never met anyone like you," he says, grinning like an idiot.

"Is that a good thing?"

"Yes."

"Good," I reply, brushing my thumb along his jaw. "Because I've never met anyone like you either."

I step back, eyes gleaming. "Now be a good boy and let me wash the rest of you."

I smack his ass for emphasis.

He yelps. "Hey! We both know who's in charge here."

He looks down at me knowingly.

"Oh yeah," I say, putting on my most innocent face. "*Definitely* you."

I feel his attention—*all* of it—as my hands move over him, slow and deliberate. I take my time, tracing muscle and skin, noting the bruises and scars that tell the story of his life better than words ever could. Proof of discipline. Of impact. Of survival.

"Make sure you clean *every* inch," he murmurs.

And just like that, the teasing shifts. Still playful, but heavier now. Loaded. The kind of moment that makes it very clear neither of us is walking away unchanged.

When we're done, I reach forward and twist the knob, the steady rush of water cutting off with a hollow echo. The sudden quiet feels loud. Steam still clings to the air, wrapping around us like it's reluctant to let go.

The curtain slides open before I even turn around.

Axel is already there, a towel stretched open in his hands like he anticipated the moment. The small, thoughtful gesture hits harder than it should. I step out onto the bath mat, the soft material grounding me, as he wraps the towel around me with practiced ease. It's not rushed, not awkward. His hands skim the sides of my arms as he tucks the fabric in place, rubbing slow circles like he's making sure I'm warm. Or maybe like he just doesn't want to stop touching me yet.

Neither do I.

He grabs his own towel and turns away, leaving just enough space for me to breathe again. I glance at the counter and see multiple items that weren't there when I came in. Lotion, a hairbrush, deodorant, Q-tips, and I can't help but smile at the sentiment.

I collect my clothes off the floor, mostly for show, and trail after him down the short hallway toward his bedroom. Water drips from my hair onto his floor, little evidence markers of what just happened. A grin pulls at my mouth.

I'm *absolutely* stealing one of his shirts. At minimum. He smells too damn good to not want to save that shit for later.

He stops just inside the room and turns to face me. The towel sits low on his hips, wrapped tight, knuckles white where he's gripping it like it's the only thing holding him together. He drags a hand through his wet hair, frustration written all over him. His jaw is tense, shoulders tight, eyes dark with something he's clearly trying to rein in.

I know that look now.

I stop directly in front of him, close enough that the air between us feels charged again, like the shower never really ended.

And suddenly, everything unsaid is standing right there with us.

"Something wrong?" I slowly run a finger down his chest.

"Yes," he croaks out.

"And what's that?" I look up at him innocently, forcing him to say it.

"I'm not inside you," he mutters, voice rough, wrecked, like the words scrape their way out of him. "And it's killing me. I can't wait another goddamn minute."

Then he's kissing me, no hesitation, no restraint left. He kisses me like oxygen is optional everywhere else but here, like I'm the only thing keeping him on the ground. Heat rushes through me as our towels slip loose and fall away, forgotten the second they hit the floor.

This, *this*, is the moment the tension finally snaps.

He doesn't break the kiss as he lowers me onto the bed, his body following mine without space, without mercy. The mattress dips beneath us. My legs find him instinctively, wrapping around his waist like they've been waiting for permission. For *him*.

He's right there. Close enough that it hurts. Close enough that every nerve in my body lights up.

Just before everything tips over the edge, he pulls back.

He looks down at me, chest rising, eyes dark and burning, like he needs to see me, to make sure I'm right here with him, before there's no stopping what comes next.

"Tell me what you want," he rasps.

"Whatever you can give me," I whisper, the words barely making it past my lips.

His eyes stay locked on mine as he swallows, and for the first time, he looks almost—*nervous*. Like he understands the weight of what I just handed him. Time stretches thin when he finally answers.

"I'll give you everything I have."

It feels like we're back at the starting gate, engines screaming, tension wound so tight it's almost painful. Then he moves, and my breath punches out of me at the same time the moment breaks wide open. I arch instinctively, fingers digging into his shoulders, the headboard inching closer behind me as my body reacts before my mind can catch up.

"Fuck, Axel," I breathe as his mouth finds my neck, slow and deliberate, like he knows exactly what he's doing.

"What?" he murmurs against my skin, a laugh tucked into his voice. "No *Mr. Milano?*"

I tilt my chin, just enough to see his face.

"Do you like when I say that or something?" I shoot back, a grin curling through the words.

His mouth drifts up to my ear, voice dropping lower, dangerous.

"Might've thought about it a few times."

The way he says it sends a shiver straight through me, my body betraying me completely as I melt beneath him.

"Of course you did," I snicker. "A fantasy of yours?"

"Maybe," he grins.

"If I called you that, would you let me in on it next time?"

I arch slightly, just enough for my chest to brush his. His gaze drops, just for a second, before snapping back to my eyes. He props himself on one forearm, his other hand lifting to trace his thumb over my lower lip like he's testing a thought.

"It's a date."

His tongue flicks over his mouth, that look on his face like I just told him he got first pick at the gates—wide, stunned, barely contained excitement flashing before he can mask it. Like he's bracing himself for the drop. Like he knows exactly how badly this could wreck him and doesn't care.

I roll my eyes dramatically, but there's no real bite behind it. Just heat. Just challenge. I hook my fingers into the back of his neck and pull him in before he can say something smug.

The kiss turns urgent, fast. There's no finesse, no patience, just need. Our mouths crash together like we're both starving, like neither of us wants to be the first to breathe. There's no careful exploration, no testing. It's all friction and fire and the unmistakable knowledge that we're past pretending this is casual.

At least I think so.

There's always been something about kissing that unravels me. It's more intimate than anything else—more honest. You can fake confidence, fake control, fake indifference. But here? There's nowhere to hide. Every breath, every hesitation, every pull tells the truth.

And Axel gives himself to it completely.

No restraint. No walls. No half-measures.

It's overwhelming in the best way. I get lost in him, the heat, the pressure, the way he kisses like he's afraid I'll disappear if he lets go. For once, I don't want to be found. I don't want to think. I just want *this*. I could stay there forever.

But today, I want everything.

"My turn."

The words come out steadier than I feel. He doesn't resist when I push him back, just goes willingly, watching me with that same reckless trust. Like he's already decided wherever I lead, he'll follow.

The new angle takes a second for me to adjust. The world reorients. Cool air kisses my skin, water still sliding down from my hair, tracing slow paths that make me shiver. Goosebumps rise in its wake, my awareness snapping sharp. Every inch of space, every breath, every millimeter of distance we're *not* leaving between us.

I breathe out slowly, grounding myself.

"Something wrong?" he asks, all smug confidence, voice lazy like he isn't watching me just as closely.

I open my mouth to respond and lose the thought entirely.

He grins like he knows exactly why.

"Too much for you?"

He moves just enough to challenge me, not touching—just *there*. My body betrays me instantly. The sound that slips out isn't planned, isn't filtered, isn't something I meant to share.

"Oh—fuck."

Stars blink behind my eyes, sharp and bright. I refuse to back down. My hands brace against his chest, solid and warm beneath my palms, steadying myself as my breath catches up to my body. My hips begin to move, the feeling way too good for comprehension. I look down to see a mutual look in his eyes.

I lean down, close enough that my mouth brushes his ear, my voice low and deliberate.

"Too much for *you*?"

That does it.

His breath stutters, a broken sound tearing out of him like I've hit something vital. The confidence cracks, just enough and, it's *delicious*. It's real. It's earned.

"Keep that up," he mutters, voice rough, "and I'm not lasting."

I straighten slowly, deliberately, letting the moment stretch. My hands slide down his torso, unhurried, claiming the space like I know exactly what I'm doing. I tuck my hair back, exposing my face, my throat, everything honest and unguarded.

He watches me like I'm the only thing that matters.

Like I always have been.

"Fuck, Stephanie... you're breathtaking."

Hearing my name like that, soft, real, stripped of bravado,

knocks the air out of me. Heat rushes to my cheeks, and I hate how much I love that he sees me. Not just the confidence. Not just my body. *Me.*

"How did we even get here?" I laugh quietly, half disbelief, half wonder.

"Because we're fucked up," he says easily, like it's obvious.

I grin. "At least you said we *both* are this time."

The joy hits me all at once when I collapse into his arms, laughter spilling free and unguarded. It's wild, how this feels reckless and safe at the same time. How we're laughing. How nothing about this feels forced or awkward or carefully negotiated.

It's just... easy.

We move together instinctively, like we've done this a hundred times in another life. Hands everywhere, breath syncing, the heat building again—tighter, deeper, more inevitable. The world narrows until there's only sensation and trust and the way he steadies me without stealing control.

When he pulls back, it's not away. It's just enough to make me ache for him. He flips me onto my stomach, my back automatically arching, arms pinned. His touch grounds me, guides me, his voice low and sure near my ear.

"I'm going to fuck you now. And I'm not going to stop until you're coming all over my dick."

My pulse quickens with excitement. It's an almost instant relief when he enters me again, a welcoming fullness. The way he takes control doesn't scare me. It anchors me. I let myself follow because I *want* to. Because I trust him.

He lifts my right hand and leans down. My body instantly reacting as I glance over my shoulder. This man...places two of my fingers into his mouth and pulls them out with a pop.

"Lift that pretty little ass, reach down, and touch yourself."
Well fuck me sideways.

I have no choice but to do what he says, because lets face it, I *want* to do what he says. I lift my ass to create some room to place my hand underneath me.

"Oh," I moan into the black fabric.

His chest rubs against my back as his fingers interlock with my free hand. He trails kisses from my cheek to my shoulder in between each movement. Every moan, pant, breath is steamy and matched with my own. With the friction of my fingers and him, it's the perfect combination. In what feels like seconds, my orgasm climbs to a new height. I begin to pulse around him as my body completely shatters. A high that is even better than the others that have happened today. If that's even possible.

"That's it. Fucking come for me," he growls in my ear as he keeps his pace steady. He lets me ride my climax out as long as I can before he flips me onto my back. I barely comprehend what's going on, when my ankles are suddenly on his shoulders.

"Fuck, Axel." I grip the comforter as he continues at yet, another new angle. We look at each other with an unspoken agreement.

"You sure?" he asks me, reading my mind. Even before I came so fucking hard, I knew what I wanted.

"Do it. I want all of you." I stare at him unblinking, unwavering.

Plus, I have an IUD so it really is a no brainer.

If I get this man, even if it's only for today, I'm getting *all* of him. Even though it doesn't feel like a one time thing.

"Good." He holds one of my legs with one hand and grabs one of my breasts with the other as he continues to fuck me.

Wait a minute. I get to *watch* him come? Not that I don't mind getting my face shoved in a pillow and my ass lifted into the air sometimes, but this feels different. I feel like I'm in the pits at a concert. Like I've just touched the artist's hand. And knowing that he's willing to let me see him, see *all* of him in this moment? It's powerful.

I see glimpses of his abs rippling behind my legs. His hands move to my hips as he drives into me. Sweat peppers his forehead, his dark hair in disarray. Eyebrows scrunch together in concentration as his eyes bore into me.

I can't look away as he begins to unravel. His eyes begin to roll back as he grunts and moans—spilling into me. His breaths are fast as he collapses, not putting his full weight on me. It's the best ending of any movie I've ever seen.

100% on Rotten Tomatoes for sure.

When the world settles again, we're breathing hard, foreheads pressed together, staring at each other like neither of us quite believes what just happened.

"Fuck," we say at the same time.

It makes us laugh.

The room settles into a quiet that feels heavier than silence. Not awkward, but charged. Like the air itself is still catching its breath.

Axel doesn't rush to move. Neither do I. Our bodies are close enough that I can feel the steady rhythm of his breathing against my side, the warmth of him anchoring me in place. My heart thuds slower now, but deeper. Like it's recalibrating around him.

When he finally shifts, it's gentle. Careful. Like he's suddenly aware that whatever we just crossed, there's no stepping back over it.

He grabs his towel, hands me mine, and disappears into the bathroom, giving me space without making it feel like distance. I sit on the edge of the bed, feet brushing the floor. The world feels tilted, like I've just landed after a jump I didn't fully see coming.

That wasn't just sex.

The thought comes uninvited. Solid. Undeniable.

When he comes back, his hair is damp and curling slightly at the ends. He reaches in one of drawers and grabs clothes. Sweatpants slung low on his hips. He looks... relaxed. Open. Like the edge he usually carries has softened just a fraction.

"Here," he says, holding out one of his shirts.

I take it slowly, fingers brushing his. The contact sparks something warm and steady, different from before. It's not frantic or consuming.

"Only a shirt?" I tease, mostly because the moment feels too real if I don't.

His mouth quirks. "I'm exercising restraint."

I pull it over my head, the fabric falling against my skin like a familiar promise. It smells like him, clean, a little earthy, unmistakably Axel. I thank him as I head towards his bathroom. I stare at my reflection, my post sex hair, the smile that is taking up my whole face.

You know the feeling of going to the bathroom after having a few drinks? That happy, slightly tipsy, giddy feeling? That's how I feel looking in the mirror except I'm drunk on a tall glass of cool, dark, and handsome.

But my eyes cast down as I re-enter the bedroom as if he'd magically regret what happened in those few minutes in my absence. When I gain the courage to look up, he's watching me like I just claimed something without asking permission.

"Fuck," he mutters, shaking his head, a smile forming.

"What?"

"You just.."

I save him from elaborating and crawl onto the bed beside him, tucking myself against his side. The fit feels natural in a way that startles me. Like my body recognizes the shape of him, knows where it belongs without instruction.

I tilt my head to look at him. "We need to make one thing clear."

His eyebrows lift, amused but attentive. "Uh-oh."

"You don't get to lose a race and say you already won because of me."

A slow grin spreads across his face, sharp and familiar. "So... what happens if I do win?"

I roll my eyes. "Then I'll be there regardless. Because it's literally my job."

He laughs and pulls me closer, pressing a kiss into my hair. It's soft and unshowy. It's sweet in a way.

"You're brutal, Switch."

We lie there for a long time after that, talking about nothing and everything. The kind of conversation that slips easily between jokes and honesty. He tells me about riding as a kid, about how black became his favorite color which then proceeded to me telling him how it matches his personality. More laughter. More teasing. And then I somehow tell him things I don't usually say out loud.

At some point, my fingers begin to trace the tattoos along his arm, following each line as if committing them to memory. I linger over the familiar skull etched into his forearm, its sharp angles softened by how often I've studied it before. Slowly, my gaze drifts upward, drawn to the larger piece on his shoulder.

A pocket watch. It's glass is cracked, the hands frozen mid-moment, time permanently stopped. The chain coils around his arm like it's holding on, wrapping itself into his skin, as if even time itself refused to let him go.

"It's broken," he says quietly, already knowing what I'm thinking.

I trace my thumb over the watch face again, the hands frozen in time. He doesn't pull away, doesn't shy away from what the tattoo means. A small step I can't help but notice.

"He'd be proud of you," I say, barely louder than a breath.

His hand closes over mine, warm and steady. "Probably jealous, too."

We laugh—soft, shared, a little sad—but it doesn't feel heavy. It feels honest.

And for the first time all day, maybe longer, I don't feel like I'm bracing for the next thing to fall apart.

I just feel... here.

With him.

25

Axel

"Hey, buddy. How was your weekend off?"

Ben's calm voice floats through the phone, steady and familiar. Exactly what I need. He's the levelheaded one, the guy who doesn't spiral when shit goes sideways.

I'm in shambles after this weekend.

Stephanie ended up staying over that night, and I'd be lying if I said it wasn't the best night of my life. Hell, best weekend. We were supposed to hate each other. That was the whole deal. It was all about the rivalry, the tension, the sharp edges.

Then she made a move that ended it.

And damn... did that feel good.

"I fucked up, man," I say, pacing the narrow balcony of my extended stay.

"I thought talking to the bosses was a good thing?" Ben says. Casual. Optimistic.

Oh, he's going to absolutely shit when I tell him.

I rake a hand through my hair and take him off speaker, pressing the phone to my ear like I'm worried someone might overhear. I glance out at the empty track below. It's silent, still, and untouched. It's Monday and there's no crews or riders today.

Why am I being so paranoid?

"That part was good," I admit. "It's what transpired *after* that."

My mind betrays me immediately—her hands, her mouth, the way she looked at me like she wasn't scared of the wreckage. *Fuck.* I glance down. My body sure as hell remembers too.

"What happened?" Ben sighs, already bracing for it.

"Stephanie-fucking-Carson."

I stop pacing and grip the railing.

"Oh, *fuck.* What did you do?!" His voice jumps straight into disappointed-parent mode.

"To be fair," I say quickly, raising my pointer finger even though he can't see it. "She made the first—"

"Damnit, Axel!"

"—move," I finish. "...and I finished it."

"Oh, for fuck's sake," he groans.

I picture a single gray hair sprouting on his perfect head in my honor.

"Please tell me the bike is clean," he pleads.

...Busted. He's really too smart for his own good.

"Why would you assume the bike was involved?" I ask, offended. "And why do you care more about the bike than me? Hello? Best friend here."

"The bike is *always* involved," he says flatly. "And I know you're fine. Or you will be."

"Nothing got on the bike," I say. "But I cleaned it anyway."

"Good. Nothing I haven't dreamed of," he huffs. "Just do it

on a bike that I don't have to maintain."

"Yes, Dad," I tease. After a few silent beats he speaks up.

"Well?" he prompts.

"She's different, man."

The words land heavier than I expect.

"I don't know how else to explain it," I continue. "She's not what I thought. None of this was supposed to happen. My plan went completely down the shitter."

And there *was* a plan. Win races. Beat Rad Carson. Keep my head down. Don't get distracted. An easy, simple plan.

"Obviously, yeah—she's fucking gorgeous," I admit. "So fucking her was always on my mind. But when it actually happened..."

I swallow.

"I couldn't let her go."

Silence on the line.

"Axel," Ben says slowly, "you didn't just fuck her, did you? You made lo—"

"Please don't fucking say it," I cut in, panic sharp in my chest.

"Made loooov—"

"Stoppp ittt!" I groan, plugging my ears like a five-year-old. "You know I hate that shit!"

"Tell me I'm wrong and I'll stop!" he laughs.

A lump forms in my throat as memories fire off like warning lights.

Washing her hair.

Kissing her like I wasn't scared.

Worshiping her without trying to win.

Letting her come first, *every* time.

Not hesitating when it came to not using protection, coming

inside her.

Holding her all night like I didn't want morning to exist.

Fuck.

Son of a bitch, he's right.

I didn't just fuck her.

It's much worse than that.

I launched straight off a jump and into a pond, drowning myself without checking the depth.

"Fine," I mutter. "*Fine.* But don't say it again."

Ben chuckles, then lets the silence sit.

"So… are you guys a couple or…?" he asks carefully.

"We didn't talk about it," I admit. "She left early the next morning. Said she had things to take care of."

"Oh. She didn't say what?"

"No," I exhale. "She still kissed me goodbye though. She seemed determined which, isn't unlike her. I'm hoping it's her parents and not some secret boyfriend she forgot to mention."

I joke, but there's a tight edge underneath.

"Honestly," Ben says, "I don't think you have to worry about her playing you. She's not like the rest of them."

"You're right," I say quietly. "She's not."

"Have you heard from her since?"

"I haven't." I glance at my phone like it might magically light up. Nothing.

"It's been two days, man," he says. "You'll hear from her."

God, I hate how reasonable he is.

"What do I do now?" I ask.

"Simple," Ben says. "Don't fuck it up."

The wise words of Ben Traymer, everyone.

"Easy for you to say," I scoff. Ben prefers going home to see his family over getting laid. Moral compass of the damn team.

We hang up, and my grip on the railing loosens.

He's right. I can't fuck this up, whatever *this* is.

I can sit here and replay every look, every touch, every unanswered question... or I can do what I've always done when things feel out of control.

I get dressed and head down to the gym.

The lights flick on, illuminating the empty room. I've trained alone plenty of times. But this time feels different. Like there's something burning instead of just grinding.

I catch my reflection in the mirror.

Something's changed.

It's not just about beating Rad Carson anymore.

This isn't revenge.

It realization.

I'm going to push myself harder than I ever have. Not because I'm angry, not because I'm chasing a name.

But, because now, I have something to lose.

I'm not just going to win.

I'm going to beat *them all*.

26

Stephanie

It's time.

My fingers curl tight around the steering wheel. I don't realize how hard I'm gripping until my knuckles start to ache.

I should've done this sooner.

I *could've* done this sooner.

But avoidance has always been my specialty.

If I want anything real—anything honest—with Axel, this can't stay buried. I can't look him in the eye knowing what I know and pretend it doesn't matter.

The crunch of tires on gravel makes my heart jump. I glance in the mirror just as Rad pulls in beside me.

Of course he's on time. Perfectly, annoyingly on time.

After a much needed therapy session with Lex—complete with a borderline meltdown and enough caffeine to power a small city—we decided Rad and I had to do this together. She screamed when I told her about my "little sleepover," then immediately demanded every detail like she was watching a live bachelor finale.

She knew something happened the second I walked in the door. My smile wouldn't quit. Couldn't. She's my light when everything gets dark, and I don't know how I'd survive life without her.

I kill the engine and step out, the morning air sharp against my skin. Rad does the same, already scanning my face like he's checking my vitals. He looks like he always does—effortless, polished, annoyingly handsome in that golden-boy way sponsors eat up, blonde curls flawless. Black shorts, Honda T-shirt, gold chain catching the sun.

"Hey," I say, forcing a smile.

"Hey, Sis." He pulls me into a tight hug. "You still sure?"

I breathe him in. Familiar and safe.

"Yes," I say, even though my stomach is doing somersaults. "If I don't do this now, I never will."

We stand there for a beat longer than necessary before walking toward the house together. Shoulder to shoulder, united. Both of us knowing this is going to get ugly.

"Mom! Dad!" Rad calls as we walk into the foyer.

"In here!" Mom's high pitched voice echos from the office that's down the hall.

Rad looks at me with raised eyebrows in a "here goes nothing" look. I know I could have done this without him, but it's comforting knowing I have Rad by my side.

As we approach the office, my mind runs through every possible scenario. She could run. She could lie or even throw stuff.

"A surprise visit?! It's my lucky day!" But, when she notices both of us her face falls. Her eyes bounce from me to Rad in a questioning look. Then she surprises us by nodding her head.

"It's time isn't it?"

We both shake our heads in agreement. She stands and waves her hand.

"Let's get on with it then. Go get your dad from the garage and make this a full on intervention," she sighs in annoyance.
Well this is unexpected.

I thought I'd have to scream at her just to get her to acknowledge me. To corner her into a conversation she's dodged for weeks. But instead, she turns and walks toward the sitting room like this is another item on her to-do list. Like she's finally humoring me.

And somehow, that makes my skin crawl more.

I follow her while Rad heads to the garage to get Dad. The sitting room is still spotless—white couches, a single minimalist lamp, too many perfectly placed plants. It looks less like a home and more like a therapist's office designed by someone who's never actually sat in one. Cold. Curated.

Mom settles onto the love seat with practiced grace, crossing her legs. I choose one of the chairs across from her, keeping distance between us. Space feels necessary right now. Protective.

The silence stretches.

And of course, my mind betrays me.

Axel fills the quiet before anything else can. The weight he carries so casually. The way his voice changes when he talks about his brother. How that loss shaped everything—his racing, his anger, his drive. My chest tightens as the reality settles in: the woman responsible for shattering his family is sitting across from me, checking her nails like this is an inconvenience.

Unbothered. Untouched.

Anger coils hot and sharp in my gut.

"Hey, what's this all about?" Dad asks as he walks in, breaking the silence as he drops onto the cushion beside Mom. His forehead shines with sweat, probably from spending the morning buried in bikes and engines—his favorite escape.

Rad takes the chair next to me, knee bouncing, fingers tapping against the armrest. Nervous energy radiates off him, even if he's trying to hide it.

I don't bother easing into it.

Patience has never gotten me anywhere in this house.

"Tell us about the accident."

Dad looks from us to Mom and I see him gulp. Mom rolls her eyes and I suddenly want to throw something at her.

"What accident? When your mom hit that deer?" The rehearsed lie coming from his mouth does little to cover up the truth in his eyes.

"You guys can drop the act now. We know the truth." I say, my patience wearing severely thin.

Mom grabs a pocket mirror from her end table and checks her makeup.

"Just tell them honey," she says, waving him off like it's no big deal.

"How did they find out?" Dad whispers to her, like lowering his voice somehow makes the truth less ugly.

"How do you *think*?" Mom snaps back under her breath, irritation sharp and practiced.

I cross my arms tight against my chest, nails biting into my skin, so I don't actually grab the first decorative object within reach and hurl it at them. The urge is violent. Visceral.

I glance at Rad, and he must read my expression because he inhales slowly and finally speaks.

"I've actually known since it happened." His chin tucks

down, shoulders sagging, like saying it out loud adds ten pounds to his spine. "I just... never said anything."

Both of our parents freeze. Their heads snap toward him in unison, eyes wide, not with guilt, but surprise.

"How?" Mom asks, bright pink lips twisting as her compact snaps shut with a sharp click.

"You weren't exactly quiet about it in the garage," Rad says softly with no accusation. Just fact. "You talked like no one was listening."

Dad straightens, jaw tightening. "So then you would have heard it was an *accident*," he says firmly, like repeating it enough times might turn it into absolution.

"What was an accident?" I lean forward, fingers digging into my forearms. "Hmm? I want to hear you say it."

Mom's eyes flash, fire meeting fire, while Dad looks between us like he's standing in the middle of a live wire.

"Fine," he exhales, placing a steadying hand on Mom's knee. "It was a dark and rainy night. After the race," his voice slows, it's deliberate. Like it was rehearsed. "And as you remember, your mom always drove separately."

Until that night, my brain screams.

"She approached the intersection and didn't see the stop sign."

"Were you too busy checking yourself in the mirror or—"

"Enough!" Dad cuts me off sharply before she has the chance to explode. His eyes swing back to me. "Do you want to hear our side or not?"

I look at Rad in disbelief. He tilts his head, gives me a subtle gesture to wait. *How* is he this calm?

The room holds its breath.

"She hit another vehicle," Dad finally says. "And that

vehicle contained the Milano family."

My pulse roars in my ears at the name. Axel's name, even when it isn't said, crashes through me. I stare at my father, unmoving. I hope this hurts them. Even a fraction.

"Everyone was taken to the hospital," he continues. "But unfortunately, the youngest boy didn't survive."

"Unfortunately," I repeat, hollow and sharp. The word tastes wrong. "That's it?"

They don't answer.

I inhale slowly, forcing myself to speak evenly. "Tell us about the court stuff."

"Why do you need to know that?" Mom cuts in, irritation bleeding through.

"It was never on the news," I say, ignoring her. "No one at school knew. *I* didn't know. How did it disappear?"

Each word lands like a thrown object. Dad sighs, then sits up straighter, like slipping into a role he's worn before.

"I did what I had to do to protect this family."

"Yes, you did," Mom says sweetly, patting his hand.

"And what exactly did that require?" My voice barely wavers, but my insides are unraveling.

"I hired the best lawyers," he says bluntly. "Called in favors, made donations. I ensured it stayed private."

"Can you imagine if it got out?" Mom adds. "The sponsors? Rad's future?"

"What about the Milano family?" I shout, hands gripping the chair arms so hard they ache. "What did you do for *them*?"

Dad pauses. "We offered compensation."

"They refused," Mom says with an eye roll. "Didn't want charity."

"But paperwork was still signed," Dad adds quietly.

Blood money. Wrapped in grief. *Wonderful.*

"What about Axel?" My voice cracks despite my effort. "What did you do for *him?*"

"He was young," Dad shrugs. "We didn't think he'd remember or notice the exchanges with his parents and the lawyers."

"And *how* is your boyfriend?" Mom snaps.

That's it.

I surge to my feet—

CRASH.

The ceramic pot explodes against the floor, dirt and shards scattering. A jagged piece skids to a stop inches from Mom's polished toes.

"That's enough!" Rad roars.

We all stare at him, stunned. I've never seen him like this— raw, shaking, furious. Relief burns hot in my chest.

"I've put my feelings aside for too *fucking* long!" His chest heaves as he points at them. "I went to the funeral! I *saw* them! Losing a son—" His voice breaks and he swallows hard. "It wouldn't kill you to have compassion for someone other than yourselves."

Silence.

"Let Stephanie live her own life," he continues. "Support her. Stop controlling everything."

Then, quieter but, still deadly serious "—And by the way? I would've gotten on the best team no matter what. My talent is why we're still here."

He drags a hand through his hair, breathing hard.

I step beside him, resting my hand on his shoulder. He doesn't flinch.

I look at our parents. I see the people I've bent myself into knots trying to please. And I let it go. Finally.

"Let's go, Rad."

I guide him towards the door, carefully stepping over the shattered pot.

Outside, the air feels lighter, the world brighter.

"Let's get a drink," he mutters.

"I'll follow you," I say, climbing into my car.

It's barely noon.

And I don't give a damn.

27

Stephanie

"Two tall drafts."

The bartender's voice cuts through the low hum of the bar as she slides the glasses toward us. The beer sloshes dangerously close to the rim, foam spilling over onto the dark wood.

"Let me know if you need anything else," she adds, her smile widening just a little too much as her eyes linger on Rad before she finally walks away, hips swaying like she knows she's being watched.

I lift my glass and lean closer to Rad, lowering my voice. "Don't you ever get sick of that?"

He squints at me. "Of what?"

"Girls," I gesture subtly toward the bartender with my glass, "Fawning over you everywhere you go."

He chuckles and takes a long sip. "It's great for my ego."

"Like your ego needs to get any bigger," I shoot back.

We both burst into laughter, the kind that feels loose and unguarded. The kind we haven't shared in... a long ass time.

I try to think back to the last time we did something like

this—just sat somewhere normal, beers in hand, no bikes, no schedules, no expectations. My mind comes up blank.

God. Our entire relationship has been built around dirt bikes.

That shit's gotta change.

"So," I say after a moment, watching the bubbles rise in my glass. "How do you feel?"

Rad pauses mid-sip, staring into his beer like the answer might be floating at the bottom.

"Relieved," he finally says, exhaling through his nose.

"Same," I nod, feeling it settle into my bones.

He sets his glass down. "What do we do now?"

I take a deep breath and place my beer beside his. "Now we live our lives. Be good people. Regardless of what our parents want us to do."

He scoffs lightly. "You make it sound so easy."

"You just need a woman to help you and calm you down," I say, wiggling my eyebrows.

He laughs. "Never. I'm having way too much fun."

We sit in a comfortable silence for a few beats, the noise of the bar filling the gaps. Music hums softly overhead, someone laughs too loud behind us, glasses clink.

"Hey," I nudge his arm. "I'm proud of you."

He shakes his head, smirking. "I thought I was the older sibling."

We clink glasses.

"To moving on," I say.

"To moving on," he echoes.

The bartender reappears almost immediately with two fresh beers we definitely didn't ask for and gives Rad a not-so-subtle wink before disappearing again.

I roll my eyes and reach for my phone as it lights up on the bar top. For half a second, excitement flares. Then falls flat.

Lex.

I was supposed to text her when I was done at my parents. A flood of messages rolls in, one after another, all variations of *are you okay* and *where are you* and *Where's Rad?!*.

When I tell her I'm with him, the questions somehow multiply.

Rad leans over, catches a glimpse of my screen, then leans back with a grin. "Alexis, I presume?"

"Yep."

"What all does she have to say?"

"She wants to know what you're wearing," I laugh, shaking my head.

"Sounds about right," he says easily.

Lex has always flirted with Rad. Loudly and too excessively sometimes. She plays it off like a joke, but I've always sensed more underneath it. A crush she's never admitted to. Rad's never noticed—or if he has, he's never encouraged it. He's always treated her like a sister.

I pretend I don't notice. Some things are easier left untouched.

"So," Rad says casually, like he's asking about the weather. "About Axel..."

My heart stutters. Always does.

"What about him?" I ask, trying to sound normal.

He studies me for a second. "Do you like him?"

"I do," I admit, swiping a drip running down the side of my glass. The condensation slick against my fingers.

It's strange—awkward, but also oddly freeing—talking to Rad about something that isn't racing. Over the years we've kept things light. Memes. Videos. Surface-level check-ins.

This feels... grown.

"Does he treat you right?" Rad asks, eyebrow raised.

Warmth spreads through my chest. "He does now."

His lips curve. "You got the upper hand, didn't you?"

"Sure did," I nod proudly.

"Nice one, sis." He lifts his glass. We cheers again.

Then his expression shifts. The protective big brother senses activated.

"He hasn't tried sleeping with you yet, has he?"

I nearly choke on my beer.

"Umm..."

"Do I have to beat him in a race again? Cut him off? Finish the fist fight that he wanted to start with me?" he adds, dead serious. "Because I will."

"No, no," I laugh, placing a hand on his arm. "There's... something going on between us."

"Oh." He visibly relaxes.

"We haven't really talked about it yet. It's new. Like days new," I say quietly. "But I really like him, Rad. I just don't know how to be with him publicly without the world tearing me apart."

He frowns. "Why would they tear you down?"

Another man that doesn't understand.

"For a lot of reasons," I sigh. "One—we work for the same team. Two—women in motorsports already deal with enough bullshit stereotypes. And three," I glance at him, "I'm your sister."

He hums thoughtfully, then shakes his head. "I've never really thought about it from your side." He wraps an arm around my shoulders, pulling me into a side hug. "I'm sorry, sis. That sucks."

"It's okay," I say softly. "I don't know how, but I'm determined to change things. For myself... and for other women."

"Well," he says confidently, "you've got my support."

"Thank you," I smile. "I'm going to keep Axel and I, a secret for now. Until I figure it out."

"Your secret's safe with me," he says. Then smirks. "But seriously... if I need to kick his ass, I will."

I laugh. "I know. But you better watch your back, Radley Carson. Axel might just win the title this season."

Rad throws his head back, laughing loud enough to turn heads.

I laugh with him, but hope blooms quietly in my chest.

Unlike most people, I believe in Axel Milano. I believe Team Green deserves to be on top.

I unlock my phone and start typing.

Me: *Your ass better be training today.*

28

Axel

It's finally my favorite day of the week.

Race day.

The two weeks off were fine—necessary, even—but I've been pacing like a caged animal since the moment the last checkered flag dropped. Too much time to think. Too much time to replay things that don't belong in my head when I should be riding.

Today fixes that.

Today, I get to line up again. I get to shut everything else out. I get to win.

Unadilla greets us with crisp morning air, a sharp contrast to the dry California heat that usually clings to my skin like a second jersey. The dirt here smells different too, damp, rich, almost sweet. East Coast soil. It grips harder, punishes mistakes, and rewards commitment.

I like that.

The trailer hums quietly around me as I go through my routine. Boots tightened, gloves laid out just right, helmet resting where I can grab it without thinking. Everything has its place on race day. Order is control.

"You ready?"

Her voice cuts through the noise like it always does, soft, familiar.

I turn, already smiling. "For what?"

Stephanie stands just inside the trailer doorway, sunlight catching the edge of her blonde braid where it hangs over her shoulder. Her lanyard pass rests against her chest, the Kawasaki polo tucked effortlessly into black shorts. It's the same outfit she's worn a dozen times before.

Doesn't matter.

She still knocks the breath out of me.

She rolls her eyes. "Jokes already this morning?"

"I wouldn't want you getting bored with me now, would I?" I say, stepping toward her.

Her eyes flick around the trailer, quick and cautious. Always aware. Always thinking three steps ahead. The reality of whatever *this* is, hums unspoken between us—close, but not too close. Seen, but not obvious.

"I'm never bored with you," she says quietly. Then, softer still, "Axel, I need to talk to you."

I stop right in front of her, then glance past her shoulder toward the open paddock. Mechanics move in the distance. Radios crackle. No one's paying us any attention.

I lean down and press a quick kiss to her forehead. It's safe and innocent, but still ours.

"I'm all ears," I say as I give her braid a quick playful tug.

She straightens, shoulders squaring like she's stepping into work mode. That confidence, I've gotten to know pretty well. I respect it.

"Here's the deal," she says. "Today, we are all business.

Absolutely no touching. No kissing. Nothing that turns into a PR nightmare."

She pokes a finger into my chest and leans in, voice dropping. "Got it?"

I raise an eyebrow. "That's it?"

She smirks. "That's it."

"But," she adds, eyes glinting, "You bet your ass I'll make sure you're on your A-game today."

I step closer just to mess with her. "What? No sweet words of encouragement? No promise of a dirty little treat to motivate me?"

Her palm lands flat against my chest, stopping me cold.

"Not happening, *Mr.* Milano," she says. "It's like you don't even know me."

I stand there, stunned, as she turns and heads for the door.

Then, right as she steps out, she glances back and winks.

A shit-eating grin spreads across her face.

And I'm done for.

Yeah, we're not normal. Whatever this is between us doesn't fit neatly into any box. She's sharp and unexpected and pushes me in ways no one else ever has.

If that doesn't add fuel to the fire burning in my chest... I don't know what does.

I roll up to the gate, the shade feeling damn near holy as Ben holds the umbrella over my helmet. The sun's not brutal today, but every degree matters. It's all about regulating your heart rate, focus, precision.

I hear him and his fan club before I see him.

Rad Carson.

Of course I get the gate next to him.

Lucky me.

Ben shifts beside me, brow furrowing. "I thought you'd gotten better with that."

I know exactly what he means.

"I have," I say calmly. "Doesn't mean I don't want to beat his pretty face in."

Rad's helmet turns slightly. "You think I'm pretty, Milano?"

Cocky as always.

I reach for my goggles, realization hitting me mid-motion.

If I'm going to keep things going with Steph, Rad isn't going anywhere. He's going to be in my orbit, pressers, podiums, team events, holidays.

I don't hate him like I used to.

But he still pisses me off.

"Only when you're behind me, Carson," I shoot back.

Ben lets out a short laugh. "That's the spirit."

Rad leans closer. "Hey."

I stiffen.

"Just don't break her heart, alright?" he says quietly.

I turn and meet his eyes. There's no trash talk there, just sincerity. Big brother protectiveness overpowering the rivalry. It stings. But I respect it. She must have told him.

I nod.

Rad settles back into position like nothing happened.

Ben eyes me. "What'd he say?"

"Just some shit talking," I lie.

Ben doesn't buy it, but he lets it go.

"Get your head back on track," he says, clapping my shoulder. "It's go time."

I grip the bars, fingers tightening around the grips. The bike hums beneath me, alive, eager. The familiar calm washes over me. The quiet right before chaos.

The thirty second board goes up.

Because I'm a dickhead, I glance sideways. Rad's already looking at me.

"See you on the podium, pretty boy," I grin.

The gate drops and everything narrows to sound and motion.

I launch clean, front wheel skimming just long enough to remind me not to get greedy. I tuck into the first turn with bodies pressing in on both sides—AJ on my left, Zane's front wheel flashing in my peripheral on the right—engines screaming, dirt flying, adrenaline flooding my veins.

The track comes at me fast. Ruts are deep, braking bumps buck me, but my body knows what to do before my brain catches up. Instinct takes over. Muscle memory. I pick lines that feel risky but right, commit fully, because hesitation is the only real mistake out here.

By lap three, I'm gone.

The lead settles into my hands like something solid, something earned. Zane hangs on for a few laps, smart and patient the way veterans always are, but I'm flowing. Every corner is a conversation between throttle and traction, every jump timed just enough to keep momentum without giving anything away. I don't look back. I don't need to.

When the checkered flag waves in Moto One, it hits me like a rush straight to the chest. Relief. Fire. Proof. I take the win, raise a fist, hear the crowd explode, and still, I know it's not over.

Moto Two is a war.

Rad launches harder than anyone, elbows out, riding like the track deserves it. He's aggressive in a way that's calculated, not sloppy, and he stays glued to me from the first lap on. AJ tries to insert himself early, but Rad shuts the door. It's clear—this one's between us.

He dives inside mid-moto, forces me wide, and for a split second I have to decide: push it and risk everything, or live to fight another lap. Rad doesn't hesitate. He never does. He takes the line, takes the lead, and I tuck in behind him, heart pounding, refusing to fade.

I throw everything I have at him. Pressure. Different lines. Late braking. But Rad is riding possessed, smooth where it matters, ruthless where it counts.

The checkered flag comes too soon.

Second place.

When the dust settles and the points are added up, it's enough for him. Moto win. Overall win. Championship still in his sights. I sit on my bike under the canopy, chest heaving, sweat dripping down my neck, staring at the scoreboard like it might change if I look hard enough.

I was right there.

One position away.

One decision from rewriting everything.

Rad won the day.

But I made him earn every inch of it.

29

Stephanie

He did it.

And he didn't.

Axel won the first moto, and for a while, it felt like the world tilted in his favor.

I stand under the canopy behind the stage, heart still racing like I was the one on the bike. He rode Moto One like something had been lit inside him. Calm, aggressive, untouchable. He pushed harder than I've ever seen him push, riding with that dangerous mix of confidence and desperation that makes legends or wrecks. No one even sniffed his rear wheel.

By the time Moto Two rolled around, the air felt different.

Rad stayed glued to him. Close enough to be a shadow. Close enough to matter. There was one moment, half a lap where Axel had the line, had the edge, and I thought, *this is it.* But Rad forced the issue and took the inside. Made Axel hesitate just long enough.

Second place.

Not a loss.

But not enough.

They might have each won a moto, but winning the second one beats the tie. Rad takes the overall.

I already have the water ready when Axel rides under the tent, stopping inches from my toes. He swings a leg over stiffly and hands the bike off without a word. I grab the bars, steadying it, while he collapses into the chair like his body finally remembered gravity exists.

Sweat pours down his temples. Dirt streaks his jaw. His chest rises and falls hard, uneven. He looks wrecked—physically, emotionally, beautifully—and still, that smile is there. Smaller than before. Tighter. But real.

"You were flying out there," Ben says, gripping Axel's shoulders like he's afraid letting go might make the whole thing sink in. "Hell of a ride."

Axel lets out a breathy laugh. "Couldn't quite finish the job."

I step in smoothly, already twisting the cap off the water bottle and pressing it into Axel's hand like muscle memory. Like this is what I'm supposed to do. Which technically it is.

"You were right there," I say, keeping my voice even. Professional. Neutral. The way it has to be knowing cameras are most likely nearby.

His eyes flick to mine, quick, loaded, full of everything he's not saying. My stomach flips traitorously. I smile before I can stop myself.

"Yeah," he says quietly. "We were."

The asshole mask slides back into place as he turns away, jaw setting, focus snapping forward.

Good.

Right?

It shouldn't sting. I asked for this. I needed this. Still... the space between us suddenly feels larger than the crowd.

I force my attention elsewhere and spot Rad a few yards away, helmet off now, bent toward his mechanic. He's calm in that unnerving way, like the anger has already burned off and left satisfaction behind. When his eyes meet mine, we exchange a small nod. Mutual respect during a complicated situation. I'm sure we'll talk later. Probably with sarcasm. Possibly with drinks.

Past Rad is Zane Ryker, Yamaha blue from head to toe, grinning like he just found an extra year in his career. Third in Moto Two and loving every second of it. He's the first called to the stage, jogging toward the ramp as the crowd explodes, air horns, cowbells, flags whipping in the air.

He comes back a few minutes later, still glowing, like the noise hasn't worn off yet.

Then it's Rad's turn.

I watch him shift gears the moment before he rounds the corner, anger from a tough win tucked away, public smile locked in place. Years of parental training on full display. Losing never sits right with him, but winning? Winning looks easy on him.

I glance back at Axel, half-expecting a sharp comment. A smirk. Something defensive.

He doesn't give me anything.

I hand him his hat and podium goggles instead. Our fingers almost touch. Almost. He slides the goggles around his neck, pulls the hat down low. His attention stays fixed on the far side of the tent where Rad reappears, champagne already in hand.

A moment later, Rad steps in close.

"Hell of a fight," he says, hand extended. "You had me sweating."

Every muscle in my body goes tight as my eyes bounce between them, waiting for it, trash talk, a shove, something reckless.

Axel takes Rad's hand, grip firm.

"You earned it," he says evenly. "Today was yours."

Rad's mouth curves into a slow, knowing smile. "For now."

Axel's lips twitch. "Yeah. For now."

Their hands drop. No theatrics. No blowup. Just two riders acknowledging the truth of it. I didn't realize I'd been holding my breath until it rushes out of me.

Then it's Axel's turn for the stage. Second overall.

I pass him the Monster can, and this time our fingers do brush. Just barely.

Electricity snaps straight up my arm.

I look up at him, and for one heartbeat, the walls drop. His expression softens. Just for me. He leans in like he's adjusting his gloves and murmurs so low I almost miss it.

"I fucking hate pretending."

My chest tightens.

Then he's gone.

The crowd still roars as Axel steps onto the ramp, lifting a hand in acknowledgment. Not a victory wave, something more restrained, earned, respected. He doesn't have to fake the smile, even if it costs him.

Ben and I move to the edge of the tent, watching as Rad takes center stage, champagne spraying, cameras flashing. This— *this*—is the part fans don't see. The thin line between winning and almost. The way it can change everything without looking like it did.

Being behind the scenes is different. You don't just see the results, you feel the fallout. Ben bumps his fist into mine. A steady presence that I've grown to know.

A team.

That's what I found this summer. Even if one part of it has to stay hidden, for now.

"Rad Carson takes the overall tonight!" Charlotte shouts into the mic as the crowd detonates again.

Rad grins, lifting the trophy high.

I glance back toward Axel, just in time to catch him looking at me from the edge of the chaos.

Not broken.

Not defeated.

Just hungry.

And somehow... that feels even more dangerous.

30

Axel

I'm still reeling as the team filters back toward the trailers, the night thick with noise and motion. Champagne hangs in the air like a ghost, sweet, sharp, everywhere. Laughter spills from every direction, easy and unrestrained, the kind that only comes after someone else finally gets what they came for.

Almost.

The adrenaline hasn't worn off yet. My hands are still buzzing, my chest still tight from pushing the limit, from riding like the outcome might bend if I wanted it bad enough.

I didn't beat Mister Perfect tonight.

Not the way it'll probably read on paper.

But, I didn't roll over either.

I made him work for it. Every lap. Every line. Every mistake he thought I'd make that never came. And that knowledge settles heavy in my chest. Not warm exactly, but solid. Earned.

This wasn't a collapse.

This wasn't a fluke.

It was close enough to taste. Close enough to know I belong

right there.

And as the noise swells around me, as the champagne keeps spraying and the crowd keeps cheering for someone else, one thing is painfully clear...

Next time, I won't miss.

As I walk, I glance back over my shoulder and spot Steph near the edge of the group, deep in conversation with a couple of crew members. She's animated, smiling, completely in her element. The lights catch the braid over her shoulder, the lanyard at her chest, the way she gestures when she talks. She's so confident, sharp, and undeniably magnetic.

I shake my head, still not entirely convinced she's real. That somehow, she helped me get here. Believed in me when she didn't owe me a damn thing. When I didn't even fully believe in myself.

My steps slow. The smile fades.

Because the high has an edge to it.

I get *why* we're doing this. I really do. But not being allowed to touch her? Not kiss her? Not even look at her too long without thinking about who's watching?

It's fucking torture.

Pretending there's nothing between us feels wrong in a way I can't quite explain. I had to act like she didn't exist when I crossed the line. I had to keep my eyes forward, my hands neutral, my face blank. Because if I looked at her, really looked, I would've blown the whole thing wide open. Her career, her reputation, everything she's worked for.

And for the first time in my life, I care enough to stop myself. That scares me more than anything else. I just hope I don't have to wear this mask until I fucking retire.

I duck into the trailer, the door closing behind me and

muffling the commotion outside. The space is quiet, tight, and familiar. I peel off my gear piece by piece, the adrenaline slowly bleeding out of my veins. I barely manage to pull my T-shirt over my head when—

Knock. Knock.

I freeze.

Of course.

I let out a breath, running a hand through my hair, trying to steady myself. I wanted a minute. Just one.

"Yes?" I call, irritation slipping into my voice despite my best effort.

"Axel?"

Her voice.

The door opens slowly, and there she is. Stunning green eyes and barely contained nerves. That look she gets when she's not sure how something's going to land but does it anyway. My heart stutters, hard.

"Your parents are out there."

The words don't register at first.

Then they hit.

My *parents.*

Here. Now. Of all days.

My chest tightens as a thousand thoughts crash into each other. Why today? What do they want? What am I supposed to say after all this time?

"You sure it's them?" I ask, grasping for denial.

"Positive." She straightens, fingers tightening on the door frame like she's bracing herself too.

I nod slowly. There's no running from it, I guess.

"You okay?" she asks softly. "Want me to have them leave?"

I shake my head.

"No. I'll... I'll talk to them."

We hold each other's gaze for a beat, something unspoken passing between us. Support and understanding. She steps aside, and I follow her down the trailer steps.

They're standing just outside, and the sight of them steals the air from my lungs.

The people who taught me how to ride, who cheered at my first races, who believed in me... until they didn't.

They're also the ones who walked away after the accident. Who couldn't understand why I needed the bike to survive. Why riding was the only thing that kept me breathing when everything else fell apart.

My mom grips my dad's arm, tears already forming. My dad stands tall, chest out, pride written all over him.

They look... good. They appear to be healthy, normal.

"Son," my dad says.

That's all it takes.

My mom pulls me into a hug, tight, and desperate, like she's afraid I'll never see them again.

"Oh, Axel," she chokes.

I hug her back for the first time in years. My dad's hand lands on my shoulder, firm, and familiar.

"We missed you," she says into my chest.

When I pull back, I don't even know where to start.

"What are you guys doing here?"

They share a look. My mom wipes her cheeks and nudges my dad.

"We thought it was time," he says.

"For what?" I ask.

"To tell you how proud we are of you."

The words land heavier than any trophy ever could.

My mom starts to apologize, but I cut her off before she can finish.

"Sorry?" I snap, turning away, anger flaring fast.

"I know it doesn't make up for—"

"No," I interrupt, voice low. "It doesn't."

I swallow hard.

"Maddox would've kept riding. If it were me who died that night, he wouldn't have stopped. He loved it just as much as I did. As much as I still do."

"We realize that now."

The room spins, but I hold it together.

My dad pulls an envelope from his pocket and hands it to me.

The Mad Madds Moto Foundation.

My heart stops.

"We saved every penny," he says quietly.

A tear slips free before I can stop it.

"How did you know it was me?" I ask.

"It wasn't hard to guess," Dad chuckles softly.

He clears his throat.

"We know it'll be a lot of work, but we want to do what we should've done years ago," he continues. "Support young riders who need it. You in?"

I don't hesitate.

"Of course I'm in."

For the first time in a long time, it feels like something's been stitched back together. We catch up as much as possible in the time that a few minutes allows us and promise to meet up on another day. When they leave, I stand there for a moment, stunned. Whole in a way I didn't know I was missing.

I head back into the trailer, past the emotional roller coaster, past the noise, needing air. I shut myself into the tiny bathroom, staring at my reflection, trying to recognize the guy looking back at me.

Knock.

"Just a minute," I call, breathing deep.

The door opens anyway.

Blonde hair and my favorite set of eyes. The lock clicks.

"Shh," she whispers. "It's just me."

The space is too small, forcing her close, her body pressed to mine. Normally I'd want whoever it is to leave but her? She can stay. She exhales softly.

"You okay?"

I lift my hands and cup her face, thumbs brushing her cheeks.

"I think so."

I kiss her, slow and deep. She melts into it. It's like we've done it a million times, perfect.

I pull back just enough to whisper, "Even better now."

She smiles.

"You've been killing me all day, you know."

"I don't like pretending either," she murmurs.

"Then let's stop."

"We can't," she says softly. "Not yet. At least not until after the season."

I drop my forehead to hers, frustration burning, but I get it. And that somehow makes it harder.

I kiss her again, knowing I'd burn the world down for her if I had to.

And that thought?

That scares the hell out of me.

I slide my hand to the front of her shorts, firm but restrained, my other hand lifting to cover her mouth as her breath hitches. I lean in, voice low, steady.

"Now, be a good girl for me."

Her eyes darken.

And in that moment, *I know*, how much I need her in my life.

31

Stephanie

"Done."

I shut my laptop, the finality of it echoing louder in my head than it should. The screen goes dark, but the weight of what I just sent doesn't. I set it on the coffee table like it might bite me if I keep it too close and look over at Lex.

She's already watching me with that look, soft, sympathetic, but sharp enough to see straight through me. Her long, curly red hair spills perfectly over her shoulder, like she hasn't been pacing this apartment with me for the last hour.

"How do you feel?" she asks.

I blow out a slow breath, rubbing my palms together.

"I don't know yet."

She nods like that's exactly what she expected.

"It's not a guarantee," I add quickly. "So, I'm not letting myself spiral over it. Not until there's something real to react to."

That part is half true. What I just sent could change every-thing or absolutely nothing. The waiting might be worse than the outcome.

Lex moves closer, plopping down beside me on the couch. She hooks an arm around my shoulders in a familiar side hug, grounding me when my thoughts start racing.

"I believe in you," she says softly. "Whatever happens, it's meant to."

I wish certainty came as easily to me as it does to her. Because, hitting send felt like choosing between two lives. One I've been quietly building for years, and another that snuck up on me when I wasn't looking. One that has a name, a face, and a way of making me forget every rule I ever set for myself.

I tell myself I'm not running. I'm just... keeping doors open. But, some doors don't open without closing others.

"Are you still coming to the last race?" I ask, needing something solid. Something normal.

Her face lights up instantly.

"Obviously. I already have the cutest checkered print outfit picked out."

I laugh, the sound easing the tightness in my chest.

"Of course you do."

We sit there for a second, shoulder to shoulder, until her smile fades just a notch.

"Do you think it'll be enough to make your brother notice me?" she asks, quieter now.

There it is.

I nudge her with my elbow, teasing but careful.

"I think you're aiming a little too close to home."

She grins anyway.

"Can you blame me?"

Maybe I can. Maybe I should.

Because if things go the way they *might*, Lex will still be here, embedded in a world I may not be able to stay in. And Rad... Rad already lives in the cracks between complicated and reckless. The kind of person who doesn't mean to cause damage, but always seems to leave it behind anyway.

"I've been single way too long," she adds brightly, the sunshine snapping back into place. "It's time."

I smile, even as unease settles low in my stomach. Because timing has never been our strong suit. And whatever I just set in motion?

It's already testing everything I'm not ready to lose.

32

Axel

The heat clings to my gear like a second skin, thick and unforgiving. Maryland dirt cakes my boots, creeps into every seam, every crease, until it feels like the track has claimed me before I've even lined up. The air is heavy. Humid enough to choke on and every breath tastes like clay, sweat, and race fuel.

I crush the empty bottle in my hand, plastic crumpling loudly. The electrolyte mix did its job, but the buzz in my veins has nothing to do with hydration.

I'm ready.

Today is the last race of the regular Pro Motocross season. Then there's a few weeks to prepare for playoffs. So, technically SMX isn't entirely over, but who doesn't want to win every championship title there is? Especially after losing the Supercross one this year.

And somehow, against odds I probably shouldn't have beaten, I still have a shot at this one.

I need first in both motos. All Rad needs is to get tenth place or better.

It won't be easy, or likely, but not impossible.

And a chance is all I've ever needed.

A sharp, high-pitched screech slices through my focus, followed by laughter. It's loud, reckless, and completely out of place among the tense hum of race prep. I yank the trailer door open, instinctively annoyed, ready to bark at whoever's losing their mind out there.

Instead, I freeze.

Steph is halfway swallowed by a blur of red curls and flailing limbs. Whoever this girl is, she's bouncing on the balls of her feet like she's had three energy drinks too many, arms wrapped tight around my little Kill Switch as if she belongs to her and not me.

The girl wears a black crop top and a checkered skirt that leaves very little to the imagination. She's all legs, drowned in confidence. A damn near walking exclamation point.

The polar opposite of Steph, minus the confidence part.

Steph laughs, genuine and unguarded, the sound hitting me square in the chest. It's a laugh I don't hear often, not lately anyways. Not with the careful way she's been carrying herself.

"What in the hell is going on?" Ben mutters beside me, stepping into the doorway.

Then he sees her.

And absolutely locks up. Straight up statue.

Oh am I going to enjoy the hell out of this.

"Let's go meet her," I say, already moving.

My voice barely registers, so I nudge him with my elbow. "C'mon."

He stumbles after me down the trailer steps like his brain forgot how legs work.

As I approach, I tilt my head, cocky grin slipping into place.

"Should I call security," I ask lightly, "or...?"

The redhead looks up at me, eyes sharp and curious. She nudges her thumb toward Steph without breaking eye contact with me.

"Is this the famous Axel Milano?"

Steph smiles softly and looks up at me.

"Sure is."

God.

She looks the same as every other race weekend. And yet... something's different. There's a tension beneath her smile, like she's wound just a little tighter than usual. Like she's bracing for something I don't know about.

I file the thought away.

Touching her is off-limits. Has been for a few weekends now. And it's *still* fucking torture. In case you were wondering. Standing this close, feeling the urge to claim her in front of everyone in this goddamn parking lot. It takes more discipline than riding ever has.

"This is my best friend, Alexis," Steph says, gesturing between us.

"Call me, Lex."

I take Lex's hand, giving her a polite shake. She studies me with a knowing look. A look that tells me Steph's told her more than just my name. There's an edge to her gaze, protective and sharp. Like she doesn't mess around.

Noted.

"Lex," I say, smirking, "Steph never mentioned she had friends."

Steph slaps my arm.

"Rude."

Lex gasps dramatically.

"Wow. I can't believe you!?"

I chuckle, then glance over at Ben.

Bad idea.

His eyes are glued to Lex like she's the only person left on earth. Borderline creepy.

I grip his shoulder.

"This," I say proudly, "Is my best friend and mechanic, Ben."

"A.K.A. Benji," Steph whispers beside her.

Ben steps forward and—*Jesus Christ*—kisses the back of her hand.

They both freeze.

Total silence.

Steph and I exchange a look that says *you seeing this?*

Loud and clear.

"Hi," they both mumble at the same time, dropping their hands in practically slow motion.

"Well," I say, clearing my throat, "Ben and I have a race to win."

I steer my now-limp mechanic away.

"Nice to meet you, *Alexis*," I toss over my shoulder, using her full name to mess with her.

Inside the trailer, I spin on Ben the second the door shuts.

"What the fuck was that?" I whisper shout.

He collapses onto the couch, elbows on his knees, palms pressed into his eyes like he's trying to reboot his brain.

"I don't know, man. I feel like I blacked out."

I laugh.

"I've never seen you that speechless and... weird."

"I know! Fuck!"

I grin wider.

"So... you like her? Or—"

"Shut the fuck up."

I raise my hands, backing off. This conversation can wait. If Steph and I keep doing whatever this is... Alexis is going to be around. And things will get a lot more interesting.

Qualifying comes and goes in a blur.

"Third's not bad."

Ben hops on the back of my bike and we ride back to the trailer. He pats my shoulder like it's supposed to soften the blow.

Not good enough.

No one expects me to win this title, not really. And that thought lights something dangerous in my chest.

Fans cheer as we weave through them, hands outstretched, voices calling my name. Call me an asshole, but I don't look at them. Today, I don't have the luxury to mess around. I park and head straight inside.

Steph's already there. She has my water ready, snack in hand. Prepared. Always prepared. Our eyes meet for half a second. Something flickers there. It's not fear or doubt but, resolve. Our masks unfortunately on. The trailer buzzes with movement as I sit, trying to get my breathing under control. Her presence nearby is distracting in ways that have nothing to do with racing.

"Pull yourself together," her whisper is sharp enough to cut through the noise.

I look up. She's standing in front of me, arms crossed. That stubborn look etched perfectly in place.

"Excuse me?"

"You're acting like qualifying third is a death sentence."

She's stern and unapologetic. Even borderline rude. And

somehow... I like it. Everyone else uses the same, typical, disgustingly positive encouragement.

"There's a lot riding on today," I say evenly. "I won't accept anything less than first."

She nods once.

"Good. Save that for the motos."

She turns away, already moving on to the next task, like the conversation is finished.

She's right.

But as I watch her walk away, that tight, unfamiliar pull settles in my chest again. The one that has nothing to do with lap times or points standings. It's the same feeling I get when she's near and I'm not allowed to reach for her. When I have to pretend she's just another team member instead of the one person who can steady me without even trying.

She moves with purpose, head high, like she always does, strong and unshakable. And it hits me, hard, that somewhere along the way she stopped being just my anchor on race days and became something a hell of a lot more dangerous.

Someone I care about.

I don't know what she's carrying, or why it feels like she's hiding something, but I know this much... I want to be the one standing there to help her through it.

And suddenly, the title isn't the only thing riding on today.

33

Axel

Budd's Creek always feels alive before a gate drop. It's like the dirt itself is holding it's breath, waiting to see who it's going to swallow. I glance down at the watch strapped to my wrist, the monitor fastened securely around my chest. The numbers steady despite the noise, the heat, the tension humming in the air.

70 bpm.

Lower than it should be. Lower than it has any right to be with thirty-nine bikes snarling beside me and a title hanging in the balance. While everyone else is burning adrenaline, my body settles. Calm snaps into place like muscle memory. Control. This is where I'm sharpest. Right before everything explodes.

The gate buzzes with tension. Mechanics shape up the dirt in front of tires, reporters hassle riders with questions, and riders gear up for a strenuous first moto.

The track layout is considered one of the fans' favorites. There's a step up leading to a sharp turn that tests out even the most experienced riders. If I can get the holeshot then that's one advantage to use against everyone else.

Out of my periphery, I see Rad-fucking-Carson, the red plastics unmistakable. He tilts his visor just enough that I know he's looking at me. That signature Rad smirk radiates even through a damn helmet.

The bastard thinks he won already.

He always does.

He was fastest in qualifying, so it's already looking up for him. We may be on better terms than before but *God*, it still sucks losing to him.

Today I'm done carrying the weight of everyone whispering about Kawasaki's losing record. I'm done being a great rider that can't win a championship. Not this year. Not this track. Not against him.

His mechanic stands there holding an umbrella like one of his goddamn butlers that I'm sure he has at home. Probably has Taylor Swift playing through his brand new AirPods too.

I shake my head.

I'm sure he's a nice guy but during race day, he can suck my dick. Nobody is friends on the track.

90 bpm

I go through my typical pre-moto routine. I stretch my fingers, arms, and neck while Ben looks over the bike. My hands move to the break and clutch making sure all is good there after starting the engine. The bike roars to life underneath me and my body instantly eases. That's one stress out of the way.

Ben nods to me, confirming that everything checks out. Next, is waiting for the officials to make final checks. Air horns pierce the air as the fans gear up for the gate drop. I feel everyone dial in beside me. It's my queue to block them out and focus on the dirt ahead of me.

Nothing will distract me today, not even my little Kill Switch.

"Hmmf," I mumble under my breath. She would keep me straight. Probably shove me back into reality when my head gets too far up my own ass. And somehow, instead of irritating me, that thought settles something deep in my chest. Fuck... it's refreshing. Scary too, but I don't dwell on that.

"All set, Axel." Ben's voice cuts through the noise as he smacks the seat behind me, the familiar signal that everything's dialed.

"You already know the speech I'd give you."

I huff a breath that's halfway to a grin.

"Don't worry, buddy. I'm gonna win regardless of the speech."

I turn my head to look at him. He meets my eyes, pride written plain as day, the kind he never tries to hide anymore. It hits harder than any pep talk ever could. I shoot him a look that says *don't you get soft on me, fucker*, and he laughs, shaking his head before jogging off toward the mechanics' area.

80 bpm.

Steady. Controlled. Right where I want it.

Now, the only thing between me and winning this moto is the last thirty seconds before the gate drops. Thirty seconds where everything slows down and sharpens all at once. I click the bike into second and give it a quick test, feeling the engine respond beneath me. It's solid. I'm Ready.

I pinch my shoulder blades together, head hovering just over the front number plate. My fender blocks my own gate, so my eyes lock onto the one beside me instead. Peripheral vision tuned in, waiting for the slightest twitch.

I bring the revs up slowly, deliberately, letting the engine scream just enough while easing the clutch halfway out. The vibration hums through my arms, through my spine, a familiar and welcoming feeling. The world narrows until there's nothing left but sound, tension, and timing.

No doubts. No distractions.

Just control.

90 bpm

The gate drops.

Like a cannon, the bike lurches forward. It's a perfect clutch release, front wheel skimming the dirt. The Kawasaki tips up slightly like it wants this as much as I do.

120 bpm

Forty bikes cram together as they begin to funnel towards the first turn. A few get bumped and tip over before they've even had a chance to begin. My knees clamp tight against the bike as instinct takes over. I see it. The smallest opening on the inside, barely there, the kind you either commit to or miss completely. There's no time to think.

I commit.

145 bpm

The throttle snaps open and the bike surges beneath me, rear tire clawing at the dirt as it launches forward. The front end gets light, skimming the ground as I muscle it back down and drive straight through the chaos. Roost sprays, engines scream, and bodies crowd in from both sides, but I'm already past them.

I hit the first turn clean, inside line locked, elbows up, daring anyone to challenge it. They don't. The bike lurches ahead, perfectly planted, and when I glance up, there's nothing but open track in front of me.

Holeshot.

The crowd erupts somewhere beyond the noise, but I barely

hear it. All I feel is the rhythm, the suspension working, the power beneath me, the rush of knowing I got exactly what I came for. Now it's mine to lose.

170bpm

By the second lap, Rad is right behind me. Close enough I can hear him, even over my own engine.

Too fucking close

He dives inside before the roller section on lap three, forcing me to play it safe. It's either that or lose the front end.

He rockets past me. Dirt slams into my chest from him roosting me.

Fine.

185bpm

Let him lead.

I pass the mechanics' area. Ben's arm stretched out, the green board waving. *Right there* written on it.

I follow Rad, practically breathing down his neck. I watch every mistake he doesn't know he's making. He's too jerky in the ruts, over jumping the table top by a foot, and drifting wider each lap. He's fast, yeah, but reckless fast.

Time does its thing.

170 bpm

With four laps to go, lappers pile up on the uphill double. Rad hesitates.

Here's my cue.

The outside berm hugs the bike as I feel like I can fly off the edge at any moment. But, I see a blur of one lapper.

Then two. Then Rad.

I passed him.

I fucking passed him.

The atmosphere erupts as the crowd confirms I'm not

dreaming.

Checkered flag.

190 bpm

I peel off toward the post-race tent, the bike rattling beneath me as adrenaline still hums through my veins. As I slow, I glance back.

Rad is two bikes behind me.

Even from here, I can see it. His shoulders are tight, head shaking as he yanks his helmet loose. The kind of anger that simmers hot and stupid. The kind that eats at you long after the checkered flag.

He's fucking pissed.

Good.

Steph is already there, right on cue, water in hand. I keep my face neutral, my body loose, like this was just another moto. Like my heart isn't still hammering. Like I didn't just take something Rad thought was his.

I take a slow drink, letting the water distract me, and force the calm to stick. Winning is one thing, but watching him unravel? That's the real reward.

I might've won the first battle.

But the war's still on.

The sun's lower and that comes with changing shadows that are long enough to swallow front wheels if you pick the wrong line. I'm sitting on my bike, at the gate, for the final moto of the outdoor season. It's all comes down to this. My last chance.

Rad takes breaks from being the pretty boy to stare daggers at me. It's conveniently only when the cameras aren't on him. Imagine that. I decide to piss him off even more when I see him hand his Airpods to one of the team members.

"Hopefully that Justin Bieber song got you pumped up for this moto," I say just loud enough for him and Ben to hear. I try my best to hold in my laugh, but it's difficult. Ben shakes his head, but stays silent. He's used to my mouth getting me in trouble.

"Good one Milano. I'll be sure to play one at your funeral," he says with a fake laugh while looking down. He adjusts his gloves with what I can only guess as frustration.

"Oh how the tables have..." Ben murmurs beside me, barely containing it.

I glance over, already knowing where he's going.

"Why are you the way that you are?" I ask flatly, fixing him with my most serious stare. He loses it and I follow.

The laughter feels wrong, too human, too easy and the riders in the neighboring gates glare at us like we've broken some unspoken rule. Let them. I've waited too long to enjoy moments like this. Not the time and place, I know, but you have to live a little.

Ben, the rule follower he is, puts his no nonsense mask back on and gestures for me to do my final checks. It's game time anyways. If I beat Rad again, even by one spot, I take the overall. All he needs is to get in the top ten to have enough points to win the championship.

The gate drops.

Rad explodes off the line like someone set his bike on fire. He slams the first corner, elbows high, as I settle behind, opting for efficiency over chaos. He may have gotten the holeshot, but that doesn't mean I've lost the race. I won't panic and overthink this time. I know this track. I should know him too at this point.

But, halfway through the opening lap he checks up in a

corner he normally rails. On purpose. I almost spear his rear wheel. My front tire kisses the side of his bike and the bars jerk in my hands. The bike snaps sideways and I save it on instinct alone, boot skimming dirt. Rad looks back and *smiles*. Not a grin. Not celebration. A warning.

This isn't normal.

Sharp edges forms in all the wrong places on the track. And looming ahead each lap is Henry Hill. It's steep, fast, and unforgiving. The kind of downhill that turns mistakes into highlight reels or nightmares.

By lap eight, I can see Rad's desperate. He's riding tight, revving the Honda like he's trying to wring blood out of it. He starts drifting across lines that aren't his. He cuts inside mid-corner, slamming his rear tire into my front wheel. My bars slap sideways. The crowd gasps. I muscle the bike upright, heart detonating in my chest.

He's not defending. He's trying to take me out. I breathe, loosen my shoulders, and settle into the track. The ruts are deep now and carved like train tracks. I let them carry me.

I tail him like a second shadow, watching the tiny errors multiply. Rad keeps glancing back. That's when I know he's rattled. When he fears I'm coming. When he fears his title is at risk. His clutch pulls are late causing the rear tire to float sideways in a rut. He's pushing too hard. Let him burn himself out. I'm not in a rush.

Four laps to go and the battle escalates.

Rad brake checks me heading into a downhill chute. For absolutely no reason. Just a sudden stab at the lever. My suspension compresses so hard my chin smashes the handlebar. I barely miss his rear fender. He wants me over the bars and on the ground.

Why?

I swing wide to avoid him and he drifts with me, cutting the lane off. Our handlebars collide. The impact shoots lightning bolts up my arms. We're inches from hooking and cartwheeling together. The crowd is screaming now. Not cheering.

Screaming.

Ben flips the pit board. One word.

Careful.

I'm so close I can smell his clutch burning. He's riding past the edge of control, revving the bike like he's trying to blow it up just to make a point. We launch a tabletop side by side and he leans into me mid-air. Our boots collide. My bike wobbles when we land. For half a second the world tilts and I see the dirt rushing at my face. By some miracle, I save it.

Barely.

Rage flashes hot in my chest. This isn't racing. This is attempted murder with a scoreboard.

We land and he veers over nearly colliding with my front tire. We swap lines, our bikes inches apart. This isn't just a rider that wants to win.

He wants to destroy me in the process.

Three laps to go.

Lappers crowd the uphill double again. Rad hesitates a split second. I use it as an opportunity. I blow past on the outside berm, which is wide open, riding the edge of traction like it's a razor blade.

I feel the roar of the fans as they can't get enough of this fight. Rad catches up on a downhill turn. He inches ahead and just when we come up on a straight away he tries cutting me off. I dodge him, knowing it was coming.

His bike falters as he corrects himself.

"Fucking idiot!" I yell even though he probably can't hear me. He can't just take the loss with dignity he has to make a scene. He'd still win the championship for fucks sake. But instead, he has to try and kill me. But, fuck him. I'm going to outsmart the bastard.

Final lap.

We rocket toward Henry Hill, engines screaming. The noise fades into a high ringing whine inside my helmet. It's just the two of us and the drop. It's a game of chicken. Rad doesn't brake. So, neither do I.

We fall into Henry Hill together. The bike chatters beneath me, suspension hammering through the dirt. I take the outside line. It's longer, but cleaner, setting up the pass at the bottom. Rad dives inside like he's got something to prove. Halfway down he drifts toward me again. Even here, even now, he wants to try this bullshit.

He tries to crowd me into the roughest part of the slope, front tire hunting my line. One more shove, one more attempt to end it. I hold steady and refuse to move. He runs out of room.

His rear wheel hooks a blown out rut, and the Honda snaps sideways so violently it looks unreal. He throws a foot out, tries to wrestle it back, but momentum doesn't care about pride. The bike bucks and launches. Rad suddenly separates from the machine. And time fractures.

He's airborne before ragdolling down Henry Hill. His helmet smacks the dirt once, twice, maybe three times. I lost count. His bike cartwheels behind him, red plastic exploding like shrapnel. The crowd gasps. My gut wrenches.

Not good.

Yellow flags begin to wave.

Growing up in this sport forces you to never give a second glance to wrecks. The worst thing I can do is freeze and cause another wreck on this slope. I keep the bike steady, heart hammering in my chest. But, it's human nature to... care. To want to look, to help. But, stopping on Henry Hill is suicide. I force myself to ride past, staying upright, hands shaking so hard I almost miss a shift.

He's not moving.

As if he's, dare I say, lifeless.

Medics are already sprinting toward him. Something isn't right. Rad's limbs aren't curled or braced they're just... still. The kind of still that makes the whole world tilt wrong.

I finish the final lap numb. The checkered flag waves, my name announced in the background, as I cross the finish line, but all I see is what I left behind. It's a mix of emotions.

I finally did it. I got what I always wanted. The title is mine, but the hill took blood for it. Victory sits heavy in my chest, tangled with the image of him crumpled in the dirt. No win is clean. But this one is filthy. Earned in inches and hatred, and a final mistake that can't be undone. Sometimes beating your rival means surviving the thing he was willing to become.

And carrying the weight of it anyway.

34

Stephanie

"He won," I whisper, the words leaving my mouth like they belong to someone else.

He actually did it.

The crowd is still roaring, the speakers still screaming his name, but the sound feels distant, like I'm underwater. My chest should be bursting with pride. Instead there's this sick, crawling feeling in my gut that won't settle.

Something is wrong.

I see Axel cutting through the infield toward the tent, riding way too fast for a victory lap. No wheelie. No waving. No celebration. Just a straight line, aggressive and urgent.

"Why is he going so fast?" I murmur.

The other media personnel glance at me, but don't answer. One of the Honda crew members suddenly stiffens. A hand presses tight to their headset. Their face drains of color as they stare toward the track. Half the crowd dies. Then I hear it.

Sirens.

Not celebratory air horns.

Sirens.

Cold dread pours into my bloodstream. Axel skids to a stop in front of me, engine still snarling. He doesn't kill it, doesn't even take his helmet off.

"Listen to me," he says sharply over the bike. "I need you to hear what I'm about to tell you."

Why isn't he getting off?

My heart slams so hard it hurts. I look up at him and I already know. I don't want the words, but they're coming anyway.

"It's Rad," he says. His voice breaks on the name. "He crashed on the final lap. It's... bad. They're taking him to the hospital. I can get you there."

Rad.

Crash.

Sirens.

The world fades.

I grab his hand without thinking and swing onto the bike. The spilled water at my feet doesn't even register. My arms lock around his waist and we launch forward. I've seen Rad wreck before. The broken bones, torn ligaments, blood. That's racing. But Axel offering to take me to the hospital? That thought claws at my throat.

The ride is a blur of noise, wind, and panic. My brain replays the sirens over and over. I don't realize we've reached the parking lot until Axel taps my knee.

"Where'd you park?"

I blink back into reality and point. Another bike slides in beside us.

"As soon as I saw, I had someone grab your stuff," Ben says gently. His voice sounds far away, like it's traveling through water.

Axel answers for me. "Thanks, man. Thanks, AJ."

AJ nods as Ben hops off the back of his bike. Axel takes my bag and gestures for me to get off the bike. And that's when it clicks.

"What the fuck are you doing?" I snap.

He rips his goggles off, eyes blazing. "I'm driving you to the hospital."

"You just won the championship!" My voice cracks. "You need to go back."

He stares at me like I said something stupid.

"No."

"You can't just— no?" I shake my head. "I'll be fine. I can call my parents. They're here somewhere." My fingers fumble for my phone. "Go back, Axel. Please. You deserve this. Don't give the press a reason to twist it."

The boys stand frozen, watching us like they're witnessing a bomb about to go off.

"It's just a trophy," he says.

"It's not just a trophy."

His jaw tightens. "I know what it's like to lose a brother. I'm not letting you walk into that alone."

The words hit like a slap.

"You think he's dead?!" I shout.

His face softens instantly. "I'm not saying that. I'm saying it was bad. I was there, I witnessed it."

Silence stretches between us. I meet his eyes one last time and force steel into my voice.

"Go do what's expected of you. I'll talk to you later."

I turn before he can argue again.

"Steph, wait!"

"Let me go, Axel."

I don't look back. If I do, I'll break. I'll drag him with me and steal the moment he's spent his entire life chasing. I won't be the reason his win gets swallowed by my family's disaster.

The exhausts putter behind me, then fades. I walk to the car on shaking legs. My phone rings the second I sit down.

Mom.

I answer on Bluetooth while backing out.

"Hello?"

"Where are you? Rad—" Her voice splinters.

"I know, I'm— I'm on my way."

The GPS says forty-five minutes.

I make it in thirty.

Mom texted me the room number but I didn't need it. I could hear her as soon as I got off the elevator.

"Why can't we wait in his room? Do you know who we are?"

Of course she's hassling the hospital staff.

When I approach them, Dad gently lays his hand on Mom's shoulder.

"I'm Rad's sister. What's going on?" I ask.

The nurse exhales slowly, like she's said this a hundred times today already.

"Your brother is in surgery. He suffered a subdural hematoma and required an emergency craniotomy."

The words bounce off me. Medical jargon. Sharp and meaningless. I stare at her.

She softens. "Your brother has a brain bleed. A craniotomy means we had to open part of his skull to relieve pressure. It was caught quickly, which is good. Things look promising."

A brain bleed.

The hallway suddenly feels too bright.

"A brain bleed?" I echo, my voice smaller than I expect.

"Yes. That's the main concern right now. The doctor will meet with you after surgery and explain everything." She gives a tight, professional smile and turns away.

Mom lunges after her with another question, but I grab her arm.

"Mom. You have to respect their rules."

"Why can't we wait in his room?" she demands. "I want him to see us. I want to make sure he remembers us."

I whip my head toward her. "You think he lost his memory?"

Her eyes flick away. "I might have Googled head injuries."

Of course she did.

"We were concerned, honey—" Dad starts.

"And guess whose fault this is?" Mom snaps, cutting him off. There's a wild edge in her eyes now. The kind that means she's already decided the villain and just needs the audience to agree.

"Who?" I whisper.

I already know, but hope she doesn't say it.

"Axel Milano."

There it is.

"All this to get revenge, no doubt!" She paces the tiny waiting area, hands flying. "He's been waiting for this. You could see it in the way he rides, reckless, calculated—"

I tune her out. It's not like he's going to put on a Ghostface mask and show up to finish the job. I shake my head not having the energy to argue with her.

The room feels smaller by the second. Beige walls, cheap framed landscape art, a stack of outdated magazines fanned across a table. A TV mounted in the corner that's definitely muted and probably stuck on a news channel no one can change. A holding cell for bad news.

My brain replays Axel's face at the track. The urgency he had, the fear in his eyes, the way he didn't care about the trophy, the cameras, the crowd. He wanted to drive me here, not celebrate. That's not revenge. That's... concern.

I sink into a plastic chair. It creaks under me. My hands are shaking and I tuck them between my knees so no one sees. I feel Mom staring, waiting for me to agree. She wants me to take her side, to light the torches with her. Dad speaks first.

"You know... it is racing," he says quietly. "Things happen."

"This is our son!" she fires back. "What if his career is over?"

"Then it's over."

The words land. Final. At least I can agree with Dad on that.

She huffs, offended by the simplicity of it, and drops into a chair across from me. The silence stretches. It feels like hours. Every time footsteps echo down the hallway my heart kicks into my throat. Every time they pass us, it drops again. It's exhausting.

Finally, a middle aged man in light blue scrubs walks in. He's calm. The kind of calm you only get from delivering life-altering news on a daily basis.

"Hi, I'm Doctor Hatfield."

We all stand at once.

"Good news," he says immediately. "The surgery went well. Radley might suffer with temporary side effects like headaches, balance issues, and weakness. He will need phys-ical therapy, neuro rehab, and time for those broken ribs to heal, but we expect a full recovery."

My knees almost give out. He's going to be okay.

The tension drains out of my body so fast it leaves me dizzy. I collapse back into the chair, laughing a breath I didn't know

I was holding.

"When can we see him?" Mom asks instantly.

"He's in post-op right now. Once he's settled in his room, a nurse will come get you."

"Will he be able to race again?" she asks, while Dad leans in to listen.

"Yes," the doctor says. "But not until he's cleared. Healing properly is non-negotiable. If you rush it, it'll be detrimental."

"Thank you," I say quickly, before she can interrogate him further.

The doctor nods and leaves. The door hasn't even fully closed before Mom speaks.

"I'm so glad he'll be able to race again."

The words hit wrong. They're sharp and hollow.

"What if he couldn't?" I ask quietly. "Would you still love him?"

They both stare at me like I've spoken another language.

"Well, of course we would," she says, already pulling out her phone.

"Who are you calling?" I ask.

"Shh. Don't worry about it, honey." She waves me off.

Then into the phone:

"He's stable. Surgery successful. Brain bleed. Yes, alert the media. Do the full statement."

Clinical, efficient and polished, like she's done this before. Like we're managing a press release, not a son. And the worst part? I'm not surprised. She's already spinning the narrative. She's making sure Rad is the headline. Making sure the Carson name always *stays* in the headlines. Even though he lost. Even while we are in a hospital waiting room. Even after brain surgery. Those are her priorities.

The numbness settles in deep and heavy. I glance at my father who is looking at a magazine as if I'm the only one that feels this is wrong. They'll never change. I know that now.

I stand without a word and walk out before I say something unforgivable. The hallway air feels cooler, quieter, and cleaner. I lean against the wall and finally breathe. And all I can think is, Axel tried to come with me. He didn't care about the cameras. He cared about me. And I left him standing in a parking lot with a trophy he didn't even want anymore.

I walk back down to the main floor lobby on autopilot. The fluorescent lights hum overhead, too bright, too clean, too normal for what just happened. My legs feel hollow. I don't remember pressing the elevator button. I don't remember crossing the floor. I just know I'm suddenly standing near the vending machines, staring at my reflection in the glass like I'm trying to recognize the girl looking back.

I pull my phone out with shaking fingers.

It rings once.

"Steph! How are you? How's Rad? I saw everything."

Lex's voice comes out like a machine gun, fast, loud, and terrified. It hits me all at once how far away I am from the track, from the crowd, from the life that was happening a few short hours ago. She's still in it. I'm in this sterile in-between space where time feels warped.

"I'm okay," I say automatically, even though I don't know if that's true. "Rad is going to be fine. He had surgery to fix a brain bleed. We haven't been able to see him yet."

There's a sharp inhale on the other end.

"What?! That is crazy. Oh my God. I'm so glad he'll be okay." Her voice cracks with relief before bouncing right back into motion. "I ran to the team's rig and didn't see you. By the way, this place is fucking huge and I'm sweating."

A tired laugh slips out of me before I can stop it. I picture her in that checkered skirt, fighting through crowds of fans, mechanics, and camera crews, probably yelling at anyone who gets in her way. The image feels so absurdly normal that it almost hurts.

"I can only imagine," I say quietly.

There's a pause, small, but heavy.

"Hey," I add, forcing my voice steady. "Did you take some pictures or videos of the championship ceremony?"

"The what?"

I close my eyes and rub my forehead, suddenly aware of how far removed she is from this world. From Axel's world.

"Never mind," I sigh. "Actually, go find Benji and he'll help you find your way. I'm going to be here for a little while."

The words taste wrong. I should be there. I should be watching him celebrate. This is the moment he's worked his entire life for. And I'm sitting under buzzing hospital lights counting the seconds between updates on my brother's brain.

The guilt creeps in from both sides and squeezes.

"No, no, I'm coming to see you," Lex says instantly.

Of course she is.

"Lex," I say gently. "I love you and appreciate you, but I'll be fine."

A beat.

"You're not fine," she mutters. "You're just good at pretending you are."

Is she right?

"Why do you have to be so stubborn?" she sighs, softer now.

"You should be used to it by now," I say, trying to keep it light.

"I swear to God I'm going to fight you later."

I smile at the floor. It's the first real smile I've felt since the crash.

"Love you, bitch," she says, her voice thick with worry she's trying to hide behind attitude.

"Love you, too."

The call ends, and the silence rushes back in. The lobby feels bigger now, emptier. Somewhere down the hall a monitor beeps steadily. A nurse laughs at something I can't hear.

Life keeps going.

I stare at my phone like it might ring again, like something else might break if I look away. My reflection stares back at me in the dark screen. Mascara smudged, hair still stiff from track dust, team polo wrinkled from the day. I'm still wearing it. Probably for the last time. The thought slips in quiet and cold.

I didn't walk out with the team. I didn't stand behind the podium. I didn't do the job I was hired to do. Cameras were rolling, sponsors were watching, and I chose the hospital over the ceremony without even thinking twice.

And I'd do it again.

But that doesn't mean there won't be consequences.

I lean back against the wall and let my head tip toward the ceiling, a shaky breath leaving my lungs. Weeks of pretending. Of balancing lines I wasn't supposed to cross. Of telling myself I could keep everything separate.

Work, family, Axel.

Something was always going to snap. Maybe it already did.

For one split second, my brain flashes to Axel — champagne spraying, the crowd chanting his name, the win he's chased his entire life finally in his hands. I wonder if he's smiling. I wonder if he's looking for me in the crowd out of instinct. I wonder if he wished I was there. The ache that follows is sharp and immediate. I shove the thought away before it can root too deep. Right now, I only have room for one fear at a time.

And my brother is on the other side of a hospital door.

Everything else can burn later.

35

Axel

oes she ever shut the fuck up?

D   I don't think Alexis has taken a breath since we pulled out of the parking lot. Words tumble out of her mouth like they're racing each other, bouncing from one thought to the next—Rad, the crash, the crowd, how terrifying it looked, how she *knew* something bad was coming. I glance over at Ben, silently begging him to look as annoyed as I feel. Instead, the idiot looks... entertained.

He's nodding along, half-smiling, like this redheaded chaos tornado is the best thing that's happened to him all day. Maybe it is. It's not like we have a trophy in the trunk or anything. He keeps shifting in his seat though, restless, fingers tapping against his thigh like he's wired on adrenaline or nerves or both.

"First time?" I whisper, leaning just enough toward him that she can't hear.

"Shut the fuck up, man," Ben mutters through clenched teeth, eyes flicking to the rear view mirror.

Alexis doesn't even notice. She's completely unfazed in the

back seat, snagging fries, the smell of fast food filling the car. Like this isn't the aftermath of the most brutal race of the season.

We pull into the hospital garage, concrete walls swallowing the sound of the engine. There was never a version of this where I didn't come. Not after what I saw. Alexis didn't hesitate either. She'd decided she was coming with or without us. So, here we are.

If my little Kill Switch wasn't so damn stubborn, I would've skipped the podium entirely. Hell, I almost did. But she was right. She always is. Walking away would've turned this into a circus, and she saved me from lighting that match. Still… it didn't sit right with me. It's my fault he's here anyway.

The thought hits hard, knocking the air out of my chest. I shove it down, bury it under logic and instinct and everything racing has drilled into me since I was a kid. But fear doesn't care about logic.

Is she going to hate me when she sees the footage? When she sees the battle? The last lap?

I picture Steph's face. It'd be confused at first, then tight and guarded. She didn't see the crash happen. Not yet. But I know her parents already did.

Reporters are probably swarming the front of the hospital by now. I don't have to see it to know. Phones lighting up, headlines already written before the medics even cleared the track. I can picture it without trying—Rad's name first, mine right beside it, stitched together like we were always headed for this collision.

I don't care enough to look.

Alexis leads the way down the hallway, her energy finally dimming as we get closer to Rad's room. The air here is different, heavy, buzzing with machines I can't see yet. Before Ben or I can step inside, she spins around and stops us with a hand to my chest.

"Let me go first," she says quietly. Not a request. "Stay here."

She takes the food from Ben's hands and slips through the door. Him and I stand there, useless and wait.

I can hear voices through the wall. Steph's, tight and controlled, like she's holding herself together by muscle memory alone. Mrs. Carson cuts in sharp and agitated, every word edged with accusation even when I can't make them out. There's a muffled male voice too, low and steady. That's the room I'm walking into.

The only one in there who can really make this worse is her mother. She's been waiting for a moment like this, something tangible to pin on me, something she can point at and say *I told you so.* She doesn't want history to be brought to the light. I know how this ends.

Rad's the story now. The crash, the surgery, the what-ifs. My win is background noise at best, erased at worst. And honestly? I don't give a shit.

I stare at the closed door, jaw tight, knowing this is the part that actually matters. Not the season. Not the title. It's about what happens when she looks at me again.

I lean towards the door when I hear..

"Did you drive here yourself?" Stephanie's concerned voice echoes from the room.

"No. I, uh, got a ride." Alexis responds nervously.

"With who?"

I smile to myself as I picture furrowed brows and arms crossed on the other side of the door. Stephanie has always been sharp, too sharp for her own good. I know her clever little brain already pieced it together. The silence stretches just long enough to be dramatic before I take it as our cue to stop hiding.

"Ah, Mr. Milano." Stephanie says. Her voice dripping with mixed emotions. Her eyes look from me to Ben.

"Hi, Benji."

"Steph." He lifts his chin at her, attempting to act cool.

"Ah, the one who caused this whole mess!" Mrs. Carson butts in.

How can Paul deal with this woman on a daily basis? If Cruella de Vil had a blonde sister, it'd be her. I look around and almost laugh as I notice he isn't here. Probably rushed back to work already.

"Clear the room," a low, rough voice says. "Everyone except Milano." We all turn towards the hospital bed.

Rad-fucking-Carson

The room goes quiet in that way only hospital rooms ever do. We glance at each other processing what he just said. Someone makes the first move. Mrs. Carson walks over to his bedside as she whispers.

"You sure, sweetie? I can get security."

"Yes," he says, firm, and this time his eyes lock on mine. There's no joking in them. No cocky smirk.

Here we go.

I keep my face neutral as Mrs. Carson brushes past me, though I can't stop the corner of my mouth from twitching. Ben's hand lands on my shoulder in quiet, solidarity. I turn to nod at him. It doesn't look like Rad wants to kill me anymore, not that he could with his current condition. But regardless, this conversation is happening. The silence is deafening as the door clicks shut.

"Pull up a chair," he says as he points to an empty spot beside the bed.

I do, and the second I sit, the reality of him hits me. I'm used to seeing Rad in gear—helmet on, shoulders squared, adrenaline practically leaking out of him. Or used to seeing him in his bright red Honda polo kissing the media's asses. So, seeing him like this feels wrong.

The room is dim, lit by the soft glow of monitors. Machines hum like tired insects in the corners. He's propped up slightly, a thick bandage running along his hairline, an IV taped to his arm. The blond curls at the top of his head have lost their bounce, drooping like gravity finally won. There's dark bruising around his right eye, swollen and ugly. A jagged scrape cuts across his cheek. His lips are dry and cracked.

He looks... human.

"How you feeling?" I ask, mostly to break the tension.

He stares straight ahead for a second before answering. "I'll live."

I huff a quiet laugh. Injuries are nothing new in this sport. As long as you're still breathing, you're winning something.

"Didn't expect you to be here," he says, his voice flat.

"Listen, I—" I start.

"Did you win?"

The question lands heavier than I expect. He turns his head just enough to look at me.

I pause, then take a slow breath. "What do you think?"

A ghost of a smile tugs at his mouth before he winces. "Of course you did."

"Pretty easy when your only competition almost dies on the last lap," I say, knowing damn well he'll appreciate the dark humor.

He snorts, then regrets it immediately.

"Do you remember anything?" I ask.

"Nah," he says quietly. "Nothing after the wheel caught. Everything after that is... static." He reaches up and touches the bandage like he's checking it's still real. "Feels like someone else lived it."

My throat tightens. "I'm sorry."

He shoots me a look—tired, but still sharp. "Don't you start that shit."

"What shit?"

"Guilt. Worry. Remorse." He lifts a shaky hand and gestures vaguely at me. "You didn't push me off the hill. You didn't even touch me. I went down because I rode like an asshole and made a mistake. I wanted that win so bad I forgot to respect the track... and the other riders."

"Rad—"

"Axel, shut up and listen, for fuck's sake."

I close my mouth and lift my hands in surrender. He exhales slowly, like it hurts just to breathe.

"That last moto took my focus. I didn't mean to take things that far. I don't know what got into me," he trails off. "It took my season. Took a piece of my damn skull, apparently." He tilts his head slightly. "But it didn't take your win. That's yours."

My chest feels tight, like something's caving in.

"I didn't want to win like that," I say.

"I know," he says. "And I respect that."

The silence that follows is different. Heavier, but calmer. I don't think he's angry. Everything just feels... real.

Then he smirks, a weak, crooked version of his usual one.

"Even though it pisses me off to say this… if anyone was gonna beat me this season, I'm glad it was you."

I laugh, because somehow that's exactly what I need right now. "That's the nicest thing you've ever said to me."

"I've always been nice to you," he says, pointing at me. "You're the one who's always been a complete douchebag."

"Yeah, you're right." I shrug. "And don't think that's ever gonna change."

For a second, he smiles like the guy I know. Then it fades. "Did she tell you?"

"Who?" I frown. "Tell me what?"

"Steph. Guess you haven't had much time to talk today."

"No," I say, my pulse picking up. "What did she tell you?"

He looks at me with something close to pity. "Just promise me you'll do the right thing."

My throat goes tight. "I promise."

Even when, I don't know what that means yet. We sit there for a few moments before he speaks again.

"You'll race next season, right?" he asks, his eyes already getting heavy.

"If you do," I shoot back.

He opens one eye. "Dude, I'm not gonna die. It's a bleed, not cancer."

"It's still pretty serious."

"Not my first major injury." He swallows. "But I'm coming back. And when I do… you better be ready. I won't lose again."

I lean back and grin. "I wouldn't want it any other way."

His eyes finally close. Before he's fully out, he murmurs, "Axel?"

"Yeah?"

"Don't let my crash mess up your win. You earned it. That's

racing."

Then he's asleep.

I sit there a few more minutes, watching his chest rise and fall. Listening to the machines. Letting it all sink in.

I filter through the flood of emotions. Fear, relief, respect.

Something like brotherhood has begun to build out of rivalry, dirt, and danger.

When I stand to leave, I tap the foot of his bed once, like a promise.

"I'll be ready, asshole," I whisper.

And I will be.

36

Stephanie

The apartment was lit by the kitchen's dim overhead light and the soft glow of the lamp beside the couch. Outside, the city hummed, muted, and distant. My legs are curled under a blanket as I practically shake with anticipation, twisting my checkered ring.

My eyes fall to the coffee table where a folder lays there like police lights. The Fox Sports offer letter. Crisp, official, and absolutely terrifying.

"When is he supposed to be here?" Lex asks.

I glance down at my wrist.

"Thirty minutes," I say nervously.

The adrenaline of the past forty-eight hours was finally fading, leaving behind a raw ache in my chest. Rad was going to be okay. That weight was gone. But the other weight? Not so much.

Lex is pacing the living room like a general prepping for battle.

"So let me get this straight," she said, pointing her water bottle at me. "Your brother wrecks, gets emergency brain surgery, Axel wins the freaking championship, they have their bro reconciliation moment, and *you*—" she stops pacing to stare at me "—you decide tonight is still not a good time to tell Axel you're moving across the country?"

I groan and cover my face with the blanket.

"Lex, please."

"Nope," she says, yanking the blanket down. "You've held this secret for days and you two are practically vibrating with unspoken feelings."

"I'm scared," I say as I bury my face in my hands.

"I know you are," she softens, dropping onto the couch beside me. "But hiding it won't make the decision easier. And it won't make the feelings go away."

"I thought I finally found my place in life. On my own. But, I'm going to uproot everything and start over? Again? And if I tell Axel, what if everything changes between us?" I sigh.

Lex nudges my shoulder. "Maybe things need to change."

I glance down at the folder again. I hate how heavy it feels, but I'm not blind to see the potential it can have.

"You love him," she says gently.

I close my eyes. My mind floods with images of stormy blue eyes that have somehow seen the real me. Those pair of strong arms that have held me when they didn't have to. The heart that has stole mine.

"Yeah. I do."

My shoulders sag. The weight of finally admitting it out loud, lifting off my shoulders.

"I can guarantee he feels the same way. I thought he was going to follow us home like some lovesick golden retriever," she says with humor in her tone in an attempt to lighten the mood as always.

"More like a Doberman," I let out a shaky laugh. "He cares about me, Lex. We both care about each other. But caring doesn't fix logistics. Or PR nightmares. Or—"

A soft knock interrupts my spiraling.

Two knocks.

"And that would be your Doberman."

My heart jumps into my throat. "I thought he'd text first."

"He probably did," Alexis said, already standing and straightening the living room, which meant she moved one pair of abandoned sneakers and tossed a hoodie over the back of a chair. "But your phone's buried under that emotional support blanket."

I scramble to my feet, palms suddenly sweaty. "Lex—"

"Nope, you've got this," she gives me a quick hug, grabs her purse, and heads for the door.

"I told my parents I'd visit them today anyways. Call me if you need me."

"Wait a minute.." I say following her.

She gives me a knowing smile as she opens the door. Axel stands on the other side, black T-shirt hugging his toned body, eyes immediately flicking past Lex to find mine.

"Alexis," he says softly.

"Still Lex," she says, brushing past him. "And Champ? Try not to be an asshole, okay? She's already had enough drama this week that could last a lifetime."

Axel blinks, confused but amused. "Uh... okay?"

She wiggles her eyebrows at me behind his back while mouthing the words, *tell him*, before slipping out into the hallway. The door clicks shut. And suddenly it's just Axel and I in the quiet apartment. The weight of everything suspended between us.

Axel takes a slow step toward me, concern flickering across his face. He reaches up and gently tucks a loose strand of hair behind my ear. His touch is careful, already bracing for it.

"You alright?" he asks.

"We should uh.. talk," I stammer out.

I twist my fingers in the hem of my shirt as Axel takes in the apartment. His eyes gaze over the blanket, the faint smell of coffee and *Love is Blind* paused on the TV. His gaze finally settles back on me. His face holds a soft expression and one that's searching for answers.

I don't blame him.

"Tell me what's wrong." he says more sternly. "Are you okay?"

"No," I admit. "But, I will be. Just... sit with me?"

He nods and follows me to the couch. We sit close. Close enough that I can feel the heat coming off him, but it still feels like miles. My heart pounds so loudly I swear he must hear it.

"I need to tell you something," I start.

His brows draw together. "Alright."

I reach for the dreaded folder and place it in his hands. He takes it slowly, carefully, like it might explode.

As his eyes scan the heading, the breath he was holding slips free.

"Fox Sports... next season of Supercross and Pro National reporting?"

I nod, throat tight. "They want me to start filling in as an on-site reporter. Interviews, track-side features... eventually commentary in a few years. They think I can grow into it."

Axel's expression is at first unreadable. Then it quickly moves to a look of pride mixed with shock, mixed with something deeper.

"This is huge, Steph." He looks over at me. "This is what you've always talked about. Moving up. Having a voice. Your *own* voice."

I swallow hard. He really does know me. Which makes this all the more difficult.

"It also means stepping away from Kawasaki, from the team. Not working alongside you anymore."

Axel's breath hitches. The words hung between them, heavy, hopeful, terrifying.

"I'd still be working in the sport," I continued. "Still be at the races. Still *around* you in a way. But for it to work, I'd need to do three weeks of training in Connecticut."

He drew in a slow breath. "Three weeks."

"Then maybe, *maybe*, they'd place me back in California. It depends on where they need someone long term and obviously I'd travel for each race same as you."

Axel leans back, hand scrubbing over his face. He doesn't look angry. He isn't even upset. He just looks... overwhelmed.

"Why didn't you tell me sooner?" he asks quietly.

"I didn't know how."

I move closer to him, folding my legs under.

"Everything was already so chaotic with Rad, the championship, us," I motion with my hands. "I didn't want to throw another grenade into the mix."

He sets the folder down and turns fully towards me.

"You shouldn't have to go through this alone."

Emotion stings my eyes. "I'm not trying to shut you out. I'm just... scared. If I stayed because of you, I'd resent myself. If I left and it hurt us, I'd resent that too."

"Hey." His hand touches my knee, tentative, and warm. "This doesn't have to be an either-or."

My breath trembles. "Maybe. But, I know you can't come with me. Training starts soon, and you'll have Playoffs. And I don't want to be a distraction or risk your career."

Axel's eyes lock onto mine, slow and deliberate. "I'm not throwing anything away. This Pro National championship was everything I've ever dreamed. You know that."

"I do," I whisper. "But you deserve to be SMX champion, too."

"I got that in the bag," he waves it off. "And who says I can't afford a few weeks off of training to come with you? But, you didn't even ask." He smirks. "But you're not nothing, Steph. You're not this... side thing I fit in when it's convenient. You matter more to me than I ever thought possible."

I blink away tears that have threatened to fall. "I know. I mean, I was hoping you'd say that, but that's why this is killing me."

He moves closer and gently places his hand on the side of my face. His thumb lingers, brushing my cheek.

"Three weeks," he murmurs. "It's not forever."

"It could be longer if they place me only on East Coast events."

"Then I'll deal with time differences and crappy hotel Wi-Fi and missing you like hell." His voice lowers, a teasing smile at the corner of his lips. "Whatever gets you in that announcers booth."

Maybe someday.

I chuckle softly as we stare at each other for a few moments.

Then, I inhale sharply. "So... you think I should take it?"

"I think," he says softly, "you should do what's right for you."

My mind instantly goes to him. What if he's what's right for me?

"What if it breaks us?" My negativity showing through.

"It won't." His voice is firm, unshakably certain. "Not unless you let it."

My chin quivers. "Axel..."

He leans his forehead against mine. "I don't care if we have to hide or not hide, or if you're in California or Connecticut. I just care that at the end of all this, you're still mine."

A single tear finally falls. He swipes it with his thumb.

"I hate to say it," I whisper. "but, I want to always be yours."

His breath hitches. Relief, gratitude, something fierce, and warm as a smile grows on his face.

"Was that so hard to say?" he jokes.

I nod slightly and he chuckles.

"Then we'll make it work," he murmurs.

I close my eyes, letting the truth settle in my bones.

My heart belongs to a rider.

When I open them again, I find him watching me with something like awe.

"So," he says gently, "Are you going to tell them yes?"

I swallow and exhale slowly, bracing for his reaction. "I already did."

"And you didn't even ask me to run away with you?" A look of exaggerated shock shown on his face.

"I guess we both want what's best for each other," I say as I lean back so I can see him fully. "Or maybe I'm sick of standing in a rider's shadow." I shrug.

A small smile tugs at his mouth, proud and pained all at once. "That's my little Kill Switch."

I lean into him, burying my face against his shoulder. His arms wrap around me instantly, holding me tight, steadying me.

"When do you leave?" he asks.

"In two days," I say, my voice muffled.

He sighs.

"Guess, we better make the most of it."

"Hey!" I squeal as the world tilts and suddenly I'm weightless. I laugh, startled, instinctively bracing my hands against his shoulders as Axel lifts me clean off the couch. I halfheartedly kick, pretending to fight him, but my body betrays me immediately. I relax. I point down the hall toward my room, because where else would we go.

"Ow!" I yelp when his hand smacks my ass, playful, and familiar. The sound echoing in the quiet apartment.

We hit the bed in a tangled heap of limbs and laughter. The kind that feels a little too loud, a little too desperate, like we're trying to outrun something closing in behind us. I don't know who moves first. Maybe it's him. Maybe it's me.

One second I'm sinking into his arms, breath still unsteady from laughing, and the next I'm underneath him, heart racing for an entirely different reason. Axel's hands are on my waist, firm but careful, like he's grounding himself as much as he's grounding me. His fingers are warm and steady as his black cross hovers over me. Always steady with me, even when everything inside him feels like it's burning.

"Hey," he murmurs, voice barely there, like saying anything too loud might shatter the moment. "Look at me."

I shouldn't. I know I shouldn't. Because the second I do, the dam breaks. Every fear I've been carrying—every deadline, every rule, every carefully constructed wall we've been hiding behind just... dissolves. He's looking at me like I'm something fragile and unbreakable all at once. Like I matter. Like I'm something he refuses to lose.

"I don't want tonight to be the thing that pulls us apart," I breathe.

"It won't," he says, thumb brushing my cheek, my jaw, my lower lip. "It doesn't have to."

His touch ignites sparks under my skin. I feel my resolve slip, melt, and dissolve entirely.

He leans in slow and deliberate, giving me time to pull back. I don't.

Our lips meet in a careful kiss, soft at first, like he's afraid I'll break. But I've been breaking for months. Quietly. Silently. Every time he walked into the Kawasaki trailer and pretended like I was nothing to him. I knew it wasn't real, but it hurt all the same.

I fist my hands in the front of his shirt and pull him closer. He exhales against my mouth, a small, helpless sound that shoots straight through me. His fingers slide up my spine, curling into my hair, and suddenly the kiss isn't careful anymore. It's hungry. His forehead presses against mine, breathing hard.

"We don't have to," he whispers. "Not tonight. Not because everything's emotional. I don't want you to feel—"

"Shut the fuck up." I slide my hand down the inside of his pants, wrapping my fingers around his hard shaft. He shudders.

"Is that how you wanna play? Huh?"

His expression shifts, every protective instinct, every ounce of restraint fades away for a second before his worry surfaces again.

"Switch..." His voice breaks. "Tell me this isn't, because you're leaving."

"It's, because I'm staying," I whisper. "With you. Even

when I'm gone."

For a moment he just looks at me. Really looks. Like he's memorizing every angle of my face, before I disappear.

Then his lips crash into mine, stealing the breath from my lungs. The kiss deepens, hot and consuming. His hands slide beneath my shirt, fingertips brushing my waist, just below my breasts, sending shivers everywhere. I arch into him instinctively and feel him inhale sharply against my mouth.

"Fuck..." he groans, voice low, wrecked. "You're killing me."

My laugh is breathless. "Then don't make me wait."

He pulls back just enough to meet my eyes again. His pupils are blown, his breath uneven, his hand still stroking slow, deliberate circles against my bare skin.

"Are you sure?" he asks, voice rough.

"Yes, for fuck's sake," I say as I roll my eyes.

That's all it takes.

Clothes fall to the floor leaving nothing between us. His mouth trails along my jaw, down my neck, slow, and reverent in a way that makes my whole body tremble. My breath catches as he begins rubbing my clit. His fingers moving in slow teasing circles, before finally entering me.

His hands then slide under me, lifting and guiding me until I'm straddling him, taking my breath away as I sink down. I gaze at the perfect picture below me, clutching his shoulders, refusing to separate from him.

Every nerve sparks. Every inch of me feels alive, ignited, wanted as I grind my hips. If only I could stay right here. To always have him this deep inside of me. To never let go.

It doesn't take long until I'm pulled down, my chest now laying on his. His hands grab the sides of my face like he couldn't wait another second without his lips on mine.

"Steph," he whispers into my skin, "I've waited so long for someone like you."

"Hope it was worth it," I smile against his lips.

"You're damn right it was. It'll also be worth the amount of caffeine you'll need tomorrow," he says seductively.

"You really think you can go all night?" I say, unable to resist.

"You say that, like I don't thrive under pressure," he says softly against my ear.

Goosebumps spread across my skin.

I meet his eyes, and it feels like stepping too close to the edge of something I won't survive falling from. Axel's gaze holds mine, steady, and unguarded in a way that makes my chest tighten. There's no teasing there, no bravado, just him. Just us.

And then we're lost in each other again, no edges, no clear beginning or end. Everything blurs into heat and breath and the soft, broken sounds we pull from one another like confessions.

His hands move with purpose and reverence, like he's afraid and fearless all at once, and mine follow instinctively, knowing him in a way words never could. Time slips sideways. The world narrows to the rhythm we find together, bodies moving as one, like this has always been where we were meant to land. I breathe his name like a promise, like something sacred I'm afraid to say out loud, and he answers with a sound that tells me he hears it, that he feels it too. The rest of the world slips away, the hospital, the job offer, the distance, the fear. The night folds around us as we drown ourselves in each other.

Hopefully, not for the last time.

37

Stephanie

The overhang for the airport drop off looms ahead, all concrete and final. I wish Axel would turn the truck around. I wish he'd miss the turn, ignore the signs, do something reckless and stupid and undeniably him. But no. Here he is being fucking supportive.

I want him to beg me to stay. To fight me on it. To tell me to just stay with the team for another year. To make this hurt less by making it messy. I know there's a chance I'll be back in California after training, but that doesn't change the fact that I'm about to get on a plane without him.

I don't do relationships. I especially don't do long distance ones. This really sucks ass.

The brakes screech as the truck comes to a stop. Axel shifts into park and looks over at me, calm like he isn't about to crack my ribcage open.

"You ready?"

"Yeah," I say, which is a lie we both politely ignore.

He grabs my luggage while I step onto the curb, the air already smelling like jet fuel and regret.

"You sure this is all your stuff?" he asks, eyeing my single suitcase and carry-on.

"Three weeks of training how to talk to riders doesn't require many outfits," I say with a weak chuckle.

He steps closer—too close—and instinct takes over. My arms wrap around his waist like muscle memory. I breathe him in, that stormy, familiar scent, and for one terrifying second I think this might be the last time.

I don't cry. I won't cry, I refuse.

"I wish you could come with me," I mumble into his chest.

"I know, Switch," he sighs, hugging me tighter. "But you know how this life is. There's never, truly, an off-season."

He pulls back, glancing over his shoulder at the temporary parking signs, looking like he might say a certain phrase.

"I—"

"Don't," I cut him off fast. "We're not doing a corny curbside goodbye. This will not be a Hallmark movie."

A smile tugs at his mouth.

"Fine."

"I'll text you when I land."

He leans down and kisses me, slow, deep, and devastating. The kind of kiss that feels like an ending even when it isn't. My heart free-falls, but I don't let it show.

Our eyes meet one last time. I reach for my luggage, my fingers wrapping around the handle. His hand covers mine.

"You're going to do great," he says softly. "Kick some ass."

"Don't tell me things I already know," I wink trying to lighten the mood. "And no slacking! Being an SMX champion isn't guaranteed."

He laughs and then kisses me again, harder this time, like he's imprinting himself into my bones. Then he pulls away.

"You don't want to miss your flight."

"Yeah," I say. "You're right."

We nod awkwardly, like strangers pretending we're not everything to each other. I turn away. The sound of my luggage wheels behind me does little to mask the sound of my heart breaking.

"Fuck!" I mumble to myself.

People do this all the time—distance, schedules, FaceTime calls at ungodly hours. But my gut twists like it knows something my head doesn't. I replay his face over and over as I weave through the airport, the way his jaw tightened, the words he didn't say sitting heavy between us. He looked like someone holding himself together with sheer discipline. Like if he cracked, he wouldn't stop.

Maybe I imagined it.

Maybe I wanted him to stop me so badly that I saw ghosts in his eyes.

By the time I clear security, my throat is burning. I swallow hard, forcing it down. I refuse to cry in public. I refuse to be *that girl* sobbing at an airport terminal like I'm starring in some melodramatic rom-com. I'm no weak bitch. I tell myself. It's not like we broke. We're grown adults.

I check my phone.

Nothing.

No text. No joke. No *I already miss you.* That stings more than it should.

I never told him I love him.

I find my gate and sink into one of the hard plastic chairs, my carry-on wedged between my feet. People mill around me, families, couples, business travelers, everyone moving forward while I feel like I'm almost moving backwards.

I picture Axel driving away from the curb. The truck disappearing into traffic. Him gripping the steering wheel too tight, jaw twitching, doing the right thing like he magically does now all of a sudden.

I hate him for that.

Boarding starts. I barely hear my zone get called. My body goes on autopilot. I stand, scan my ticket and step onto the plane.

This is it.

This is what I get for letting myself fall in love with a rider. I finally let one tear fall. Thank *God* I have a window seat. I watch the crew load the luggage onto the plane when I hear the rustling of others boarding the plane behind me.

I refuse to look, to be kind with whoever is unlucky enough to have to sit beside me. And honestly, I don't care at this point. Once again I'm on a plane flying across the country, either running from something or starting over or both. It's hard to tell at this point. Hopefully, it's worth it this time.

The aisle fills as passengers board behind me. Bags bump seats. Someone knocks my elbow.

"Ow," I mutter without turning, already resigned to being trapped next to a stranger for the next five hours of quiet misery.

The person sits and I finally look. And my entire world stops.

Navy blue eyes. Cocky grin. The audacity of him sitting there like he didn't just emotionally wreck me two hours ago.

"Axel-fucking-Milano," I whisper, breath leaving my lungs in one violent rush.

He looks way too pleased with himself.

I hit him, *hard*, in the shoulder, then fist his shirt and drag him into me, kissing him like I might die if I don't.

"Ow," he laughs into my mouth.

"What the fuck are you doing here?!" I demand, pointing at his chest.

"You can't get rid of me that easy," he grins. "I figured surprising you on the plane was better than chasing you through TSA."

"I thought you left," I snap, my voice cracking despite my best effort. "I thought that was it."

His smile softens instantly. He reaches up, thumb brushing under my eye like he knows exactly where it hurts.

"Never," he says quietly.

I stare at him, stunned.

"Are you really flying with me to Connecticut? No bullshit?"

"Yes. But, I can only stay for a week and then I have to fly back for playoffs."

I nod my head in understanding.

"And we just have to hope I'll be back here after training," I say softly.

"We'll figure it out," he says confidently as he gives me a knowing look. "We don't have to hide anymore." He gently traces my hand with his thumb.

"Yeah, I've decided I'm over that shit." I give him a small smile as my shoulders sink in relief. "That will be nice."

Our eyes meet and he smiles.

"You know your nickname isn't just because you turned my bike off right?"

I tilt my head in confusion. He takes a deep breath as his face grows serious. My heart starts beating faster as I wait for him to elaborate.

"You.." his voice drops slightly as he pauses. "...killed everything I thought I knew. You ended the old me and switched my whole outlook on life. In a good way." He huffs a laugh and I can't help but join him.

The tears I've tried to hold back start to slowly fall down my cheeks. He reaches up and tenderly wipes them away.

"I love you, Stephanie Carson," he says finally. "I have for awhile now." My full name on his lips giving me butterflies.

His thumb continues to stroke my cheek as my emotions tumble over. I feel like I'm the one that actually won the championship. Where's the flight attendant? I need some champagne.

I got the guy and I'm not hiding it anymore. The moto world is about to shit their pants and I can't wait. It's time for the women in the industry to get some recognition and expand the sport for the better. And if they happen to fall in love along the way? Who gives a shit.

I take a deep breath and slowly exhale as I grab his face with both hands. I look deep into his eyes as a huge smile breaks out across my face.

"I love you too, Axel Milano. Now, kiss me you asshole."

The End

Epilogue

Axel

10 years later

I know what you're thinking.

That winning didn't matter anymore, because I got the girl. That I'd have been happy whether I won or lost.

No.

I wanted to win more, *because* of her. It *mattered* more. She made me better.

And, I didn't just win for Stephanie. I won for my parents, for Maddox, for Ben, for our daughter, and for myself. For the kid I used to be, who thought success only came with a trophy and a bottle of champagne.

"Don't forget to keep your toes pointed in, okay, honey?"

"Daddy! I *know* how to do it!" she yells back, her tiny voice full of attitude as she twists the throttle and takes off.

I shake my head, already smiling. Her long dark hair, tangled, wild, streams out from beneath her helmet as she zips around the track. I glance over at Steph, her hand resting instinctively on her growing belly, pride written all over her face.

"She sure is stubborn," she says.

"You wouldn't want it any other way," I reply with a wink.

She rolls her eyes, of course.

"How are the boys today?" I say as I lean over planting a kiss at the top of her belly.

"They're kicking the shit out of me," she groans, rubbing her stomach.

I laugh. "Just wait until they tear it up on the track."

She groans louder. "If they're anything like you and Rad, we're fucked."

We both lose it, laughing as we watch our daughter carve through the dirt like she was born for it. My hand finds Steph's, and everything settles into this quiet, perfect moment.

Complete bliss.

I breathe it in and let my mind drift—past championships, podiums, trophies stacked in corners, shelves, collecting dust, until all of it fades beneath something far more important.

Her.

Stephanie wrecked my life in the best way possible.

After flying with her to Connecticut, everything changed. We were unstoppable. Still are, if I'm being honest. Kawasaki never wanted to let me go. I became the SMX champion that year. Breaking that losing streak for them mattered, but having my Kill Switch beside me for every step mattered more. They sent her back to Cali after training. Everything aligned and worked out, how it was always meant to. Just how I told her it would. Her stubborn ass.

She was the one who convinced me to get my own place instead of living in a bunkhouse like a frat boy with a factory ride. I still laugh thinking about how nervous I was asking her, like I was proposing instead of apartment hunting.

But it forced me to think about *our* future, not just mine.

Every time I said, "I want what's best for you," she'd throw it right back at me. We never stopped competing. Never stopped challenging each other. I loved those arguments. Mostly because they always ended the same way, breathless, satisfied, and grinning like idiots.

Stephanie kept everyone on their toes everywhere she went. Including me. Even to this day.

She started as a trackside reporter and then absolutely stole the announcer's booth. Not actually steal. She did, legally, get hired. The haters talked. They said it was the Carson name, said it was me.

Ridiculous honestly.

A name only gets you in the door. Talent keeps you there. And Steph was born for that job.

Now, she and her co-anchor, Derek, own the box every weekend. There's no favoritism. No bullshit. Just sharp insight and real love for the sport. She earned the respect of the community the hard way, and I couldn't have been prouder.

After every win, I'd look up toward the booth, wait for the camera, and give her a wink or say something completely unhinged. Once I said, *"I had to win or else I'd have to sleep outside tonight."*

She hated it. The fans loved it. And honestly? Getting under her skin has always been one of my favorite hobbies.

Sharing this life with her, knowing she loved it as much as I did, made everything else feel secondary. That's why, after one year in, I asked her to marry me. Her response?

"It's about damn time."

Fire. Always fire.

A few years later, our daughter was born. A chapter I never saw coming when I was a kid with nothing, but a bike and a chip on my shoulder. And now, with twin boys on the way, I've never been more grateful. Especially knowing they've got the best mother on the planet.

Watching Stephanie thrive in the career she fought for gave me a new perspective when it finally came time to retire. I didn't need racing the way I once thought I did. I just needed to change my perspective. I needed *this*. Her. Our family. And a new have dirt bikes in the mix.

I still support the Mad Madds Moto Foundation. I still teach classes. Still help kids chase dreams the way dirt bikes once helped me. But our most popular class? The couples class. The one Steph and I teach together.

Fuck... I'm proud of what we built.

I used to think the best feeling in the world was a bike between my legs.

I was wrong. I mean, yeah, it's pretty damn close.

But, the real dream is right here—my wife, my kids, dirt under our boots, laughter in the air. Watching my daughter fall in love with the same sport that gave me everything is just the cherry on top.

Ring

"Open the door, old man."

"You know the code. Why don't you open it yourself?" I say as Steph smirks beside me.

"Because I'm not an asshole, that's why. *And* I refuse to risk another incident where I had to bleach my eyes after what I walked in on."

"That was years ago, buddy," I laugh. "You got the crew with you?"

"Do I ever leave home without them?" he says sarcastically.

I snort. "Alright, I'll be there in a sec."

I hang up and check my watch.

"Benji and the fam?" Steph asks.

"Yeah, they're here and he still refuses to just come in."

She smiles and shakes her head, walking inside.

"Madds! Race is about to start!" I yell, waving her over.

She skids to a stop, already talking a mile a minute about the WMX, women's motocross, she watches on TV. Says she wants to be just like them someday, strong, powerful.

Pride swells in my chest.

And if she wakes up tomorrow and decides she hates dirt bikes? I'll still be proud. I'll support her no matter what she chooses, because that's the kind of father I promised I'd be. And because she's got a mother who would never let us forget it.

I glance at where Stephanie was standing, the love of my life, the woman who changed everything.

Life will knock you down and drag you through ruts you swear you'll never climb out of. But, don't quit. Keep pushing and chase your dreams until you see that checkered flag.

And if you're lucky, someone might just be waiting for you on the other side.

Acknowledgments

If you've made it this far, then I truly can't thank you enough. I hope you enjoyed the ride and love the characters as much as I had a blast writing them. If you smiled once, at any point, then I will go to bed happy.

My goal wasn't just to create another sports romance. To not just write about something that I loved. Although I wanted it to be fun and exciting, I also wanted it to mean something. I wanted to represent and shed light to the women in the industry. There are a few (like Haley and Will) that are badass and I love to see them track side or in the booth on race day. I'm also excited for the growth and expansion of WMX and women in the sport. I feel great things coming!

So, I hope that I created that unique mixture. And dual POV novels are always my favorite to read, so obviously I had to do it for my own. Because, what woman doesn't want to know what goes on in a man's mind? Even though it's fictional and in real life it's probably just "boobs" and dirt bike noises.

But, fun fact about me is that I can be quite nerdy. So, if you haven't noticed some characters and quotes are inspired by some of my favorite movies. Are any of these movies relevant or similar to any of these characters? Absolutely not. Is Love is Blind (that I mentioned once) one of my guilty pleasures? Yes. It's just small personal details in my book from my real life. Almost like having an inside joke, but with yourself. So, if your curious then feel free to continue. Oh, and I thank some people after that.

Axel Milano, got his last name from the Marvel movie *Guardians of the Galaxy. The Milano* is Peter Quill's (Star-Lord) spaceship, which I also have a tattoo of. Ben Traymer is named after a character mentioned in the classic movie *Halloween*. A movie I watch religiously every year. His nickname, Benji, I got from the movie *Pitch Perfect*. A movie I've seen so many times I could sing the songs word for word. Much like the songs mentioned throughout the book as well. I'm really showing my age here...

I had a blast creating these characters, their personalities, their story and making it my own. Never did I think I'd have the courage to write a novel, let alone a motocross romance. And I had a hell of a lot to learn. And honestly, it all started with Tiktok (booktok). I started posting about the books I was reading in 2024 which led me to meet some amazing fellow readers and authors. I had the privilege to work with independent authors, create book covers, merch, read their work, and learn so much from them. I still love collaborating with authors and helping them with whatever they need.

And with those connections and friendships included Amber. If it wasn't for her, I wouldn't have put the words that were in my head and actually put them on paper. She gave me the courage to start and continues to give me the support, and is always there when I need her. I'll forever be grateful of our friendship.

Now, a little back story. I wasn't always a fan of motocross. I loved sports in general. I played softball and lacrosse growing up and have always loved watching and going to football games. My husband introduced me to the moto world in 2019, took me to a race, and I was hooked. From there, it led to more races, dirt bikes of our own, and trips to the local track. And there was just something about Team Green...

Then one day while watching a Supercross race on TV, I got the idea for this book. The idea turned into words, then characters, then chapters, then a whole ass novel. And after doing some research, I found that there isn't many motocross books out there. There are a few amazing ones like *The Moto Crush Series by Afton Seeser,* with the first book being called *Perfectly Untamed.* I read it and I was inspired (thank you Afton!) and committed to finish/perfect the story and follow my dream.

But, there are so many people to thank for this whole writing journey. Autumn for the beautiful pics for the back of the covers (@a.purdypics on instagram). To my brother and sister-in-law—cheers! My parents for hearing me yap about it and saying you'll read it. My in-laws, brothers, aka second family. To the rest of my family and family friends for being supportive. To my kids for only messing with a few sentences and being as excited as I was when my first proof came in the mail. I had no idea how to explain the "not for resale" line to them, lol. They were so confused, but I'm so grateful for the time they allowed me to write.

Anyways, I appreciate you all so much!

And last, but not least, my husband. The one person I truly couldn't have done this without. Thank you for answering my million moto questions, constantly hearing about this story, for going on this crazy adventure with me, and being my real life ride or die. It means the world to me, that you took the time to read each and every word even when you're not a reader. You're my dream come true even... when Honda red is your favorite ;).

If you've seen my Goodreads or my bookshelves at home, then you know that I like to read multiple genres. Will I be the same as a writer?? Stay tuned...

About the Author

A. Anthony is an independent author that lives with her husband and two children near Pittsburgh, Pennsylvania where she was born and raised. She attended Penn State New Kensington for Radiological Sciences and works part-time as a Radiologic Technologist. When she's not writing, she can usually be found reading, collaborating with fellow authors, riding dirt bikes, going on adventures with her family or fueling her days with hot coffee and corny jokes. She writes romance filled with grit, heart, and just enough heat to keep the pages turning.

Be sure to follow her on social media!
  Tiktok: @allison_onederland
  Instagram: @a.anthonyauthor

www.ingramcontent.com/pod-product-compliance
Lightning Source LLC
Chambersburg PA
CBHW031118160726
47991CB00004B/1446